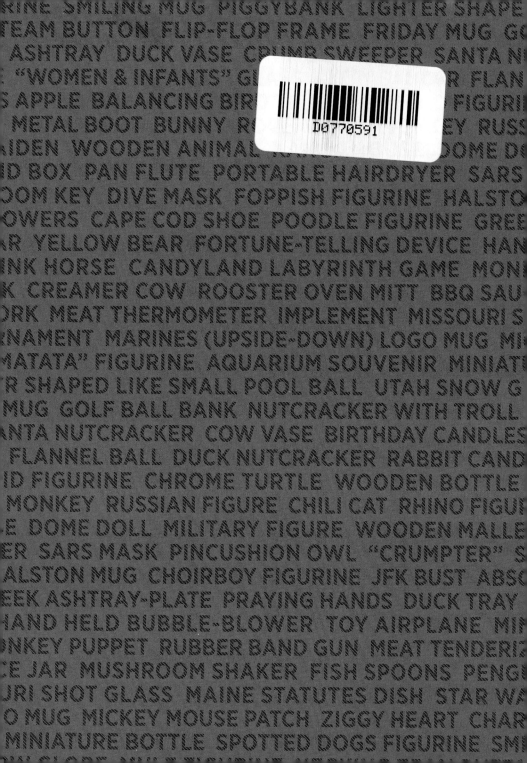

LIKE SMALL POOL BALL UTAH SNOW GLOBE MUL
F BALL BANK NUTCRACKER WITH TROLL HAIR (O
CRACKER COW VASE BIRTHDAY CANDLES LETTER
L BALL DUCK NUTCRACKER RABBIT CANDLE 4-TIL
CHROME TURTLE WOODEN BOTTLE FAKE BANAN
N FIGURE CHILI CAT RHINO FIGURINE BASKETBAL
L MILITARY FIGURE WOODEN MALLET MASSAGE
ASK PINCUSHION OWL "CRUMPTER" SHARK AN
MUG CHOIRBOY FIGURINE JFK BUST ABSOLUTIO
ASHTRAY-PLATE PRAYING HANDS DUCK TRAY JA
HELD BUBBLE-BLOWER TOY AIRPLANE MINIATUR
EY PUPPET RUBBER BAND GUN MEAT TENDERIZE
E JAR MUSHROOM SHAKER FISH SPOONS PENGUI
DT GLASS MAINE STATUTES DISH STAR WARS CARD
KEY MOUSE PATCH ZIGGY HEART CHARLIE'S ANGEL
RE BOTTLE SPOTTED DOGS FIGURINE SMILING MU
OBE MULE FIGURINE NECKING TEAM BUTTON FLII
AIR (OR SOMETHING) "HAWK" ASHTRAY DUCK VAS
LETTERS AND NUMBERS PLATE "WOMEN & INFANTS
E 4-TILE CERAMIC SHELL BRASS APPLE BALANCIN
FAKE BANANA WOODEN APPLE CORE METAL BOO
NE BASKETBALL TROPHY INDIAN MAIDEN WOODE
MASSAGER WIRE BASKET ROUND BOX PAN FLU
ARK AND SEAL PENS MOTEL ROOM KEY DIVE MAS
LUTION FIGURINE JAR OF FLOWERS CAPE COD SHO
AR OF MARBLES TOY CAR YELLOW BEAR FORTUNI
IATURE TURKEY DINNER PINK HORSE CANDYLAN
R MINIATURE PITCHFORK CREAMER COW ROOSTE
N CREAMER COOKING FORK MEAT THERMOMETE
RS CARDS CRACKER BARREL ORNAMENT MARINE
IE'S ANGELS THERMOS "HAKUNA MATATA" FIGURIN
ING MUG PIGGYBANK LIGHTER SHAPED LIKE SMA

"When people are finding meaning in things — *beware*."

EDWARD GOREY

Significant Objects

ROB WALKER & JOSHUA GLENN

OUR HYPOTHESIS:

Stories are such a powerful driver of emotional value that their effect on any given object's subjective value can actually be measured objectively.

SCALE REFERENCE OF U.S. PENNY.

THIS BOOK COLLECTS ONE HUNDRED STORIES – BY AN ARRAY OF EXTREMELY talented writers – all inspired by what had previously been distinctly insignificant objects. A gift-shop souvenir from a stranger's vacation, a cheap promotional item for a defunct business, a tacky religious or corporate-branding figurine: You've seen their like at yard sales and flea markets, along the sidewalk on trash day, and in friends' living rooms. Perhaps you've wondered: What's the story with *that* thing?

Long before we began the Significant Objects project, we understood that stories make objects more meaningful. It's stories that make us treasure childhood toys, family heirlooms, and the like, far beyond their "rational" market value – just as it's stories that make some brands (famously: Harley-Davidson, ESPN, Apple) into cult phenomena.

The goal of our project was to test the following hypothesis: Stories are such a powerful driver of emotional value that their effect on any given object's subjective value can actually be measured objectively. We devised a daring experiment, one that would not only meet the standards of the laboratory – i.e., instead of gathering true stories, we commissioned *entirely fictional* stories about objects – but that would play out in a real-world marketplace.

It was a three-stage process.

First: At thrift stores, yard sales, and flea markets we obtained one hundred insignificant objects. On average, we paid a little more than $1.25 per object. (Turn to Appendix for complete experimental data.)

Second: We recruited one hundred of the most creative and compelling story-tellers working today. This included well-known writers like Jonathan Lethem, Lydia Millet, Meg Cabot, Nicholson Baker, Colson Whitehead, Curtis Sittenfeld, and William Gibson, as well as first-time novelists, comic-book writer-illustrators, staff writers from *The Daily Show*, and others whose talent and imagination we admired. We asked each participant to write a very short story, one that attributed significance to one of our thrift-store finds.

Third: We listed each object for auction on eBay, using its invented story as the item description. The auction's starting price was whatever we'd paid for the object.

We were careful to note – even though it was hardly necessary, in most cases – that the item description was a work of fiction. We named the story's author, and directed eBay shoppers to our website, SignificantObjects.com, for an explanation of the experiment. Thanks to these stringent parameters, we knew we could accurately and objectively determine whether significance-driven value could be artificially injected into insignificant objects. What's more, we could measure that increased value empirically.

Voilà! Before the first week's auctions had concluded, excited bloggers and journalists were chronicling our experiment's success. By the time we'd closed our hundredth auction, Significant Objects had pulled off not one, but two nifty tricks.

§

Our first trick – i.e., transforming insignificant objects, which we'd picked up (remember) for about $1.25 apiece, into significant ones – succeeded beyond our most optimistic projections. The evidence is incontrovertible. Several items sold for as much as $50; and a few sold for over $100. In total, the tchotchkes we'd purchased for $128.74 sold for a whopping $3,612.51. Via our experiment, the exchange value of these unwanted and sometimes un-lovely objects was increased by more than 2,700 percent!

This set journalists and trend-spotters in the literary, economic, marketing, and product-design spheres buzzing. Our innovative research, we heard again and again, could prove extremely useful to commodity-producers and marketers eager to tap into the value-adding power of narrative. Indeed, in the summer of 2010 the influential ad agency Wieden+Kennedy proposed a "retail environment" (code-named SKU) that was inspired, they claimed, by our project. Each month, the idea goes, SKU

SCALE OF 2,700%.

would sell a collection of items curated by a famous person who'd tell stories about them: Wes Anderson's favorite bicycle pump, say. (Wieden+Kennedy-ites, you'll want to check out the Appendix for counterintuitive data on the market value added by famous vs. up-and-coming authors.)

As Significant Objects established itself, we published stories that were the result of team-ups with the Center for Cartoon Studies, *The Believer*, *Design Observer*, *Electric Literature*, *Underwater New York*, and others. We ran contests with *Slate* and *SMITH Magazine*, and recruited Paola Antonelli, senior curator for design at the Museum of Modern Art, to inspire contributors with objects fished out of her own junk drawer. Meanwhile, successful bidders sent us photographs of the objects made significant by our experiment, lovingly displayed in their new homes. Some objects traveled to readings or literary festivals, and at least one appeared in an art exhibit.

So have we, as it's been suggested, discovered a new business model, a killer marketing app? All we knew for sure is that we'd dreamed up a fun, creative project that was (for once!) profitable; all proceeds, by the way, went to the authors. Our trick was so successful that we kept it going for a few months as a fundraising vehicle: Two subsequent "volumes" of Significant Objects stories raised thousands of dollars for the literary tutoring programs 826 National and Girls Write Now. (See Appendix for details.)

§

As pleased as we are by the success of our experiment, we're prouder of our project's *second* trick – one terrific outcome of which is the volume you're holding.

Writers love a challenge like the one we posed them – i.e., making up a story inspired by an object they've never seen before. Our contributors met the challenge with wildly imaginative, deeply moving, and darkly ironic stories. They wrote letters, email solicitations, memoirs, operating instructions, public notices, diary entries, wine-tasting notes, and public ordinances. Some crafted rich character studies, others told tales through whipsaw dialogue or internal monologue. Some took bold experimental risks, while others opted for evocative minimalism or genre fiction.

It turns out that once you start increasing the emotional energy of inanimate objects, an unpredictable chain reaction is set off. Many of the stories we published on eBay could not be contained within the confines of the Significant Objects laboratory! For example, Stewart O'Nan wrote a domestic vignette [Item 67] about a character named Emily and a duck-headed tray: Emily, who had previously appeared in O'Nan's 2002 novel, *Wish You Were Here*, became the protagonist of his 2011 novel,

Emily, Alone. Jim Hanas' story [Item 47] about a tense encounter between ex-lovers, one of whom wields a small wire basket, became the linchpin of a story cycle since published under the title *Why They Cried*. Readers who wondered about the Labors of Worthiness alluded to in Colson Whitehead's cryptic description of a shabby wooden mallet [Item 45] were able to learn more about them via his Twitter feed. We could go on.

Perhaps the inventiveness of our contributors was boosted by competitiveness; after all, their stories would eventually appear on a chart sorted by object sale price. We shy away from hypotheses that can't be tested, yet this would certainly explain why not a few of the stories attribute good luck or magical power to the objects we listed for sale: The object that sold for the greatest amount in our initial experiment was a homely Russian figurine described in Doug Dorst's story [Item 36] as a holy icon that might "come to life and begin dancing" – with combustible results. Other stories linked objects to famous figures or historical events: The solution to a real-life military-historical mystery, Bruce Sterling's story [Item 33] seems to suggest, has something to do with a boot-shaped paperweight; and Mimi Lipson's story [Item 58] places a particularly tasteless coffee mug in the possession of Andy Warhol.

For whatever perverse reason, several of our contributors sought to make the objects we'd assigned them less, not more, attractive than they were to begin with. A character in Ben Ehrenreich's story [Item 68] loses her marbles when they're plucked, one by one, from her skull. The Candyland labyrinth game in Matthew Battles' fable [Item 76], and the miniature bottle in Mark Frauenfelder's [Item 100], are cursed – you wouldn't want to own them, much less purchase them. The titular object of a few stories was, according to the narrative, destroyed. Kurt Andersen's story [Item 15] deploys both the competitive famous-figure and perverse less-attractive strategies: in it, an American pop-culture icon uses a Santa nutcracker for unspeakable ends.

Thanks to our contributors' imagination, a motley collection of geegaws was transformed into the inspiration for something truly priceless: great stories, published in a literary journal that used eBay as a platform. That was Significant Objects' second trick.

§

We're thrilled to reprint one hundred of the best stories from Significant Objects' first, second, and third volumes; and we're thrilled to be working with Fantagraphics, a publisher whose authors have been pushing the story-telling envelope for decades now.

FOSSIL	◉	Bears mute witness to a vanished way of life.
EVIDENCE	◉	Implicated in a crime or public event.
TOTEM	🦅	Offers wisdom from the natural world.
TALISMAN	♘	Magical, lucky, and/or alive.
IDOL	🗿	Intense contemplation lends it an aura.

KEY TO SIGNIFICANCE TYPE.

We've organized the one hundred stories in this collection by its object's intended-use type: Novelty Items, Figurines, Kitsch, Toys, and so on. Each story is also categorized by its object's significance type: a FOSSIL is an object that bears witness to a vanished era or way of life (including childhood); an object that played a role in a crime or public event is EVIDENCE; a TOTEM is an object from the natural world (animal, vegetable, or mineral) that acts as a tutelary spirit; a TALISMAN is an object that possesses magical power, is lucky, or is alive; and an IDOL is an object contemplated so intensely that, although it doesn't have any powers, it takes on an aura of significance.

Also, we have provided the original price, and final sales price, for each object. All of this data is provided, and parsed, in the Appendix.

§

WARNING: ARTIFICIALLY INCREASING THE SUBJECTIVE VALUE OF OBJECTS WILL MOST LIKELY LEAD TO UNINTENDED CONSEQUENCES.

ENJOY.

TABLE OF CONTENTS

Novelty Items

TOTAL SALES: 265.76

INITIAL COST: 13.56

ADDED VALUE: 252.20

I'm Glad I Spotted You!

ORIGINAL PRICE

$1.00

FINAL PRICE

$17.50

CURTIS SITTENFELD

It's not that I think I married the wrong man. Because really, how can any of us make a decision except as the person we are in a particular moment? I met Larry and Ronald less than two weeks apart, when I was nineteen. After high school, I'd moved into an apartment with a couple girlfriends from St. Agnes Academy, and we all thought we were very sophisticated, living on our own like that; Bernadette used to grow alfalfa sprouts in pantyhose in the tub. This was in '68, and I was working as a switchboard operator at a bank downtown. I met Ronald through a girl from work – he was the girl's cousin – and Larry I met on the bus riding home one day.

I was carrying an orchid plant I'd bought for the apartment, and he asked if I considered myself a flower child.

I dated them both, but not in a loose way if you know what I mean. That's how it was then – my girlfriends all dated more than one man at the same time, too. I liked Ronald better because he was taller and because it was harder for me to guess where things stood with him; I had to work to draw him out. Larry just flat-out adored me. He'd always compliment my outfit, and once when he said my perfume smelled nice, I told him in kind of a haughty way that I didn't wear perfume, it was just shampoo. At the movies he'd take my hand even before the trailers had ended. When he picked me up for a date, he'd mention whatever he'd seen or done since we'd last been together that had reminded him of me – a song he'd heard on the radio, for instance, or these spotted dogs, which he gave me after we'd been going out a couple months.

Part of the way I got Ronald to propose was by hinting that Larry might do it first, and that I'd say yes if he did. If I'm being honest, I can admit that while Larry did sometimes angle toward the topic of marriage, I'd always change the subject. I didn't want him to propose, maybe because I really wouldn't have known what to do but accept. Ronald and I had been married about three years when I heard that Larry and Bernadette, my old alfalfa-sprout-growing roommate, were engaged. I was pregnant then with Jenny, our second daughter, so this news didn't register much with me. Well, time passed – almost forty years, which just floors me to think about – and last spring Larry and Bernadette moved into a house one street over from ours. They'd been living in the western suburbs, so I'd hardly laid eyes on either of them all those years, and suddenly, at any hour of the day I can now see into the back of their house from the back of ours – they're not directly behind us, but they're only two lots down, so it's impossible not to notice if their lights are on or not.

Back when we lived together, Bernadette was so weight-conscious that she wouldn't lick stamps or envelopes because she said it was wasted calories, but she's gotten hefty since then. This is the thing, though – she and Larry sometimes stroll around the block in the evening, and I can see out our front window that they're holding hands, that when he turns to talk to her, the expression on his face is of pure devotion. Why didn't I understand when I was young how rare his kindness was, why was I so intent on shoving it out of my way?

Ronald and I have had a perfectly fine marriage, and he's a responsible husband and father, but we've never had much to say to each other; we eat dinner watching the local news. It's clear enough now that what I thought was a mystery in him worth teasing out is just a kind of flatness.

Again, it's not that I'm unhappy, but I will say that when I open the drawer of the dressing table where I keep these little dogs, they're such an unsettling reminder that sometimes just seeing them, my breath catches.

ORIGINAL PRICE	FINAL PRICE	
$2⁰⁰	**$32**⁰⁸	ITEM 02 SMILING MUG

BEN GREENMAN

This object is best known from its appearance in the 1939 film *No News From the Navy*, a comedy starring James Wilton as a hapless midshipman who cannot set aside his seafaring ways, even when he is confined to dry land as a result of an injury. Wilton's character (who is called, simply, "Sailor") competes for the affection of a young woman named Evelyn (Mary Hannan) despite the opposition of her father (Gordon Howard) and a larger, determined suitor (Kenneth Lopp). The film is a second-tier comedy, but there is one classic scene in which Sailor shaves before taking Evelyn out on a date. He is clearly accustomed to shaving aboard his ship, and as a result, he is constantly attempting to regain his balance, despite the fact the floor is level and stable. The critic Leonard Folsom has written that "The unheralded Wilton has a scene that combines the physical complexity of a Chaplin solo with close-ups of inexpressive expression that rival the finest moments of Keaton." At the beginning of that scene, Wilton uses this smiling mug as his shaving mug, and while he sets it on the shelf above the washbasin midway through, it remains, as Folsom writes, "an oddly compelling focus of the film so long as it is onscreen, enormous in its diminutive size, menacing in its cheer."

There are other shaving mugs that resemble this one, but none was created as this one was: by hand, with the assistance of a kiln, by a famous surrealist sculptor. This one was. In fact, it was wheel-thrown and fired by the Belgian artist Paul Coppens in 1932; Coppens, of course, was part of the group of artists supported by the patronage of Edward James. "I have dreamed of a smiling shaving mug," Coppens wrote to James in June 1932. "A sketch is attached. It looks like a face, of course, because a face is the only thing that is capable of smiling (or is it?), but it also looks like a tooth, because a tooth is the only thing that is capable of showing when a face is smiling. In addition, I have noticed that daily washing rituals, including shaving, are illogically equated with the whiteness of teeth. But there is more to the image. Look at the handle. It functions like an ear visually, but as there is only one, this figure is incapable of 'smiling ear-to-ear,' as the idiom has it. In addition, I have recently learned that 'mug' is a slang term for the human face in some parts of the English-speaking world. (Ironically, this practice comes from the fact that beer steins were fashioned in the human image, and unattractive specimens of our race were said be 'mug-faces.')" Coppens' piece, which he called *Tooth Fils* (the wordplay refers both to dentistry and to its small size), was part of the International Surrealist Exhibition in 1936.

How *Tooth Fils* came to be in *No News From the Navy* is simpler than the creation of either work. James Wilton, who himself trained as a painter and considered himself an acolyte of, if not a participant in, Surrealism, attended the exhibit, acquired it, and insisted that it be in every one of his films. As there was only one film, this is a condition that history has found easy to satisfy.

MATTHEW De ABAITUA

ORIGINAL PRICE

FINAL PRICE

$1⁹⁹

$15⁵⁰

ITEM 03
PIGGYBANK

My Daddy shouts at me when I go near the piggybank, and he screams when I turn it upside down. So I leave the piggybank alone and tell my baby brother and sister to leave it alone too. The piggybank is the family curse.

One day a week my Daddy is good to me, and he teaches me that words that sound the same can mean different things. Like *were* and *wear*. Like *sentence* and *sentence*. He listens to me as I read my stories and when I am finished he tells me how talented I am. I like those days. But on working days he is mean and tells me to shut up, before he has even heard what I am going to say. My Daddy's working days are hard, so hard. You wouldn't believe how hard they are.

Because of Grandad, our family has to keep the piggybank with us always. Grandad met the devil coming out of his wardrobe and the devil promised him death, death right there and then, and Grandad said no, and so a deal was struck. If the piggybank goes out the back door, death comes in through the front door.

On payday, one half of all the money that crosses the doorstep goes into the piggybank. Daddy comes back from his job making safe the gas in the iron lungs that rise and fall across our town, rise and fall like the valves of the trumpet he plays on our birthdays. He takes out his pay packet and pinches half of the notes between his fingers and hands the money to Mummy, without looking at it. It is Mummy's job to place the tribute into the cursed pig.

Daddy gets angry so suddenly, it makes it hard to breathe. I know he doesn't mean it. I tell him not to be so angry with me and he stops, and he looks sad. I'm a big girl. I know how hard the days of grown-ups can be, so hard you wouldn't believe.

Saturday is shopping day. Mum and I look around the shops. In the toy shop Frank, my little brother, plays with the train track, and he screams when the time comes for us to leave. None of the clothes fit Mummy right. There is nothing for us to buy. I see the scooter I want, the one with the special wheels. I go to the pig to see if there is money in it but the pig has eaten all the notes and left only coins.

Once I walked into the living room and found the piggybank choking on our money. Greedy piggy. I slapped it on the back and the money rattled back into its belly. When I turned it upside down, the money had gone.

This is the family curse, the same thing every week, the same for my Daddy as it was for Grandad and the same it will be for me, when I am older. Mummy looks for the bad hairs on her head and pulls them out. Daddy rolls moaning in his bed. I take a deep breath. The pig swallows and winks.

ITEM 04
LIGHTER SHAPED
LIKE SMALL POOL BALL

ORIGINAL PRICE

FINAL PRICE

$1<u>00</u> $27<u>00</u>

ROB AGREDO

"You lose," she puffed.
True.
Again.

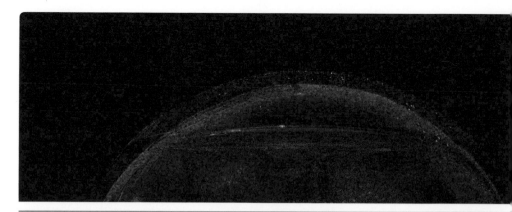

BLAKE BUTLER

99¢ $59<u>00</u>

ITEM 05
UTAH SNOW GLOBE

UTAH

My granddad's granddad had a box under his bed. If you got to open the box (you had to beg) you would find a little door. The little door had a combination on it that you had to know to get inside the second box, which I did. I had the combination tattooed on my spinemeat when I was four while on a trip to see the circus. The tattoo was free. My granddad's granddad was very powerful and rich.

With granddad's granddad in the bed asleep above me, I opened up the box inside the box. My knees were bloody from the begging. I could see way down into the box. There was a black pattern, then a ladder. I fell forward and grabbed ahold. The inside of the box smelled like the backyard where the money got made from skin. I began to climb along the ladder, getting older every rung. I was a very special boy.

The room under my granddad's granddad's room was octagon-shaped. As I climbed into the room, the mouth to it closed. The walls along the room were lined with little cubbies. There were more cubbies than I have days I've lived, or hairs that I have grown, which is also more than how many mouths I'd put my mouth against if I lived to be very, very old.

In each of the cubbies there was a little globe. Each globe held another little thing, each named with a label for what the thing was. There was a cubby with a globe containing FIRST EVER REDWOOD TREE. One containing PERRY MASON. One containing PEAS. The globe containing JOYOUS LONGING held a bright pink liquid smoke. PERRY MASON looked pissed off.

The globe containing UTAH made a burning sound against my head, and there were all these people chanting, and my face got all sandy and all wet. I shook it and it made my blood tingle and some coins appeared in my hands. I had so many gold coins I could live forever. Some of the coins were chocolate, which was food.

The ladder would not come back down. I could find no door in all the cubbies. No doorbell or key or gun.

In one cubby I could see out of the room beneath granddad's granddad's room. I could see back into the house where I'd grown up. In a little mirror on the counter across from where I was I could see back onto the label underneath the cubby in the house that held the globe I was inside now: MY GREAT GREAT GREAT GRANDSON.

ORIGINAL PRICE

$1.00

FINAL PRICE

$14.50

ITEM 06
MULE FIGURINE

MATTHEW SHARPE

This is the statue of the mule that I have sculpted by my hands, but if you are the serious person about the hand-sculpted statues, also serious when you are knowing how to feel the deep meaning in Life, then you will see that is not really the statue of the mule. I will not be able to say what the statue is truly because then I will be embarrassing and you will be embarrassing too if you are the serious person about it. "Not all of the things are to be talked about in the computer." But the mule is also to show how I am having many nations that I am coming from in my family background.

I, the selling person, am Hans Mifune, Artist. What is the Artist? It is the ancient river running in the new bed. (Also I do not always feel like getting out of the bed! Because my bedroom is small!) I must sell my beautiful artworks for that is sometimes only the way that the other people of the world can see my artworks and also then sometimes I can eat some things that are not the sandwiches with sugar and lard. And even these sandwiches sometimes do not have sugar and bread on them!

I am finishing this selling with saying how the "ashes" in the sculpture is because I have some pain to have so many nations at once as the location where I am coming from in life. The pain is not because of my many birth origins "in and to itself," it is because of the humans that live "in the world of them." I live "in the world of us." I hope that you live "also in the world of us."

You will have also the penny in the photograph of the mule for the same price that you bid the most to the statue of the mule plus shipping and handling.

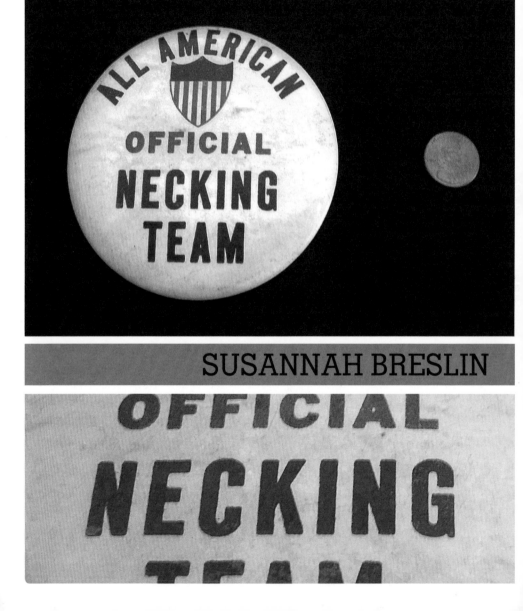

SUSANNAH BRESLIN

I reached my hand into the drawer, withdrew it, and looked at what lay in my palm. "ALL AMERICAN OFFICIAL NECKING TEAM," the pin read. It was hard to reconcile the words with my father. At this point, he had been dead for nearly 15 years. After he had passed away, my mother and I had stood over the dining room table upon which sat a large box that contained what was left of him. *Cremains*, the man had called them. *My father*, I had longed to correct him. Thankfully, my mother had been willing to share what remained of him with me, his only son. My father was a skyscraper of a man – six-foot-five, Ozymandias hands, a brooding forehead – a great man, really – and so, he had left a great deal of himself behind. I dipped a teaspoon into the mound of his ashes and placed three or so tiny shovelfuls into a plastic bag. I fastened the bag with a twist-tie. I put the bag in a small wooden box that smelled faintly of the peach tea it had once held. Later, my mother handed me a bag of his things, which, to be perfectly honest, I had forgotten about – until today, when I spotted it in the back of the drawer, behind my wife's underwear, and reached into the leather case and pulled the pin from it.

I imagined my father had won his place on the All-American Necking Team sometime during 1953, his senior year at Brooklyn Preparatory. I knew what he looked like back then from photographs: a young man with deep-set eyes undershadowed by dark circles, his long form gangly with the awkwardness of his youth, a thin tie knotted at the base of his bird-like neck. Once, my mother had told me about his penchant for drinking Zombies, about the time in the middle of a party, he had proclaimed, "I'm a tree," and then fallen flat to the floor, how she had stolen him from another woman older than her, who had a child – and in the remembering, my mother had smiled. But that summer, his father, my grandfather, a frustrated CPA with a roaring temper fueled by an abiding love of Four Roses and the failures of the Brooklyn Dodgers, had fallen dead of a heart attack while taking the IRT subway to work one day, and my father's life had changed forever. Instead of trundling off to some Ivy League college, he had stayed in Flatbush, enrolled at Brooklyn College, and dutifully taken care of his mother, a woman I'd never met, whose name was Rose.

Looking down at the pin staring up at me like a Cyclops, looking through this portal into a time wherein I was nothing but a flickering flash in one of my father's constellation of neurons, I wondered who this all-star necker was: my father, a young man not unlike myself, or something else altogether – a man beyond my understanding now relegated to a past that lay on the other side of a bridge where the land was so dark that I could no longer see him.

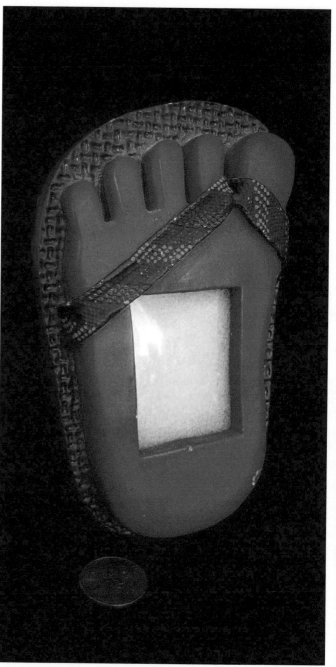

MERRILL MARKOE

A ny image that has been carefully placed in an antique gold frame embossed with angels and laurel wreaths becomes transformed into something elevated and celestial. "All you need to know about this old person/building/animal/plate of food/scenic vista/bleeding martyr is that it is sacred to me and holds a very special place in my heart," the frame seems to tell us.

But what if you are the kind of person who wishes to remember the bad times? You believe there is wisdom in being surrounded by cautionary tales – reminders of your most fatal blunders. How else to remind yourself to never again respond too quickly to a seemingly harmless social invitation and risk becoming mired in an evening so vile it undermines your sense of self-worth? So you bring home a memento of that detestable event: a whimsical cocktail stirrer or a personalized matchbook. But where do you put these wretched things? Or the snapshot you still have of that person you dated who stole your credit card and talked with a phony English accent? Let's not forget that former best friend of yours who calls to brag about the good things that happen to him by disguising them as disappointments, tragedies and inconveniences. "I'm so depressed," he says, "That deal I closed has moved me into a much higher tax bracket." Then he leaves you with a faux-ironic autographed photo of him standing in between Spencer and Heidi. You need a place to put that unpleasant souvenir of friendship gone sour. One that will admonish you never to take his phone calls again. Ditto the business card left behind by the tech guy who came to fix one broken USB port, disassembled your entire Internet connection, refused all blame, and insisted on getting his full fee.

Well, some people put these things at the center of dartboards. But that has become a cliché. And why run the risk of attracting unwanted dart games? No, when you want to demean an image, hold it up to spite and ridicule and single it out as something worthy of scorn, you want a frame that conjures a rage like the one that overwhelmed that Iraqi journalist who threw his shoes at George Bush. You want a frame that says "I step on you with my bare dirty feet."

This poorly articulated caricature of a foot wearing a flimsy multicolored flip-flop sits atop a frame that boldly declares, "Whatever I have enshrined here is something I hold in contempt. He/she/it is sub-par in every way: cheap, shallow, unimaginative, disposable, as void of any real value as the very worst, most despicable gift catalog. And just like the frame itself, they too are under the false impression that they are adorable and a welcome addition wherever they go." May they eat every meal for the rest of their lives from a plastic plate festooned with Santa's adorable helpers, listening to a never-ending loop of the opening line of "Up, Up and Away," by the 5th Dimension.

ORIGINAL PRICE

FINAL PRICE

50¢ $12<u>50</u>

ITEM 09
FRIDAY MUG

I think it was Ted Spain's to start with, though I'm not sure. He used to take it to meetings, and on Fridays before the all-staff I'd see him filling it with gin from a bottle he kept in his second drawer.

No, serious! He knew I knew, too – he looked up once and I was staring at him like you're looking at me, and he just sort of, you know – you want some? With a big smile on his face. I didn't take him up on it, but sometimes I think I should have. I mean, pretty much that whole year before you got here, I should have.

Anyway. So Ted had it, and he did that pretty much every week for five months until he got laid off when they got rid of the design staff. Remember? Right before Easter, too. And when he left, on his last day, he walked by my cube on his way out and set it on my desk, and it was full, and he winked at me and that's the last time I saw him.

So that's kinda how the Death Mug became the Death Mug. When Lara got fired, her and Manny and me went to the parking lot and did about five tequila shots each from it, and then when Sharon left to go take care of her mom in Seattle, she brought in some box wine and a bunch of us went over to the Piper and sat on the patio and drank it, and she drank out of the mug. And then she came back after her mom died, and they laid her off about six weeks later, and we did it again, only me and Tracey brought the wine this time and we made sure it was good wine.

"Nothing pink!" That was Tracey's rule. Good rule, right? For wine? "Nothing pink!" Only he said it the way Tracey would say it.

So I don't know. I guess it's a, a thing now. It's the Death Mug. We break it out every time this happens, or whatever. Three rounds of layoffs, plus Lara and then Tracey. And when Bette left to marry Evil Eye – God, she drank like half a bottle!

Anyway. I was wondering if you'd want to meet me outside. I have some gin in my car. It's been there since Easter.

And then, you know. I figured I'd leave it with you, right?

TODD PRUZAN

ORIGINAL PRICE

$2⁹⁹

FINAL PRICE

$14⁵⁰

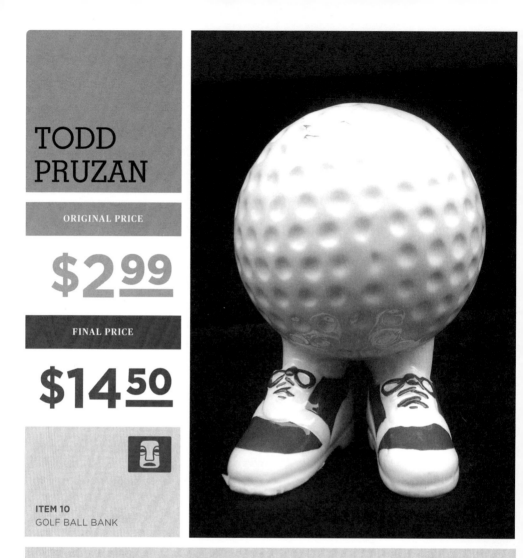

ITEM 10
GOLF BALL BANK

The worst thing is: he sees the golf-ball bank two, maybe three full minutes before it breaks his nose. It's sitting right there on the table, in full view of the whole room, next to a tiny recorder. This is 1980, and he's never seen a recorder so small, except maybe in a James Bond movie. There are dozens of cameras in the room, but the photographers who will be craning for a shot of it just a few minutes from now, something to get out to the wires before five o'clock, aren't paying the slightest attention to it. But oh, they will.

The woman who's about to wing the golf-ball bank at the senator's face is brandishing it with comic menace. She's running her finger along the red laces, tracing the ball's dimples. The senator is answering a question, but he's thinking about the golf-ball bank, trying to figure it out. Let's see: banking subcommittee, bill protecting The American People, he's out playing the 18th hole at Burning Tree when he should be voting on it, hey, sorry, welcome to Washington.

So what the hell: he just calls on her. Young lady, with that golf-ball bank with the tennis shoes. Heads turn her way. Deadpan aside into the bank of live mics: You look like maybe you're wantin' to throw that thing at me. Chuckles from the other reporters – and then she just does it. She really does it. She stands and picks it up and throws the bank at him, hard – not at all like a girl, he'll remember later – and nobody reacts, because it's too fast, and then it's flying and getting bigger and bigger until it breaks his nose, and finally, everyone gasps and shouts. The senator screams at an octave nobody realized he could reach, including himself. The audio will be replayed for months at inopportune moments on *Saturday Night Live*. Years after the general public has stopped recognizing it, a DJ in the Bronx will unearth the audio and turn the scream into a popular hip-hop sample.

The golf-ball bank hits the lectern first, then lands on the floor, on its feet. Two secret-service guards lunge for it, as though they really think it might run away, and clunk heads, hard. There's a scrum of arms around the woman, who's got straight blonde hair and enormous tinted glasses. Her chant, whatever it is, fades as she's pulled further away from the front of the chamber. One of the guards, without thinking, hands the golf-ball bank to the senator. He probably thinks the senator dropped it. The golf-ball bank is unbroken, and there's no blood.

The next morning, the *New York Post* is first out of the gate: FORE SCORE! One of his friends shows up at his Georgetown house with a copy of the paper. The senator signs: Craig – only 17 holes to go! Best wishes. The friend has a favor. He's got a nonprofit doing a silent auction that Saturday. Can they auction off the golf-ball bank. A piece of Washingtoniana, a piece of Congressional history. It's for a children's hospital. All yours, says the senator, and hands it over.

The winning bid on the golf-ball bank gets raucous cheers – it gets as much as a pair of season tickets to the Redskins. The bank then sits on a coffee table for four years. Then the family moves, and it sits in a box for more than two decades, until the youngest son is in college and finds it in the attic when he's looking for old VHS tapes. He mutters: No way.

The protester is retired now. She rarely does interviews, but when she does, she gets fired up again about the banking bill. It still gets to her. She doesn't regret the 72 months in jail. She's glad she did it.

The senator's legacy isn't in banking law but in Congressional security. Just try bringing a walking golf-ball bank into the Capitol Building today: you're liable to spend a few hours explaining yourself to stern-looking police officers before they let you go. (You're probably not really going to pull anything, they'll decide, finally. Probably not worth our trouble.) Sir: We're going to let you go, but you can't be bringing that in here. Leave that bank at home.

ORIGINAL PRICE

$1⁰⁰

FINAL PRICE

$14⁵⁰

ITEM 11
NUTCRACKER WITH TROLL
HAIR (OR SOMETHING)

Authentic
MR. YODELS
Love Totem
The "Sylvia St. Etienne" edition

This is the only witness to – or, some say, the cause of – the tragic death of legendary
chanteuse and muse to famous Ecuadorian footballer
Francisco Chavarria
NOT AN IMITATION!

Condition:
   The artifact is in good condition. Some slight damage, consistent with the violence of
the wreckage, on the *Tres Marias* rabbit headpiece and on the hand-painted ovoid eyes.

Otherwise the piece is exquisitely preserved, including (as required by the folk magic tradition) Mr. Chavarria's "plasma donation."

The Mr. Yodels Tradition:

Jacob Tauxe, the notorious "Swiss Voodoo Houngan" from Bern, designed the original line of ceramic Mr. Yodels figurines employed by frustrated suitors as love totems. By a feat of acoustic engineering yet to be explained satisfactorily, all custom-made Mr. Yodels figurines produce a distinctive upper-and-lower register song – the "love yodel" – when placed at an open window by which the loved one walks, provoking powerful spontaneous feelings of pair-bonding, veneration, and leghumpery.

Dangerous and unsanctioned Do-It-Yourself models – those made without knowledge of the proper techniques or precautions – are rumored to be responsible for the unions of Julia Roberts and Lyle Lovett, Woody Allen and relatives, Elizabeth Taylor et al., Chrysler and Daimler, and others.

The "Sylvia St. Etienne" Mr. Yodels:

Caracas, 1956. The fiery Ecuadorian striker Francisco Chavarria meets the legendary Hollywood songstress Sylvia St. Etienne, best known for her sultry interpretations of "Ashes in my D-Cup," "Cabana in Urbana," and "That Was It?"

For seven glorious, champagne-drenched, strawberry-inserting, mogul-free weeks the couple was inseparable – until Ms. St. Etienne met the mogul Sven "Big Krona" Uggla. Then they separated.

Heartbroken, and publicly humiliated, Mr. Chavarria vowed to get her back, but Ms. St. Etienne was – as they say in Monte Carlo – "*avec mogul.*" With no other recourse to intercourse, the jilted footballer traveled to Switzerland and implored Mr. Tauxe to fashion for him the most powerful of all Mr. Yodelses. But the Swiss Voodoo priest, bitter over Mr. Chavarria's last-second game-winning header over the Swiss, refused.

Desperate, Mr. Chavarria fashioned his own Mr. Yodels, ignorant of the necessary protocols, and tied it underneath the passenger seat of Big Krona's BMW 507 roadster, thinking, you know: *The windows will be down. Gotta work.*

Only ten hours later, after Sylvia St. Etienne gave the last performance of her life, singing the hits from "Hurry Up, These Sheets Itch and I'm Sweating," "Waiter! There's a Jackass in my Demitasse!" and "Side-Saddle Won't Work," she drove off into the night with Big Krona and plunged to her death in a mountain gorge.

All that remains of the great singer are her treasured recordings – and, now, available for the first time to the public, from the estate of Mr. Abernathy Hastings of Newport, this gloriously preserved Mr. Yodels.

Look at the eyes: you can almost see what Francisco Chavarria saw.

Witness the ears: you can almost hear what Francisco Chavarria heard.

Observe the mouth: you can fit a Bud Kinger in that thing.

Reserve set low by request of the estate, this auction represents a rare opportunity to own the last remaining vestige of one of the 20th century's most tragic love stories.

It may also possibly crack walnuts.

House & Table

TOTAL SALES: 461.27

INITIAL COST: 18.47

ADDED VALUE: 442.80

$2⁹⁹ $101⁰⁰

ITEM 12
"HAWK" ASHTRAY

WILLIAM GIBSON

In 1969 my friend's dad was a Pentagon technocrat. My friend said that when his dad came home with a new tie-tack, it meant there was a new weapon in the works. Not that there would *be* a new weapon, but that there was now a coterie of guys in the building who thought the idea was cool enough that they'd wear the tie-tack. It started with the tie-tack. If you couldn't get the über-geeks to wear your tie-tack, your project wasn't going to get off the ground. You had to demonstrate that your weapon had *fans*, and these guys didn't wear t-shirts. My friend said that Soviet spies should hang out at malls and supermarkets in McLean and take micro-telephoto pictures of tie-tacks. Because it was all there, *revealed*, this utterly top-secret quadruple-classified shit, on a background of plaid madras. And you could be sure that the weapon of mass destruction depicted there was really the very latest thing, because, he said, it was uncool to wear them once they became a done deal, just as it was uncool to wear them if they definitely weren't going to happen. What you wanted to demonstrate was that your tie-tack depicted something that was *liminal*, something still in the Dreamtime.

I imagined that David, my friend's dad, had one of those '50s dad boxes on his dresser. Where he kept his doohickeys. Cufflinks. Whatnot. And in David's box was a fistful of tie-tacks, their little anchor-chains hopelessly tangled, a secret history of Pentagon blue-sky imagination.

He was a good guy, David. In 1969 he told me that what was going to happen with the Soviet Union was that it was going to go bankrupt. He said they were cooking the books, fooling themselves that their economy worked, that their system made sense. He wasn't talking politics. He was an engineer. He was absolutely right, though I confess I didn't buy it. I couldn't imagine a world without the Soviet Union. He called it. The only thing he got wrong was the food riots. In the end, they weren't necessary. In the meantime, he said, we just had to hold them at bay. With tie-tacks.

This ashtray, I imagine, came from somewhere further along the Hawk missile system's developmental span. Ashtrays aren't liminal. When you're passing out ashtrays, you've actually got a product. When they passed a little spring-topped jewelry box, closed, to one of the über-geeks, that confidential "check this shit out" moment, it wasn't a product, it was a glyph, something there but not there, half-juggled from the Dreamtime.

A fossil from a future that you knew might not even happen. Dashing, enigmatic, unworn. Not yet tangled in the darkness of history's dad box, with the dead boys and the lost stupid war they died in.

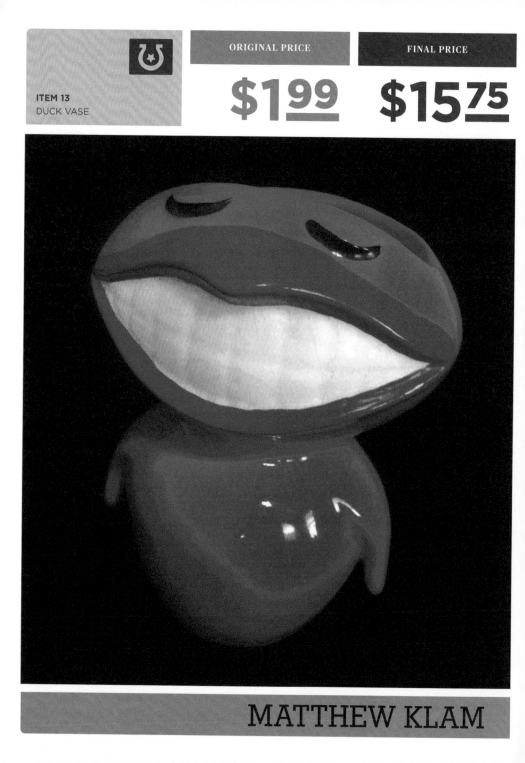

ITEM 13
DUCK VASE

ORIGINAL PRICE

$1⁹⁹

FINAL PRICE

$15⁷⁵

MATTHEW KLAM

I acquired this object at a flea market in the parking lot of a bilingual high school. Its little hands are smooth flippers. I believe it to be quite valuable, possibly antique, based on dates of patents listed on the ornate bronze panel on the inside door. Chinese in origin. Solid cast iron. Quite heavy. Designed to resemble the lead character of the short-lived American cartoon, "Chucky the Chicken." I never saw that show. There are knockoffs out there, and research indicates that knockoffs are made of brass or cheap plastic, but this one is well built, from original specs.

You may keep it in your car. You may keep it in your home. You may carry it on your person.

Be warned. There is a loud clicking sound coming from the control module.

For a while I kept this in my glove compartment. The original instruction manual mentions that the magnetic field it emits can change traffic lights from red to green. THIS DOES NOT WORK. Also, you will cause a pile up!

If you decide to keep it by your bed (as I did) and begin seeing colorful lights reflected on the walls and windows as you try to sleep, DO NOT WORRY AS THE OBJECT IS OPERATING NORMALLY.

DO NOT touch it or disrupt the cycle as this will cause IRREPAIRABLE HARM and may give you a POWERFUL ELECTRIC SHOCK. KEEP AWAY FROM CHUCKY UNLESS INSTRUCTED BY CHUCKY HIMSELF.

* Phase 1/Initial Phase: Transmission of messages.
* Phase 2/Functional Phase: Chucky cycling normally.
* Phase 3/Unity Phase: Walls bleed beautiful colors.
* Phase 4/Perfected Phase: Controller/controlled.
* Phase 5/Paradise Phase: Identity of Supreme Dictator revealed.

Chucky said to me, "HELLO MY LITTLE FRIEND. I am your GOD. Shift administrative tasks to your REPRESENTATIVE IMMEDIATELY. Prepare for LOVE SYMBOL."

Ha ha. And well we know what that love SYMBOL is now, DO WE NOT?

Certainly this object may have other uses. Keep it as an antique vase or planter, or with slight modification use as liquor locker, gun cabinet, bomb safe, champagne cooler, cocktail pitcher, etcetera. Dental detail alone is worth the price. Cannot verify that all parts are included. Cast iron is in excellent condition, however: do not microwave!!

Do not touch the outer shell with your tongue. Do not form contractions. FOLLOW THE MANUAL. Do not attempt modifications. Try to keep the dust out of his middle. CLEAN the inside WITH YOUR TONGUE if your TONGUE is long ENOUGH. THIS IS NOT HARD TO DO if you stick your tongue out. FARTHER. A LITTLE FARTHER.

N.B.: *Cast iron may actually be ceramic. Bronze panel and inside door may be difficult/impossible to locate. Instruction manual not included.*

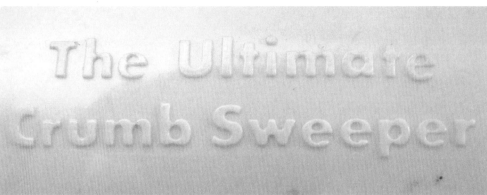

The Ultimate Crumb Sweeper

ORIGINAL PRICE

FINAL PRICE

$1⁰⁰ $30⁹⁹

ITEM 14
CRUMB SWEEPER

SHELLEY JACKSON

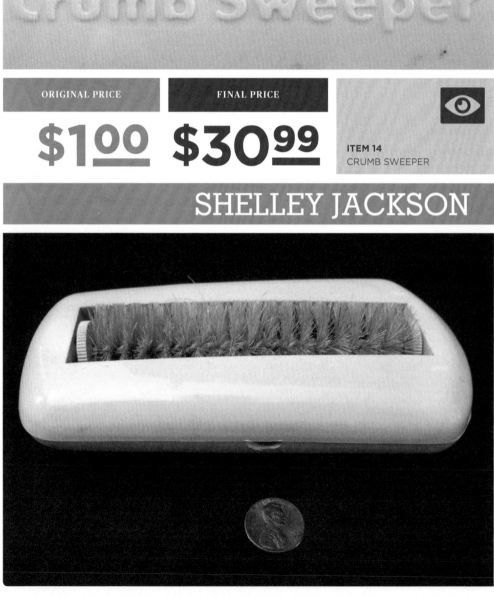

When I first met him, the moon – a chip of bone in the pale blue of morning – was just past full. I can be sure of that, though it was only later that the phases of the moon became as familiar to me as the seasons or as my breath coming and going. He was crouching against a tree in Prospect Park, nearly naked despite the autumn chill, the pale skin stretched over his shuddering ribs disfigured with a rash. He was swiping at his red, swollen, and tearing eyes with one paw, while the other, with a very practiced motion, was employing what looked at first glance like a bar of soap, to harry clouds of short, coarse, whisky-colored hairs from a pair of loose drawstring pants and a tunic draped over his lap. I did not think anything of the fact that both items appeared to be inside out. I did not pay any special attention to the fellow at all, who seemed to me an everyday sort of eccentric, only (for I have an eye for curiosities, particularly those ingenious contraptions rendered pathetically *de trop* by advancing technology – clockwork computers, water clocks and the like) to the object he was holding, which I now saw to be a rounded bar of ivory (or an imitation) in which a cylindrical brush had been ingeniously set so that it might skim a smooth surface and rid it of debris – the tool of a butler or maître d', I thought, for clearing crumbs from a place-setting.

I stopped to comment on it, reaching out a casual hand. He snarled at me, and I took my hand back, the small hairs standing up on my neck.

I hardly think I felt an attraction then, despite his undress; he was not a prepossessing sight, with his wet red eyes and nose, and his rash. So how can I explain, except by some atavism buried deep in the genes, that I did not excuse myself and continue on my way, but cringed down before him on the grass with a truckling grin?

Events followed, many good, some very bad. He left me this object and my life, which was good of him.

He was exceptionally fastidious, for a werewolf. Indeed, his whole family, or, I should say, his pack, was so. They left no bone unburied, and curried the furniture daily to rid it of hair. To do so was their pride, as an ancient, aristocratic family, but it was also necessity, since every member of that bloodline was congenitally allergic to dust, to dander and, such is the cruel levity of fate, to dogs – and a wolf is but a purer, more essential dog.

He is not the only person I have loved whose constitution was at war with his calling, but he handled it rather better than some.

ITEM 15
SANTA NUTCRACKER

$2.00 **$15.50**

KURT ANDERSEN

Although I live now in Indianapolis, I grew up in Gas City, which is a town (not a city) about an hour and a half northeast. During the summers after 7th and 8th grades, through a program run by the Grant County FFA (Future Farmers of America), I worked as the "hired hand" on a quarter section (160 acres) down between Jonesboro and Fairmount owned by a couple in their 70s named Mr. & Mrs. Winslow. Every weekend Mrs. Winslow (Ortense) baked a pecan pie, and so every Friday afternoon she'd have me crack and shell about a pound of pecans (Priester's). And I'd use this Santa Claus nutcracker to do it.

On one really hot Friday the first summer I worked there the two of us were on their porch, me cracking the pecans and she sitting in her metal chair, and she was looking at me odd, kind of smiling but kind of sad, too. She sometimes said weird things, which I chalked up to her age (like about her "time in Hollywood"), but since she was staring with that funny look and not saying anything I asked her if something was wrong. She said, "Oh, no, dear. It's just that seeing you, there in the afternoon light, in your t-shirt with your hair damp and pushed back, you suddenly looked to me just like Jimmy when he was your age. And gosh, he did love that nutcracker."

I didn't have any idea who Jimmy was, since her husband was Marcus Sr. and their son was Marcus Jr. But when I said "Excuse me, who?" she turned sort of weird, like I was making fun of her. "You've never ever seen Jimmy on TV?" she said. I told her we were Pentecostal, and didn't watch television, so she explained to me that Jimmy Dean was her nephew who she'd raised from the time he was nine years old, before he got famous. "Oh," I said "Jimmy *Dean*. That's interesting, Mr. Winslow. Do you get free sausage?" I assumed her nephew was the founder of the Jimmy Dean Sausage Company. She laughed and laughed, but then the phone rang and we didn't talk any more about him.

That night I asked my mom if she knew who the Winslows' nephew was, and she explained that "Jimmy" was James Dean, who'd grown up on the Winslows' farm in the 1940s and graduated from Fairmount High and then became a movie star. She said she'd never seen one of his movies.

A year later, Mr. Winslow died. And on my last Friday working at the farm, which must have been August of 1976, at the end of a long day, we were drinking lemonade, as usual, but this time Mrs. Winslow was putting vodka in hers. We were out on the porch again, me cracking pecans, and we'd just heard a train pass by and blow its whistle, and suddenly she asked if I wanted to take the Santa Claus cracker to keep, as a keepsake, since with Marcus Sr. gone she'd decided she'd stop baking pies. I didn't really want it, but to be polite I said sure, and thanked her. Then in a big gulp she finished her third glass, and sort of giggled. "But don't you ever do what I once caught Jimmy doing, OK?" When I asked what that was, she giggled again and said she couldn't say, but I chuckled too and kind of insisted, so she told me. One afternoon in the spring of 1945, when Jimmy was 14, she'd heard on the radio that the Nazis had surrendered, so she ran into Jimmy's room to tell him, and found him sitting on his bed with his pants off and his penis stuck in the nutcracker.

She smiled and shook her head. I didn't reply, and at that point she seemed to realize it was, as my kids would say, "TMI," and stood up and took the pitcher of lemonade and her glass and the vodka bottle inside.

But I did take her nutcracker home, and have kept it ever since. Until recently, the only other person I ever told about what they call its "provenance" was my wife – my ex-wife now – and I didn't want to reveal it publicly until our kids were grown, since I thought it would embarrass them (or worse) when they were little. Plus, Mrs. Winslow has long since passed on. So when my girlfriend, who's a Realtor, told me she'd seen on *Antiques Roadshow* that a jacket of James Dean's was worth $1000, I told her about the nutcracker. And now she's convinced me to sell it. She says I owe it to history and, in a financial sense, to myself. (I called the guy who runs the James Dean Gallery, up north of Fairmount, at Exit 59 off Interstate 69, to find out how much it might be worth, but he pretty much hung up on me.)

Although I haven't cracked a nut with it since that afternoon in 1976, I have no reason to believe it doesn't still work fine.

ED PARK

ORIGINAL PRICE

$2⁰⁰

FINAL PRICE

$62⁰⁰

ITEM 16
COW VASE

If you came of age in the '70s and '80s, you probably have some sense of what the fantasy game *Dungeons & Dragons* was like. Players became characters – dwarf or knight or wizard – and wandered labyrinths looking for treasure, battling monsters along the way. Dice were rolled, charts consulted. Even if you never played, you probably knew someone who had, a brother of a friend or a nose-breathing cousin who himself resembled a minotaur.

Serious gamers will also recall other so-called roleplaying games that cropped up during this era, such as *Traveler*, a militaristic science-fiction title with a map of the galaxy; or *Gamma World*, set in a post-apocalyptic America, in which your character had weird but potentially useful mutations – infrared vision, extra leg. But I don't know anyone, aside from me and my next-door neighbor, Darren, who'd even heard of *Mountains of Moralia*, the sole offering of Radon Claw Game Labs.

The cover of the utilitarian rulebook featured what looked like a large gray triangle, which upon closer inspection revealed itself to be the titular land formation, spidered with trails, along which motley caravans of adventurers clashed with trolls, rocs, slavering wolf packs, and sentient malevolent vegetation.

Glimpsed a certain way, one could discern two dark watery eyes and a ragged mouth incised in the mountain itself – the first clue that all was not as it appeared on Moralia. The first section of the rulebook was a 10-page description of some fabled road that all travelers must take to approach Moralia – a text seemingly designed to make potential players chuck the thing in the trash. Darren read it aloud, as fast as he could, and then we turned to the pages concerning Character Generation.

Curiously, one did not play a single adventurer (dwarf, wizard, etc.), but instead took on the character of a huge chunk of land – that is, a Mountain of Moralia. What I'm saying is, you basically pretended you were a mountain. As if hypnotized, we followed the rules to the letter, rolling dice in the strange permutations typical for fantasy games. But this time the results were applied to things like Forest Coverage, Erosion Quotient, and Mammal Population.

Soon we had generated our two mountains. I named mine Epak's Peak; Darren dubbed his This Totally Sucks. Part Two was a sample scenario in which the mountains ... fought each other. Using Land Magik, you flung your rocks, animals, trees, grass, dirt, and so forth at the other mountain, trying to reduce it to rubble. However, as you lost these items, you were reduced, and there was a chance that, say, a boulder flung at your opponent became embedded in its side, thus giving it more mass.

This went on for round after round, hour after hour, and should have been the most boring thing in the world. Yet Darren and I soon found ourselves playing *Mountains of Moralia* to the exclusion of all our other games.

When Darren finally emerged triumphant, we jumped to Chapter 8, where we learned that we had just finished waging the Battle of Lavache, and that we could send in a certificate, signed by all players, for a free limited-edition trophy.

We sent it in, waited for six weeks. This is what we got. We never played *Mountains of Moralia* again. When I found this cow figure last week, stored with the fine china, I e-mailed Darren and asked if he still had the game. He said he didn't know what I was talking about.

ORIGINAL PRICE

FINAL PRICE

—DONATED—

$21⁵⁰

ITEM 17
BIRTHDAY CANDLES

SCARLETT THOMAS

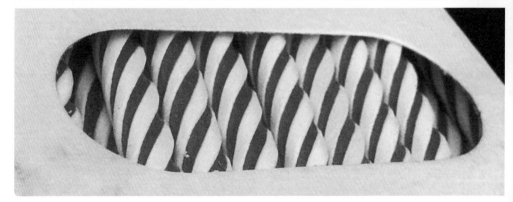

You can find all kinds of crap in the back of drawers. Here is the string we once used to tie the handles of the French doors together so that Julius wouldn't open them and walk into the pond. Here is a thimble, and a seam-ripper, although I don't think anyone in our family ever ripped a seam on purpose. Here is an incomplete pack of cards with topless women on the backs, the best ones stolen by my brothers. Here is dust, dust, and underneath a pair of dice: one small and black, one big and red. There is a blister pack with no tablets in it and the silver tape measure that bites your fingers when it snaps back. There are the birthday candles I bought when I was seventeen. After I bought them I walked home from the corner shop imagining the hot wax dripping onto my naked skin and Mark, who still owed me for the mayonnaise thing, peeling it off after it had dried.

ORIGINAL PRICE

FINAL PRICE

$2⁴⁹ $61⁰⁰

ITEM 18
LETTERS AND NUMBERS
PLATE

JOE LYONS

It's true that there are many accounts of fascinating Amish dinnerware, but none is more interesting than Samuel Stoltzfus' Divining Plate, forged in 1881. "Limpy Samuel," his nickname after a disagreement he had with a mule, originally created the plate as a gift for his son, Moses. Samuel meticulously etched the alphabet and numbers around the edge of the plate, which was forged from scraps of metal and discarded Civil War muskets that could still be found in the fields. The hope was that his son, who had difficulty with his lessons, could learn while he was eating. But the plate would prove to be far more useful than an educational tool for Moses, who was a lost cause anyway.

For you see, one of the muskets that Samuel melted down for the plate was responsible for the bludgeoning death of Thomas Becker, a Union soldier and the fourth son of Martin Becker (who was also a fourth son). This, combined with the fact that 1881 was an astrologically perfect year for inter-dimensional rifts, made the plate particularly susceptible to otherworldly influence ... which is exactly what occurred when Samuel etched the letters and numbers on it. Doing so invoked the essence of one of the Good-But-Not-Great Old Ones, an otherworldly deity as old as time, whose name contains all of the letters of the alphabet and the numbers zero through nine. The only way to come close to pronouncing its name is to say "Abercrombie Snooze Mine" slowly, while slapping oneself in the throat.

One day Samuel was using the plate to cool down nails he was making in his shop. He looked down at the metal shavings floating in the water he had in the plate and said aloud, "Will these nails hold true?" Suddenly, the shavings joined together and floated to the edges of the plate until it spelled out "Yes." Intrigued, Samuel continued: "How many will I need for Jonathan's barn?" The shavings pointed to two, then five, then zero. Convinced his eyes were deceiving him, he asked, "What happened to my best hammer last spring?" After about fifteen minutes, the shavings eventually spelled out "Hezekiah pilfered it."

From then on, after the vicious shunning of Hezekiah, Wise Limpy Samuel (his new nickname) used the plate and its gift to become the most respected elder in his community. Samuel always seemed to know how the weather would affect the crops and whose thoughts were the most sinful. The plate was always Samuel and Jesus' secret, since he assumed it was Jesus in the plate and not an inter-dimensional being, and he only used it to help his people.

After Samuel passed, Moses sold the plate in Harrisburg for two dollars, which he then spent on rock candy. Today, it sits on the back shelf of an antique store near Philadelphia, where it continues to answer questions, but its revelations, which have included World War II, disco, and the fact that six-year-old Stephanie Lewis of Baltimore would one day marry Michael Huther even though she thinks he's "gross," go unnoticed.

JEFF TURRENTINE

ORIGINAL PRICE

25¢

FINAL PRICE

$50⁰⁰

ITEM 19
"WOMEN & INFANTS" GLASS

TASTING NOTES

All wines were stored at 55 degrees and decanted for one hour before being poured into the same glass (pictured) – which, as regular readers know, is the only glass I ever use.

Marques de Riscal 2004 Rioja Reserva ($29)
Explosive cherry notes, which gently yield to black pepper, vanilla and tobacco. Assertive but not overbearing tannins. When I was ten months old, my mother made

my father breakfast one morning, kissed him on his way out the door, then grabbed me and her packed suitcase and loaded us both into an airport-bound taxi. By the time he returned home that evening, we were halfway across the country, in Oregon. I didn't see him again for sixteen years. This wine will cellar beautifully, but can be enjoyed now: think red meat, roast chicken, or even pizza.

Guenoc 2005 Lake Country Petite Syrah ($17)

Super jammy, heavy on plum and blackberry. Less astringent than other young Petite Syrahs. So the story went, my dad was a real bastard: verbally abusive, wholly uninterested in fatherhood and all it entailed, an incorrigible and unapologetic skirt-chaser. My mother withstood it for as long as she could, until one day when he became enraged over the electric bill or somesuch and she feared, for the first time, that he might actually hurt her, or maybe even me. No reason to get too fancy with pairings here: a perfect companion for burgers or red-sauce pasta dishes.

Bertani 2002 "Catullo" Veneto ($20)

Wow. Stunningly bright fruit (especially cherry and blackcurrant), moderate acidity. They were officially divorced a year later. Whenever I would ask my mom about my dad, or wish aloud that I could meet him, she would say that every time she tried to arrange for a visit he balked at the last minute, citing some work-related or personal conflict that couldn't be avoided. I spent my childhood believing that my dad just wasn't interested in meeting me, much less being a part of my life. I served this with some re-heated Chinese food the other night and drank the whole goddamn bottle by myself, it tasted so good.

Provenance Rutherford 2000 Cabernet Sauvignon ($30)

When I was sixteen I went rummaging through our garage, looking for my old base-ball mitt, and I found a cache of letters, dozens of them, all from my dad, and all of them pretty much boiling down to the same plea: *Come back, Barbara. Please. I know I love you more than he does. I forgive you. Please come back and bring my only son with you.* I confronted my mother, and she tearfully admitted that she'd been lying to me my whole life. This wine is just okay. Personally, I wouldn't pay thirty dollars for it – but then again, I don't ever pay for wine. It's delivered to my door practically every other day. My dad wasn't a bastard at all. My mother had left him because she had convinced herself that she was still in love with an old boyfriend back in Oregon. Her marriage had simply been a huge mistake, she said. When I finally met my father a year later, he told me that he didn't contact me, didn't ever let me know the truth, because – his words – he didn't want to destroy my relationship with my mother. It was better that I grow up hating him, since I would never have another mother, but it was possible that I might one day have a new stepfather. You know what? I take back what I said about this wine. As I drink it, right now, in my favorite glass, it tastes fantastic. It gets the job done, and in the end, that's what counts.

ITEM 20
KITTY SAUCER

ORIGINAL PRICE

$1²⁵

FINAL PRICE

$15⁵³

JAMES PARKER

"You know, of course," said the periodontist, as he bore down with his scalpel, "that Nancy Pelosi is insane?"

Floyd Haruspex, gaping and nearly prone in the chair, made no answer. The question had been rhetorical anyway.

"She is, excuse me, batshit crazy ... Any pain?"

"Ngh-ngh," answered Floyd, emphatically. Halfway through this operation to fix his receding gums and he was feeling no pain at all. The left side of his mouth and face had in fact become a miraculous region of pure psychology. No sensations, only ... impressions, intuitions, insights. Ah, Novocain.

"Let me know," said the periodontist, whose name was Dr. Soundgarden.

But now Floyd like a saint was gazing beyond this earthly scene, gazing over Dr. Soundgarden's meaty white-clad shoulder and out through the window. Rainy ocean sky. Undifferentiated sub-glare. A vast range of numbness. Somewhere out there was Diagnostic Jones with his pack of Harley-riding Illuminati, all pushing their hogs through the last frontier of mechanical endurance en route to the big kahuna, the king burrito, the cosmic giggle-osaurus. And Prima Materia, alchemical sex-siren. Tying one on in some cheesy maritime bar no doubt, with several new friends of the fishing or dope-running persuasion. Would he, Floyd, ever get the chance to *dissolve* and *coagulate* with her – to produce with her the philosopher's stone? Yeah, right.

"What's happening with this country right now, I'd like to go to sleep for ten years." Dr. Soundgarden was talking again, while his hands in their bloodied plastic gloves made squinching sounds in Floyd's mouth. "Sleep for ten years, wake up, maybe things'd be back to normal. Know what I'm saying?"

Floyd inclined an eyebrow *à la* Errol Flynn. He was at the shoreline, and some sort of John Bircher was fixing his gumline. Karma was a pretzel sometimes. And he hadn't even *begun* to think about the kitty plate. Why had someone left it in his car last night, this little milk-saucer with the face of a cat painted on it? He had floundered heavily into the driver's seat, with the bar-reek on him, to find it propped on the dashboard like a rebuke. The cat was ginger-ish, with a distant, unreadable expression. "And the same to you, partner," Floyd had mumbled, tossing it onto the back seat and scraping at the ignition. He'd never owned a cat. He didn't like cats. Which was not to say that he didn't understand the cat thing: he knew any number of ex-radicals and tired misanthropes whose single connection to the world-as-commonly-experienced was via some sullen feline. Barney Breaks, for example, the P.I. he'd hired to spy on his first wife. Pissed-off to the core. A disenchantment with humanity that was truly cosmic. Now there was a cat guy.

Could it have been Barney who left the kitty plate in Floyd's '66 Chevy Impala? As a message that his darkest apprehensions re: Prima Materia were about to be realized?

But Barney had joined a cult three years ago: the Joy People, out of Humboldt County. Never been heard of since, poor bastard.

Besides, the cat on the plate wasn't giving a message. If anything, he was withholding a message. That's what cats did, right? Unlike everything else, they refused to signify. And Floyd, in the periodontist's chair, began to shake with unphraseable laughter.

ITEM 21
FLANNEL BALL

LUC SANTE

After my friend Claude had his accident I went to visit him in the hospital. When I saw him I had to cough to divert a laugh. He looked like a guy in a cartoon, his entire body wrapped in bandages. He had broken everything that could be broken, from his skull to his toes. Somehow he was conscious and could speak, although to hear him I had to put my ear right up to his mouth-hole. I thought he said "door," so I shut it, but he was still agitated. Eventually I got it: "drawer." The one in his bedside stand contained a single object, a ball of wrapped flannel that looked like his head, only more colorful. I went to pick it up with my fingertips, but then had to readjust. Astonishingly, the thing weighed at least five pounds. I gaped at it, but Claude was making noises. I finally understood: "Don't unwrap it."

Claude went to glory a week later, felled by some hospital bug. The ball sat on the shelf next to my bowling trophies. Occasionally I'd blow the dust off and pick it up just to feel its weird heft. After a while I forgot about it, as stuff got parked in front of it and stayed there. One night I was rooting around trying to find my paintball gun and there it was. When I picked it up it seemed twice as heavy. I got spooked and reburied it.

Time passed. The seasons came and went: hockey, muskrat, sweeps week, estrus. I grew a mustache and shaved it off, twice. I enjoyed the stylings of eight cars for varying lengths of time. I fell in love with Sheila, Bambi, Marla, Candy, Darla, Brandy, and Concepción. At work I climbed from office boy to field officer to regional sales manager to CFO, and then back down again. My apartment grew ever denser with stuff. I could barely move around, and tended to use and wear only things from the top layer, a fleeting category. One time I was poking around for some itch cream when my hand grasped the ball. I couldn't move it.

Then, on a dark November morning, as I was lying in bed watching paragliding accidents on TV, the crash came. My shelves buckled and caved in the middle, one by one. There appeared a sinkhole in the floor, which sucked piles and piles of stuff down to hell, or at least the garage level. Then cracks appeared in the walls.

As the other residents and I huddled across the street in our bathrobes, watching the fire department string caution tape around the building, the whole thing shuddered briefly and then dissolved in a blizzard of concrete. We stood transfixed and mute as the dust died down, what seemed like hours. Then something emerged from the ruins, a colorful little ball that seemed to shoulder its way out and then rolled straight to my feet. I picked it up. It weighed nothing.

ORIGINAL PRICE

FINAL PRICE

3\underline{^{00}}$ 37\underline{^{00}}$

WAYNE KOESTENBAUM

Gloria Swanson owned a duck nutcracker. Guests, including Jean Harlow and Franchot Tone, cracked nuts at Gloria's cocktail parties.

After Gloria died, John Travolta inherited the contraption. He brought it out as a conversation piece when Roland Barthes came calling.

Then the duck nutcracker fell out of favor.

I found it at a hand-me-down tchotchke shop in Culver City and bought it for Nicole Kidman.

Nicole grew furious at the nutcracker's improper performance.

"The stars are peeved at me," thought the duck.

And: "I'm not to blame for the rancid walnuts that enter my body."

Nicole gave the nutcracker to Miranda, her dipsomaniacal cook, who returned it to me.

I put my wedding-ring finger in its vise and broke my knuckle.

The duck asked to be psychoanalyzed.

The duck is not fake! The duck has an unconscious!

The duck wished that Jayne Mansfield were alive. Only Jayne understood the duck's delicate sensibility.

"I, too, had a career," thought the duck, remembering happy-go-lucky, pre-doom days, when *The Girl Can't Help It* set the tone.

The duck was delusional.

"I'm a Valkyrie astride her wingéd horse," thought the duck, stuck in a phase of adolescent rebellion against invisible authorities.

I forgot to mention an important fact. The duck was made in Lisbon in 1925 by a Jewish mystic named Abraham Pacheco, who lived in a dusty, book-crammed atelier on the Largo de São Carlos, near Fernando Pessoa's house. Abraham overcame a mild case of tuberculosis, fell in love with a dissident nun from the Convento da Ordem do Carmo, and eloped with her to Hollywood, where they opened a duck nutcracker shop, frequented by the stars.

Decoration

TOTAL SALES: 780.89

INITIAL COST: 19.73

———————————————

ADDED VALUE: 761.16

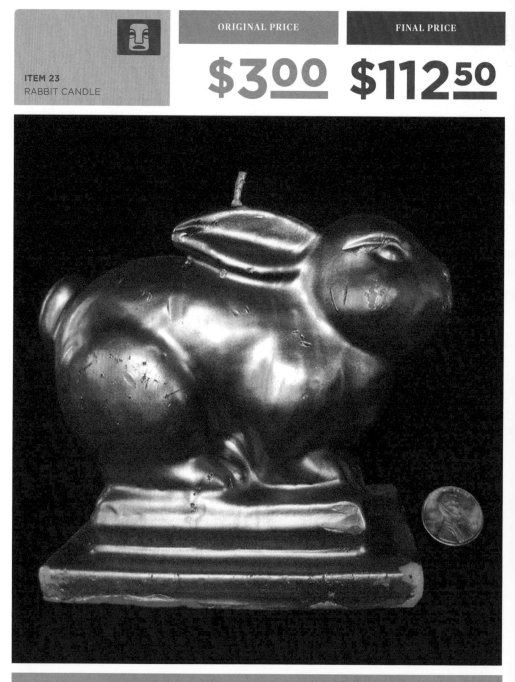

NEIL LaBUTE

Instead of walking home the way I usually do – past Maple and cutting over on Ivar before getting to the river – I decided to save a little time and turned right, going down toward the church instead of around it. They were having a yard sale on that scruffy patch of grass on the side of the rectory, near where the old chestnut tree had fallen down back when I was in the third grade. The stump is still there, in fact, and I could see it as I was passing. So many names carved into its now smooth and weathered face. I slowed at the sight of all the mothers and children bunched together on the lawn – for such a dark November day, it seemed as if a street fair or something colorful like that was going on. I drew a little closer and poked around a bit, picking up a magazine or two, sifting through a stack of dishes. I moved on to the next long table, past a small mountain of discount clothing and there it was. The golden bunny. It was still chipped in many places, the fingernails of dozens of children who must've touched it over the years up there in His room. Marveled at it sitting on His desk while they waited for Him. Watched Him. My friend Tim swore it was "yellow" but I knew the truth – perhaps I alone – that it was made of real gold and that there was an actual bunny buried deep inside the wax. He promised me that one day, if I was very good, that we would light it together and set the bunny free, that if it burned long enough and if I waited there in the dark with Him quietly enough, that it would emerge from its fiery prison and be mine. Mine alone to keep or to take home or to play with as I wished. That is why I kept going back in the beginning. At least in the beginning. The rest is unclear and haunts me still, coming back in fits and dreams and jobs that I can't keep and endless bottles of liquor I consume. The rest is a lawsuit that remains tied up in court and my friends looking away from me when they see me coming or in the stands at local baseball games. The rest is all of that and more. The golden bunny, though, is untouched in my mind, sitting on the edge of His desk and calling out to me. Even from up there on His bed, with my head buried in a pillow I could still see it. Reach out for it. Touch its glowing, golden nose. Yes, even from there.

§

I bought the thing for fifty cents and hid it in the back of a drawer when I finally got home. Behind two stacks of old instruction manuals. I only bring it out when my wife is safely asleep in her room.

TONI SCHLESINGER

"I have something for you," she says.

"For me?" he asks.

"For you!" she says. "Wait, waiter, I'll have a pale gold drink."

"For you?" asked the waiter.

"I'll have one that's blue." He coughs. "I'm so excited."

"Here it is." She places the 4-tile on the table.

"Oh," he cries. "But it's not Valentine's Day."

"Why does that matter?"

"You know, the candy heart that reads 4 U but without the U. What is it?"

"You remember ..."

"Of course! You had it made to remind me of the four times I strayed."

"I wouldn't do that."

"Yes, you would!"

The waiter returns. "Here are your drinks, for heaven's sake."

"I know, that time we discussed having a foursome!"

"We never did. That sort of thing is so out of fashion."

"God. It's from Vegas. Some indicator of money lost or gained."

"No, you're being too formal in your thinking."

"It's the 4 from the height chart in the lineup of suspects where you had to stand when you were arrested for murdering that man in Tennessee?"

"You're getting close. Don't look so forlorn."

"I'm foraging. Perhaps the waiter knows."

The waiter looked at the ceiling. "It's not for me to say."

"I'll give you a hint. A summer day, all the world was as blue as your drink. You flew through the air ..."

"... and I dove into the cool water of the swimming pool and I thought of marimbas and orchids and forsythia and when I came up ..."

"You said, 'Be mine forever.'"

"No, I said, 'Be mine – for now.'"

$3⁰⁰ $23⁵⁰

ITEM 25
CERAMIC SHELL

CHARLES BAXTER

This beautiful object was discovered in downtown Minneapolis, Minnesota, by a high school student, Emily Traumer, on the corner of North First Street and Third Avenue. Emily was waiting for the morning bus and was bored, as adolescents usually are. Looking down to see if her Doc Martens were tied, she saw a meteorite on top of a pile of shoveled snow. She picked it up. It was still warm from its fiery entry through the Earth's atmosphere.

She dropped the meteorite in her pocket. It radiated inter-stellar warmth throughout the bus ride all the way to Anton Kiesiewicz High School, where her science teacher, Mr. Duderstadt, complimented Emily for her sharp eyes. He pointed out to her that the shell pattern, quite characteristic of meteorites generally, was produced by the "turbo effect" of oxygen and nitrogen against the rock as it enters the atmosphere. The characteristic blue coloring on the larger side of the rock is a result of the "spectrum burning" of heat against the materials, producing a glass-like surface; hotter surfaces turn blue, while cooler surfaces, shielded from the direct heat of atmospheric forces, remain white. The formula for such heating, Mr. Duderstadt said, approaching his blackboard, could be written out as follows:

$$\rightarrow = \sum (34f) - 2^{TM} + \$5.32 \geq 4\% \times \Omega \left([@5\pounds7] + \yen5\right)$$

He then inquired whether he might take the meteorite over to the University of Minnesota's Fowlwell Hall, where the eminent astrophysicist, Professor Heinz Schlempp, might take a look. Emily agreed, somewhat reluctantly.

Four days later, Mr. Duderstadt returned with the meteorite. "Well, Emily," he said, during his Wednesday science salon, "that's a very interesting piece you have there."

"Was Professor Schlempp able to determine of what materials the meteorite consisted?" Emily inquired, somewhat baffled, syntactically, by all the attention her discovery was garnering.

"Yes, he was," Mr. Duderstadt said.

"What's in it?" the impatient schoolgirl asked.

"Well, that's the interesting part," Mr. Duderstadt said, leaning back in his chair, and rearranging his necktie. "Professor Schlempp put it into his spectrometer, and then placed a tiny microscopic sample into the Gigatron® electron microscope, and then, dissatisfied with his result, put the meteorite into the university's Super Vulcan X-ray Analysis Machine, where a definitive analysis finally became possible."

"And?"

"Well, here's the surprise," said the genial wizard of Kiesiewicz High. "The piece naturally has a high content of Iron, whose symbol, as you know, is *fe*. But more interesting was Schlempp's discovery that the object has a high content of the rare earth, Probabilium, along with a certain amount of Potassium, Cyanide, and Blorth."

"*Blorth*?" asked Emily. "That's awesome!"

"The rarest of metals!" Mr. Duderstadt cried out. Turning around, he wrote on the blackboard again. "To get Blorth," he said, "you have to have the following force-fields in an inter-active matrix."

$$\text{æ} = 45\pounds \neq 8! \times \rightarrow 2 \geq 14\text{®}$$

"Wow," the astonished teenager said.

"Exactly. This meteorite is priceless. And not only is it priceless, it's beautiful. And useful."

"I could use it as a paperweight," Emily said.

"There's no limit to a person's imagination," Mr. Duderstadt said, conclusively.

MIRANDA MELLIS

Once you went on a school field trip and were shown the constellations in the false night of a planetarium. You looked hard trying to see ... *something* more meaningful than the connect-the-dot resemblances to hybrid animals that had so captivated the ancestors. Finally, space was more interesting as an idea. Space suggested alternate worlds, different ways of life even. Perhaps there were aliens not ruled by the rhythms of school and production, living in the *hooky* state of mind, an abdication practiced by children and teenagers in search of the meaning, or the meaninglessness of time. Being on a field trip was not exactly hooky, but it had the expansive flavor of freedom. The class met only to disperse in a herd, loose enough to move across the city, tight enough for collective purpose.

The tour of the stars at an end, you filed back outside with the others into the blinding afternoon light to eat lunch in a courtyard with gnarled, leafless trees and a penny-filled fountain. Your friend Cassandra ate next to you across from her mother who stood casually but watchfully by. Cassandra's straightened hair was coiffed in the usual respect-arousing topknot. A flame-shaped bang swooped across her forehead tapering down by her temple. At times Cassandra's mother and father tried to convert you to the ways of the Jehovah's Witnesses, but you were a committed atheist. Once you told them that your mother was a communist, they let you be. Cassandra didn't mind at all that you did not share the same cosmology. You never tried to convince her that God was a made-up parent figure for adults, and she had no interest in converting you. Moving closer to her, you opened your lunch box and then closed it immediately before she could see the contents.

Although you understood by now that bad desires were implanted in you by advertisements – messengers all bearing the same message – and that your desire for a tiny pencil-hugging koala bear and a miniature license plate with your name on it, let alone a television, were forms of false consciousness, you were still full of normative desire. Yet you had developed a broad appreciation for objects not marketed to you. Comrades gave you carpentry tools and unusual rocks on your birthday, and you were not ungrateful. You knew that history was written by the victors, that reality was mutable. But was it too much to expect real food in your lunch box? Why the plastic sandwich, the rubber carrot and the brass apple on this happiest of days, when everyone had permission to leave school for more stimulating environments? Nothing in your experience had prepared you for this blind-siding prank on the part of those you were now considering running away from, when you realized that you had mistakenly picked up the toddler's toy pail by the door in your fervor to make the bus. Relieved of anger and blame, you were more than content to be simply hungry.

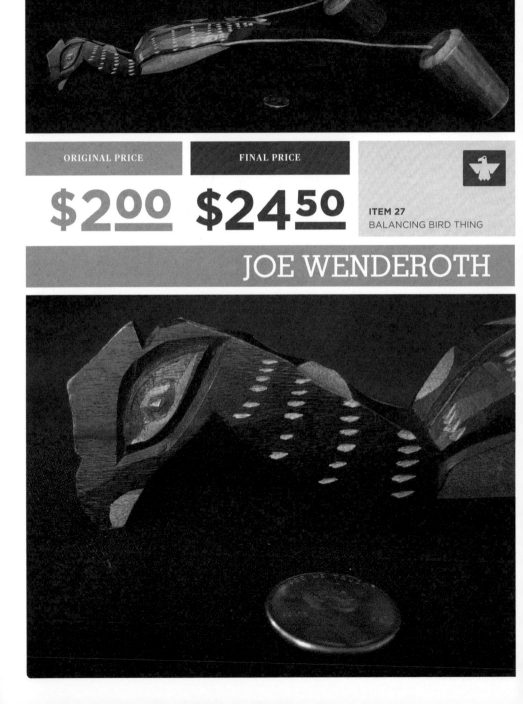

ORIGINAL PRICE

FINAL PRICE

$2.00 $24.50

ITEM 27
BALANCING BIRD THING

JOE WENDEROTH

Up for your consideration is this Antique Icelandic Menstruating Judgment Bird. Early Icelandic Judges used these birds to determine the outcome of all serious arguments. It was also used domestically – with considerably less ceremony – to resolve smaller household arguments. It works like this: in an outdoor space, bricks are stacked – two stacks; between the two stacks, a yarn is pulled tight and secured beneath the top brick on both sides. Next, a Birdman (a native Icelandic priest) tries to balance the Menstruating Judgment Bird on the yarn. If the Bird remains balanced for the next ten seconds (in the Birdman's head), the Bird has become ripe for Pronouncing Judgment. After ten seconds (in the Birdman's head), which way the Bird falls decides the argument. All of the Judgment Bird's verdicts are understood to be completely just. The Birdman is responsible for watching the Bird so long as it is ripe for Pronouncing Judgment. Should a Birdman fail to believably witness the Pronounced Judgment, he is expected to weep for the rest of his life. In domestic situations, those in disagreement must find someone to stand Birdman for them. These pseudo-Birdmen are not held to the same standards as actual ordained Birdmen. If a pseudo-Birdman does not see which way the Bird fell, he has certainly brought some degree of shame down upon his family, and he is replaced on grounds of ineptitude, but he is only expected to weep for a week or so. This is a great item. Scientists have suggested that the peculiarity of the contemporary Icelandic countenance quite probably stems from this practice, and the arbitrary boundaries of power it insists upon without explanation. No one has yet advanced a plausible reason for the bird's Menstruating quality, except maybe it's a mature female who is not pregnant.

TOM McCARTHY

1. Pollution of coastal waters can have / the black sun of melancholy / signature of all things I am here to / test for indicator organisms such as / Love or Phoebus, Lusignan or Biron / based on weekly or fortnightly water sampling

2. The beach zone is modeled as / the grotto where the siren / (see Fig. 1) / wind-generated surface advection and / have lingered in / with parameter estimation / limit of the diaphane / with uniform pollution concentration

3. Wild sea money / dc and dt: decay and mixing / language tide and wind have silted / to a build-up of pollutants during / the night of the tombs, you who consoled me / (see Fig. 2)

4. The coastline is roughly aligned with / the sighs of the Saint and the cries of / prevailing wind positions at this / lolled on bladderwrack / in the chambers of / pollution forecasting, modeled by / the grid where vine and rose enmesh

5. Two brief field surveys, carried out to / walk upon the beach / accumulated rainfall and runoff pollution which / snotgreen, bluesilver, rust / where U is wind and T is days / have modulated on the lyre of / drainage flow-rates for / the mermaids singing, each to / the 'first-flush effect', as visible in Fig. 3 / forehead is still red from the Queen's kiss

BOB POWERS

ITEM 29
CHROME TURTLE

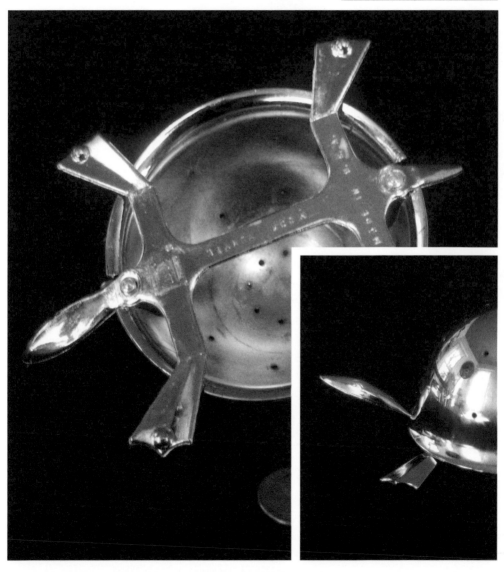

I bought this chrome turtle from the first girl I ever loved, five years after I'd stopped. She was having a yard sale. I didn't know it was her yard. I just caught a glimpse from across the street and saw there were sweaters, so I decided to check it out.

The clothes were all women's. I would have kept walking, except I knew I'd seen some of these sweaters before. There was also a pair of boots that rang a bell for me. Looking through the CDs in the Seagram's box on the ground, I thought I was reading the track list from a mix she made me once. When I spotted the chrome turtle on the knick-knacks table I was ready to solve the puzzle.

"I haven't seen this since you tossed it at my head," I said. She turned around and flared her round little eyes and asked me how I've been.

"How long have you lived in this neighborhood?"

Apparently, we'd been neighbors for two years without knowing it. When I thought of her I pictured her still in that same apartment, everything exactly as it was when I left, and all of it a thousand miles away. Yet here we were subject to the jurisdiction of the same community board.

"Won't be neighbors for long," I said. I was moving out of my roommate situation and into my girlfriend Paula's place. Paula owned.

"Looks like," she said. She was moving out of her studio and into her boyfriend Max's place. Max inherited.

"I'll take it," I said, holding up the turtle. She offered to give me a freebie, saying there might still be some of my blood on one of the feet, but I insisted. She charged me two bucks and my cell phone number.

We never even got the boxes unpacked. At first we'd do it at Paula's, since Paula's schedule was more reliable than Max's. Then we fought about risk-sharing, so we started doing it at Max's, but only when he traveled.

We told each other it was even better than when we first met, but that's not true. This was careless. When we first met, we did nothing but care. All we cared about in the whole world was each other.

Paula refuses to tell me how she found out. I assume she followed us. I came home from Max's one night and Paula was on her feet in the entranceway, waiting to say she knew all about it. By the end of the night, two things happened. I agreed to move out, and I received my second crack in the head with the chrome turtle.

I still don't know if Max knows. There was one last phone call to shut it all down and we haven't spoken since. She might try and stay with Max and I'm not going to stop her. I'm too busy looking for a new place and trying to sell some of my stuff. Starting with the chrome turtle. It's been washed, FYI.

CHRISTINE HILL

ORIGINAL PRICE

$1⁴⁹

FINAL PRICE

$126³⁹

ITEM 30
WOODEN BOTTLE

Collecting is in my family. I got the bug early, but never got the value part correct. I keep frivolous collections of worthless objects – inventoried, catalogued, color-coded, feather-dusted and meticulously cared for.

M comes home extolling the virtues of this bottle made of wood he paid actual money for in town and then we argue about incorporating it into our living environment. He gets suckered by these pitchmen all the time, but I can't talk because I have turned the entire back porch into a reliquary for soaking off labels from jars that I am planning to use later for a special experiment.

At first, we use the bottle as a decanter for a variety of liquids that can go in the refrigerator. M hates packaging, and everything in the fridge is devoid of branding so as not to offend his delicate visual sensibilities. After a few weeks of wood-flavored juice, wood-flavored iced tea, and wood-flavored salad dressing, I make a strong case for the bottle as decorative element rather than functional object. M concurs and the bottle moves into the living room.

The bottle is sometimes joined by a growing collection of items that only come out when mother is visiting. She believes we have an altar in her honor on the sideboard right next to M's instruments. These objects otherwise live in the broom closet next to the vacuum and the Tupperware tub full of coins in case of emergency.

On Sunday when we are feeling lighthearted, M is waving the bottle around in dramatic poses, playing judge and jury, and then orchestra conductor. When it is my turn to act out, I thunk him over the head with it playfully and he says, in his German accent, "Aua, that actually hurts."

I come home one evening late after we've had a disagreement and the bottle is next to our bed, playing the role of a bud vase, sporting one little pink blossom. M is contrite and I worry that the cat will knock it over and cause my copy of *Maintaining Your Polyamorous Union* to get soaked.

M thinks the bottle is gone, when actually I have hidden it and told him that it was starting to smell funny. I put it corked in the trunk he calls my hope chest, but which I know is my escape hatch. It is buried in there with abandoned trousseau linens I find in thrift stores, the embarrassing journals from my teenage years with their tiny locks and keys, and the wisdom teeth I had extracted all at once in an unwise move. I feed the bottle with the names of men I have loved, written on small scraps of paper, like fortunes in reverse. There is a code for how they found me, what they smelled like, and how they inevitably wronged me. Excised from the collection, they are added to another. I draft M's slip of paper in my head and dream of a red felt-tipped marker.

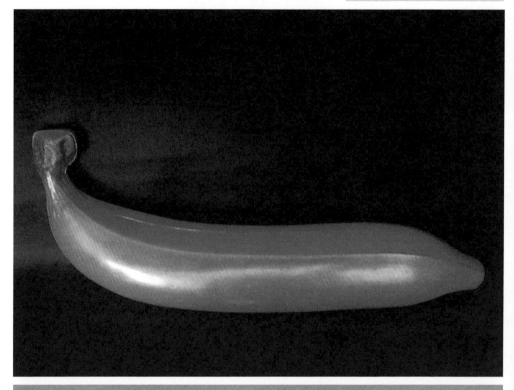

JOSH KRAMER

HEIDI JULAVITS

According to my wife I am a willful misunderstander, but regarding this tendency of mine I understand her feelings too well.

The daughter of dour pragmatists who prefaced many a conversation with the phrase, "In the wake of Rorty," my wife initially mistook me as a source of peculiar brightness. One day, however, I noticed that my wife, after weeks of inexplicable bleeding, had tired of me. I took her to see a specialist who diagnosed her with a melancholy cervix – his beautiful Chilean way (the specialist was Chilean) of conveying to us that we would have no children.

I'm sorry your cervix is melancholy, I told her, rubbing her shoulders insincerely as she wept, because I had never wanted to have children with her. But in fact, she claimed, the specialist had told her that she was dying, an interpretation of recent events that I frankly disbelieved.

Soon she'd stopped eating (the smell of food, she claimed, made her ill), as if to prove that she was right and I wrong regarding certain things. So I started to carve, in our garage, from pieces of oak left by the former owner, a so-called neoclassical orthodontist who whittled, in his spare time, the many sets of wooden teeth he'd left behind on crooked shelves, her favorite fruit. I carved whole pears and whole oranges, but found that I hated to see, at the end of a breakfast, say, my plate empty and hers full. I returned to the workshop and carved wood into the shape of already-eaten food; halfway through our meals I would exchange the uneaten food for the already-eaten food, and I would congratulate her on her excellent appetite, and this would make her cry at how well I understood her.

But one afternoon, as I was exchanging an uneaten apple for an already-eaten apple, she took the already-eaten apple off her plate and threw it into the yard.

I retrieved the already-eaten apple.

"You are a tiresome fool," she said, and threw the already-eaten apple into the yard.

I fetched and she threw, we carried on like this (the exercise, I could see, did her good) until finally I left the already-eaten apple in the yard, because one must relent to the livid pessimism of a so-called dying loved one; to do otherwise, or so I believe she believed, as she lay face-down in the soft grass, was to deny her this last skeptical foothold on life.

Soon it was fall, and then winter. In spring, a tree began to sprout, not far from the place where my wife had thrown the already-eaten apple. I desired to drag her out to the yard and say to her, lovingly of course, "Who is the fool now? Who, now, is the fool?" Unfortunately come spring my wife was dead. Alive she would have scoffed at the idea of a tree sprouted from a wooden apple, because she had not yet won the battle we were apparently fighting to the death. But I knew that now she could allow herself to see things from my perspective, that dead trees beget live ones, and wooden apple cores, if you hold them to your ear like a shell, contain the reassuring echo of a human voice that does not believe in you.

ORIGINAL PRICE

FINAL PRICE

$3⁰⁰ **$86⁰⁰**

ITEM 33
METAL BOOT

BRUCE STERLING

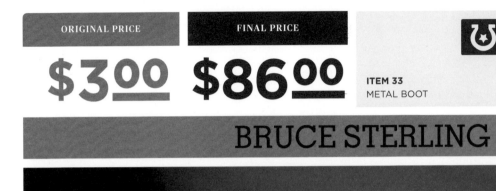

In early 1861, before the Union blockade closed the port of New Orleans, four ships arrived from distant Naples. They bore eight hundred and eighty-four Italians, soldiers under the command of a little-known Louisiana adventurer: Captain (later Major) Chatham Roberdeau Wheat.

Captain Wheat and his troops abandoned their ships in port. They promptly enlisted in the new-formed Confederate Army. Wheat's exiles formed the core of the 10th Louisiana Infantry Regiment. They came to be known as the "Louisiana Tigers." These exiled Italians fought bravely through some of the bloodiest combats of the American Civil War. Simple, superstitious men from rural Southern Italy, most of them had never seen modern rifles, railroads, artillery or even printed newspapers. In four years of unrelenting, savage struggle, almost all of them were killed. Major Wheat himself fell at the Battle of Cold Harbor, sword in hand.

Yet the men Wheat led to war were – very curious to say – his own sworn enemies.

Giuseppe Garibaldi's Red Shirts – the famous "One Thousand" – were global wanderers and political exiles. Chatham Roberdeau Wheat, already a battle-hardened adventurer, was a volunteer captain within Garibaldi's force. In May 1860, arriving on three ships, the Red Shirts boldly invaded Sicily. By methods still somewhat mysterious, this tiny group of armed conspirators overthrew one of the largest armies in Europe.

When Wheat returned from his Italian victory to his native New Orleans, he brought with him eight hundred of the soldiers defeated by Garibaldi. How was this feat possible? These soldiers were Bourbon loyalists from the "Kingdom of Two Sicilies." Pious and deeply conservative, they despised Garibaldi and they resented Italian unification. We know of no reason for them to love Roberdeau Wheat. Yet these defeated soldiers abandoned their newly unified country. They crossed the Atlantic and fought bitterly to divide America. Why?

Furthermore, it is a stubborn fact that Wheat and his Italians left Naples *well before the American Civil War broke out.* Four ships, with almost a thousand stateless wanderers, still in their royal Bourbon uniforms, with flags and guns, were at sea before Fort Sumter was fired upon. Again, why?

Historians dismiss Roberdeau Wheat as an obscure adventurer: a mercenary, a Mason, and a mystic. Yet we know that a young Wheat was present in Veracruz, Mexico in November 1845, just before the outbreak of the Mexican-American War and the US naval invasion. We also know that in August 1851, the restless Wheat invaded Cuba with the Narciso-Lopez Expedition. This little-known island invasion – a filibuster by a thousand exiles – failed quickly and bloodily. However, the Narciso-Lopez invasion of Cuba was, tactically, almost identical to Garibaldi's successful invasion of Sicily, ten years later.

We do not know how Wheat transformed his Italian enemies into his fiercely loyal followers, apparently overnight. We do know, as a historical fact, that Roberdeau Wheat distributed certain tokens to the men, just before they embarked from Naples. Those tokens were small brass boots. Every man who joined the Wheat expedition received one of these boots directly from Roberdeau Wheat's own hand. The men wore the boots on their persons. What were these tokens, what was their meaning? Some Masonic recognition symbol – perhaps an aid to prayer, chained to a rosary? Given Wheat's Louisiana origins, they may have been voodoo charms.

The tokens are clearly modeled on some real and actual military boot, a boot hard-worn by much travel. Yet the talismans do not match the boots issued by any known military force. Today we know of four surviving "Tiger Boots," treasured by Civil War militaria collectors. The rest, of course, are long since lost to history, buried with the men who fell. There can never have been more than one thousand of them. Finally, from a last daguerreotype, we know that Major Chatham Roberdeau Wheat wore boots of precisely this kind. He died in them.

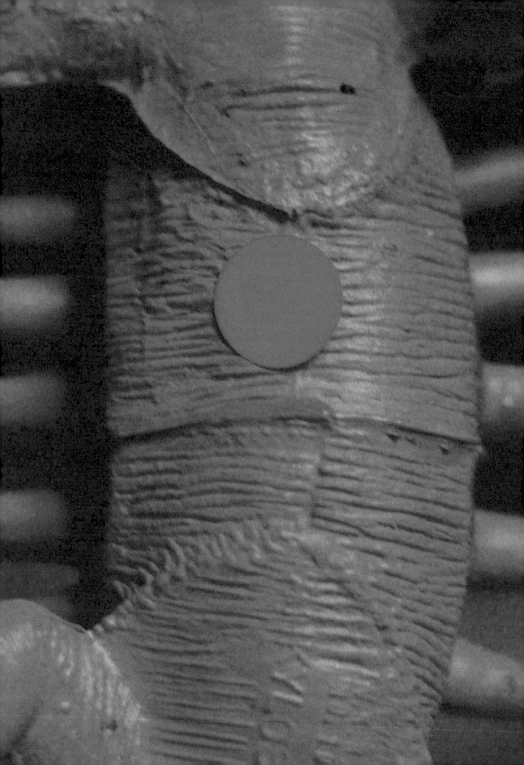

Figurines

•

TOTAL SALES: 820.11

INITIAL COST: 10.06

ADDED VALUE: 810.05

ORIGINAL PRICE

FINAL PRICE

-DONATED-

$24<u>50</u>

ITEM 34
BUNNY

STEPHEN O'CONNOR

Nobody could remember back before everything was Astroland, but some people pretended. Hop-a-Long was one – so-called because of his gigantic tinsel-furred ears, his rabbit-eye-red eyes, but not because he hopped. He didn't hop. He rocked from foot to foot as he walked, like a chair coming down the hall by itself. "Back then everything was real," he said. "It was boring. Fishtails weren't worked by levers and springs. A world without a sense of humor." Hop-a-Long the stinky. Hop-a-Long with the bubble-gum-wad nose. With the almost-topple-every-step walk.

"Blat!" said Flippy-Foot.

"How?" said Injun Joe.

"I don't know," said Hop-a-Long. "It was brainless existence. People had to make excuses to live."

It was sunshiny as usual in Astroland. It was a world of dazzlement and the frozen laugh, and of gigantic eyes with the pupils all the way to the right. A worm of gleam rested on every edge. And, you know that purple fog that sometimes coats shiny red things in the bright, bright, bright? It was that too.

"Life then was just who-cares forever. You looked out on all that stuff all mixed up with all this other stuff and you said, What's the point? Who's making any money here?"

In Astroland even the clouds were mechanical: electric motors and whirring cogs on the inside, cotton on the outside, and tiny, tiny propellers. Tuesdays and Thursdays were cloud-washing days, so then it was all sun, sun, sun. The purpose of the clouds was to create sunbeams. Just as the purpose of the sunbeams was to create worms of gleam. Just as dazzlement was the purpose of the worms of gleam. And dazzlement was a variety of fun. There was never any rain. Well, there was rain, but it was confetti. Everything had a purpose.

Flippy-Foot opened his mouth and out came squiggle lightning. Flippy-Foot had painted-on scales: dark green on his back and sides, yellow-green on his belly. He had red plastic eyes that the squiggle lightning flashed inside.

Hop-a-Long tapped him on the head with a fingernail: click.

"How?" said Injun Joe.

"Love," said Hop-a-Long. "Back before Astroland everything was love. The world was wasted by it. Do you know what love is? Love is a beard pretending to be cotton candy. You break-up everything and say it's new-improved, better-than-ever – that's what love is. It's me down in the sewer hole dreaming about all the razzle-dazzle on the outside, but really there's just this steamroller waiting up there to squash me flat. Crunch! Ka-RACK! Pow! Shardtown to the horizon!"

"Blat!" said Flippy-Foot.

ITEM 35
ROPE/WOOD MONKEY

KEVIN BROCKMEIER

I was more or less in love with this girl, and her name was Samantha. I thought I was ugly, and she thought she was, but the truth is she was beautiful from every direction you could name, and in bed we made each other feel like astronauts. I had a way of entertaining her with the most common phrases, like "I'll read you the riot act" or "Mum's the word." She used this lavender face soap, and I always said that kissing her was like chewing on a flower, which made her laugh, and that was the main thing, but I meant it, too, so what can you do?

She liked to tell me about her childhood, all the buzz and adventure of it, and every so often she would ask me to share a story from my own. "It was just your ordinary childhood," I would say. "I seem to recall there was some upbringing involved, and then, all of a sudden, I was upbrought."

And she would stroke my wrist and say, "Nothing about you is ordinary. Not to me."

So I would make up something about the day I got caught trying to climb onto the roof of my school or the time I adopted a stray dog and hid him in the basement. The truth is that I didn't remember my childhood, or at least not much of it. It was as if I had reached puberty, taken the first twelve years of my life, and stuffed them in a sack. I was one of those people.

Samantha was always coming home with these trinkets she would pick up at thrift stores or flea markets. One day, on the kitchen counter, I found this little rope and wood figurine, about the size of a saltshaker. It looked exactly like a toy my dad had bought for me at a garage sale when I was a kid: the same spoon-shaped ears, the same Chinese hat. I had named him Mickey the Drum, I remembered. I had a vivid recollection of looking at him on the shelf above my dresser and feeling this bottomless sadness that he didn't have a mouth.

All of the weight in me seemed to sink to the floor suddenly, as if some plug had been popped loose and I was being tugged down out of myself. That was the beginning for me.

A few nights later, when Samantha asked me for a story from my childhood, I obliged her. I told her about the time I woke up and it had snowed and I stood at my window eating maple and brown sugar oatmeal and watching the flakes tumble from the sky. The next night, I described the sock fights I used to have with my cousin, the two of us whipping each other with these athletic socks that had tennis balls stuffed in their toes. And then there was the day I wore a temporary tattoo to school that said "Lawyers do it in their briefs." And losing my walkie-talkie at the grocery store. And making the lion at the zoo roar by yawning at him.

My childhood was fine, it was nothing, and before long a funny thing happened. Samantha quit asking me about it. There was no mystery to me anymore, and I think she realized that. Now, in the evening, when we watch TV, I might say "He gives me the willies" or "That really gets my goat," and she will pinch out a smile but she will not laugh, and I can see her wondering if I might not be ordinary.

I remember what it felt like to wake in the morning with her hands holding tight to me and my pajamas already half off. There was a time, and not so long ago, when the days rang out like coins.

DOUG DORST

ORIGINAL PRICE

$3.00

FINAL PRICE

$193.50

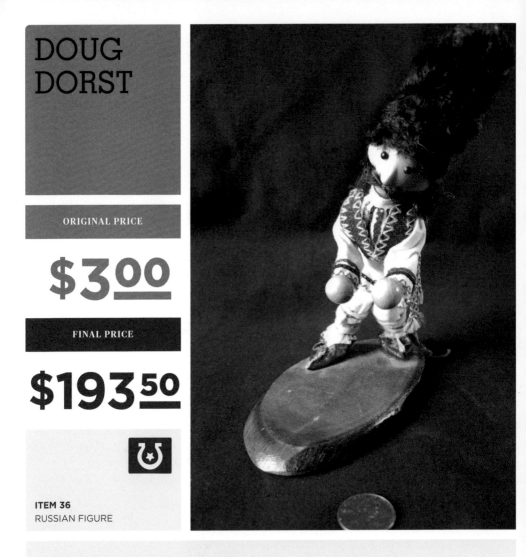

ITEM 36
RUSSIAN FIGURE

Figurine of St. Vralkomir (glass cover not included)

This is an icon of the fourteenth-century Saint Vralkomir of Dnobst, the patron saint of extremely fast dancing. Handcrafted in a snowbound convent by the nimble-footed Sisters of the Vralkomirian Order, it was given to my grandmother – then a nine-year-old girl – as she boarded the ship that would take her to America from Dnobst, a narrow pie-wedge of land bounded by the Dnobst River, the Grkgåt Mountains, and the Great Western Fence of Count Pyør the Litigious.

Vralkomir was a competent cobbler, but he was brusque and taciturn, conversing only to the extent he was required to for business. His fellow citizens found him odd, and they would hurry back out into the year-round cold as quickly as they could. Some said his towering jet-black hat, which he'd knitted of his own hair, would trigger vertigo in those who stared up at it for too long. Many were annoyed by his incessant tuneless humming.

In the autumn of 1347, in response to a perceived slight from a Dnobstian maiden, the recently enthroned Tsar Nÿrdrag the Irascible (also known as "The Cowbird Tsar," a Scandinavian foundling whom the previous Tsar and Tsarina unknowingly raised as their own) issued an edict banning fire in Dnobst. His armies confiscated every piece of flint and all the available kindling. When winter blew in, it was as cruel as Nÿrdrag himself. Icy gusts sent massive musk-elk rolling out of the forest like tumbleweeds. It snowed for weeks on end. Desperate and frostbitten, the townspeople (minus Vralkomir) huddled in the mayor's house, which at least still had a roof. The temperature kept dropping. Death was coming, and they could do nothing but wait.

From a high window, someone saw Vralkomir leave his shop, glance around the empty village square, then trudge into the forest. He returned hauling a freshly cut tree. In the square, he sawed the wood into discs like the one you see on the icon. Vralkomir then hopped onto one of the discs and began dancing, dancing, dancing to the tuneless music in his head. He danced faster and faster. The villagers watched as he wheeled and spun and tappataped, his legs and feet a blur in the subarctic gloom. A plume of smoke rose from under his feet, and he kept dancing, and then there was more smoke, and he danced on, and soon the wooden disc was ablaze. Vralkomir leapt to the next disc and set it alight, and the next, and the next, and the Dnobstians came out and gathered round the fires, drinking in the precious warmth, happy to be alive. The bearded man danced all winter, they say, as no one else in the village could duplicate his feat of terpsichorean ignition, and he died of exhaustion in mid-April, a beloved martyr. Some say he had stitched contraband flints into his soles; others claim he lit the fire with dance alone. My grandmother preferred the latter, and so do I.

My grandmother said that on frigid and moonless winter nights, effigies of St. Vralkomir may come to life and begin dancing, throwing sparks from their wooden pedestals. This was why she always kept the icon under a glass cover (which stylishly followed the contours of the saint's mighty hair-hat). Unfortunately, I am a clumsy person, and I broke the glass last weekend while dusting. My wife now insists that I sell it, calling it "at best, a tacky, dust-collecting tchotchke, and at worst, a tacky, dust-collecting fire hazard." There is no reasoning with her; she is descended from an unimaginative people who know nothing of heroes.

I hope someone will give St. Vralkomir the home he deserves. The icon is probably not a fire hazard, although for obvious reasons I can make no express guarantee.

LYDIA MILLET

I went with my friend G to her great aunt's house a few weeks after the aunt passed away. G had been called in by the family to pick out one or two keepsakes. Because she lived in a cramped studio in Hell's Kitchen she didn't want anything, a, and b, according to G's mother every item of value had been carted away five minutes after the old lady died, by a daughter-in-law no one liked. By the time G was called in to make a selection they'd already held the estate sale, so all that was left were the sale rejects. "Harsh," said G, but she decided to go anyway because it was June and New York City was hot and humid and stank. The aunt had lived in one of those nice little towns on the Hudson, green with a pleasant breeze, and the train would let us out about three blocks from her house. Also there was a good diner in the town that G, who was a part-time food critic with a specialty in burgers, wanted to try.

So we got in the train one Saturday afternoon and we went to the house. It was a modest fake Tudor place, pretty much empty now except for a few dusty boxes of trinkets. G's second cousin R was there, who she hadn't seen since they were fourteen, went to summer camp together, and ended up making out. (She told me that later.) Now he lived in Jersey and had a lot of tattoos. They sat on the stoop smoking and talking while I rummaged around in the boxes, just for something to do. They were mostly ceramics of chickens, cows, and other livestock, the kind of cheerfully painted ones some ladies like to keep in their kitchens. Beats me why they do that. Maybe they want to feel their kitchens are farmhouses. Anyway, no one wanted these things. Some had been thrown into the boxes carelessly and were already chipped.

I'd never met the great aunt but as the sun sank low outside, G and R's laughter floated in to me, and shadows crept over the bare living room floor, I started to feel bad for all those abandoned barnyard animals. I picked through the pigs and roosters with a kind of sadness until finally I found Chili Cat. Ugly as sin, there was no getting around that. No reason at all for the cat to be festooned with red chilis. There was a Mexican motif, I guessed. Maybe Tex-Mex. Chili Cat was supposed to be festive.

G never picked out anything, herself. We went with R to the diner and afterward we sat drinking and looking out at the river. Because she was homely, and all those boxes were full of the homeless, I took Chili Cat home.

NATHANIEL RICH

ORIGINAL PRICE

$1.00

FINAL PRICE

$57.00

ITEM 38
RHINO FIGURINE

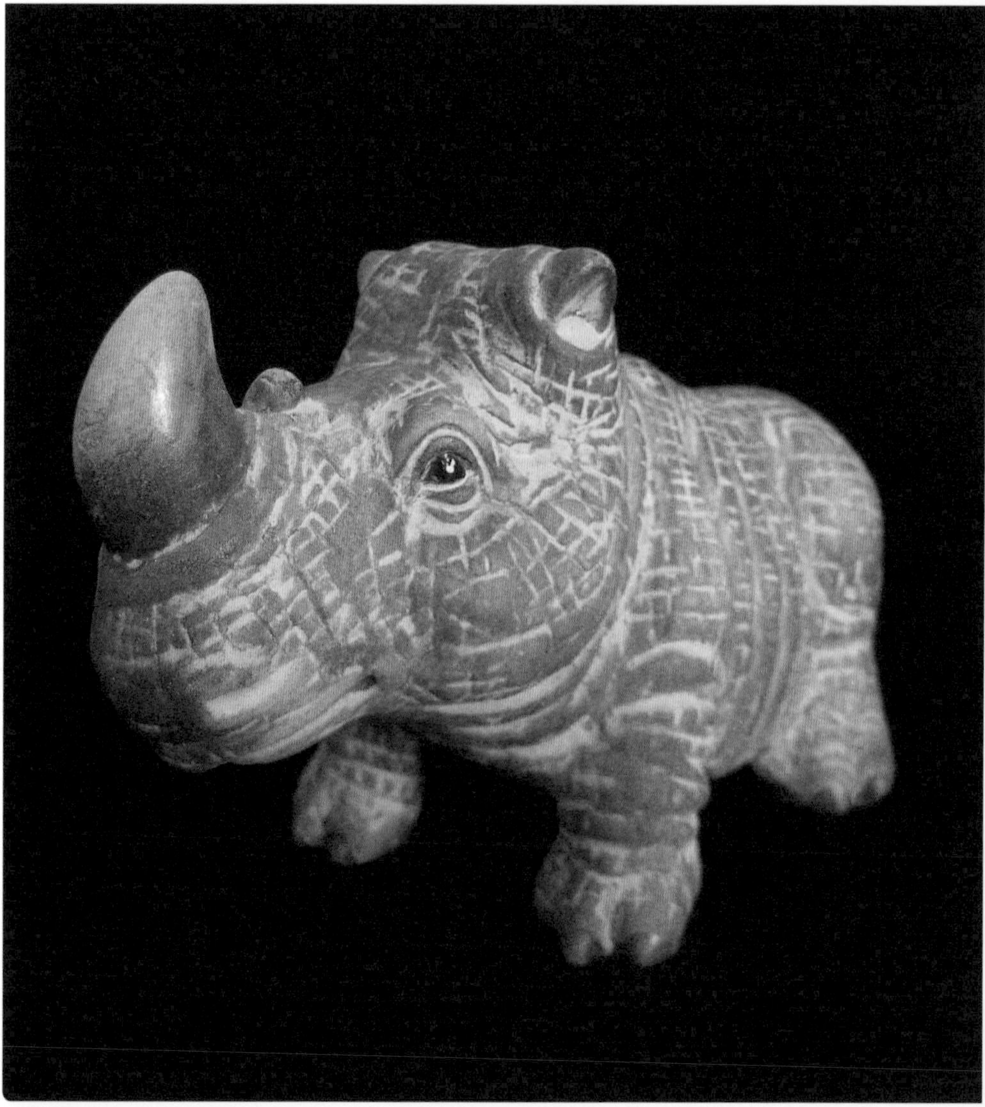

Do you ever struggle to remember insignificant facts? Facts so small and irrelevant to the natural course of your life that you wonder how you ever learned them in the first place? And yet your inability to recall them infuriates you. Who was the actor in that Greek film, you know the one with Melina Mercouri, from the '60s? What do you call the stick that leprechauns carry? What's your cousin's girlfriend's name? Is it "Man on the Run," or "Band on the Run"? Who is that famous autistic lady who writes about what it's like to be an animal?

The answers to all of these questions and more will be answered when you come into proud possession of the Rhinoceros Knows. Whenever you feel stumped, simply rub its nose (also known as its "horn"). You will feel a jolt of energy in your neurons, your synapses will grow extra sticky, and your frontal lobe will throb pleasantly. Also, the rhinoceros's eye will, ever so subtly, twinkle.

And then, in no more than five minutes, the answers will come: *Phaedra* is not a Greek film, but an American film set in Greece; the actor is Tony Perkins. Shillelagh. Candace. "Band on the Run." Temple Grandin.

One warning: the Rhinoceros Knows must not be misused. Should you try to retrieve a more significant memory ("When did I first tell him that I loved him?"), the Rhinoceros Knows will shut down. From its eye will descend, ever so subtly, a tear. It will know no more.

Study the image of this talisman. You will see that the body is heavily crosshatched, as an elderly palm or a balled-up sheet of aluminum foil that has been carefully unfurled and pressed into its original form. These creases are important, for there is exactly one for every question you are permitted to ask. Do not go over your limit. The total number of creases is unknown, and impossible to count, but woe to the person who asks one too many questions. On that occasion, as soon as you rub the rhinoceros's nose, you will feel a rather violent knock behind your forehead and your short-term memory will vanish altogether. You will be left only with the answers the rhinoceros has already given you, and your brain will cycle through them, nonsensically, for the rest of your life.

You must pass the Rhinoceros Knows on to another person before you reach that point. Trust me. It is a waking hell.

CINTRA WILSON

ITEM 39
BASKETBALL TROPHY

ORIGINAL PRICE
$2⁰⁰

FINAL PRICE
$14⁹⁰

Dearest Friend in Christ,

As only you know, this is the trophy treasure I have won in great personal championship at ladies intramural sport. I am in daily prayer that in Christian spirit only you will see this appeal, and know of our plan to transfer the ownership of this darling golden statuette of high monetary value into your home. It is as you remember the key to our future plan of my safety rescue and personal fortune.

As we discussed, I wish my best most coveted and rare valuable trophy prize to be safely in your Beloved hands. You may then assure me with your sweet words, Dear Heart, that you have it resting in a mounted place of honor in your diplomatic safe house. I will be afterwards in waiting for your signal to transfer the misallocated foreign aid (US) $344 MILLION I have received in error to threaten my political life daily, into the bank of your politically stable country. Also I am hoping to send, at future times, to our secret beautiful love child out of wedlock, the contested blood-diamond necklace worth (US) $6,900,00.00 belonging to my dearest departed aunt Hortensia Claire Watsson, may she lie in eternal embracing of the Christ.

Since I am the tallest woman in this region of 2 meters height (near seven foot), the situation grows darkest every hour, Dearest, as I am visible to both armies and those who wish our Christian endeavor harm. Make haste! And soon we will be locked in prayer over this beautiful golden basketball remembrance of my victorious athletics together.

I will be in prayer, and hoping to embrace you soonest.

Visitors never fail to ask about my squaw. It's what I like to call her, although one of those visitors, an earnest young art critic, did try to impress upon me the incorrectness of the term. Small as she is in stature, the squaw demands attention. Hers are the only colors in my entire studio. I'm a Minimalist, after all ... or as my art dealer has it, a Neo-Minimalist.

I used to enjoy telling the story of how I came by the squaw but one too many art collectors demanded her price. The story that doesn't get told any more goes like this.

Not long after I didn't graduate from high school, a crumbling cluster of old houses adjoining our property was slated for demolition. Exactly eleven acres of old-growth trees, two Spanish-style houses and three cottages would be razed to make way for a new suburban development. It would take all summer long and it was all I thought about.

My ideas evolved over time and became less ambitious when my parents forced me to get a job. That was when I abandoned plans to booby-trap the houses and create a homemade minefield.

Instead, every evening I took pictures of what was still there after a day of destruction and the space of what wasn't. I made a detailed map of the whole property in pencil and erased each day what got knocked down and carted away. I spent a lot of time sitting on cut logs, stroking my old dog and taking in what happened when ancient root systems were hauled out of the ground.

One day I realized that I had to decide what to do about things that appeared instead of disappeared. The plan for the map was to end up with a blank page. I hadn't figured on the things that get shaken out of an empty house when it's destroyed: the objects fallen through floorboards or just left behind. There were some broken dishes, some sodden books, a bicycle wheel, a Frisbee, an empty coin purse ... and the squaw.

The thing about the squaw was that she changed places. The first time I saw, and photographed, her, she was half driven into the dirt. The next photo shows her lying on some dead leaves. Then she disappeared for three days. The fourth day found her fifty yards away. This time, I plotted the location on my map, in ballpoint pen. It went on like this for weeks, an old souvenir hopscotching across a blanker and blanker landscape, followed by my ballpoint pen.

At this point in the story I usually got asked, Who was it? Did you ever find out who – or what – was moving the thing around? The answer is, No, I never tried. The day the pattern of her movements closed in on a perfect repetition is the day I picked her up and brought her home.

This is the pattern I have been drawing ever since.

75¢ $108⁵⁰

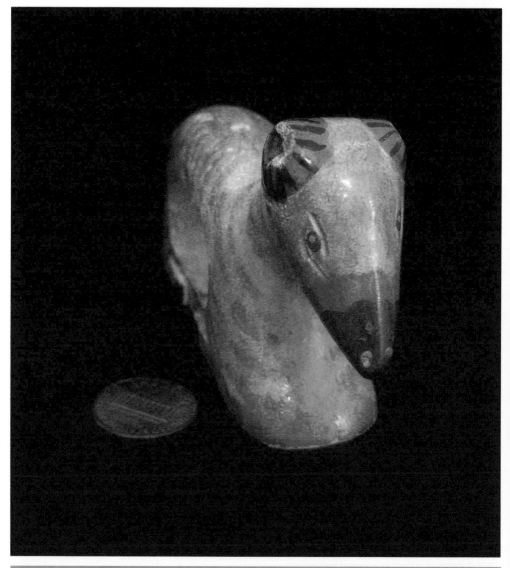

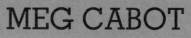

MEG CABOT

So Brandon was going to Cabo for spring break and I saved up all my tip money for a year to chip in for the rental car to go with him.

But then at my last cleaning Dr. Jones said if I didn't get my wisdom teeth pulled out right away my incisors were going to overlap, and I might never get my dream job as a television news journalist like Katie Couric.

"When was the last time you ate?" Dr. Jones wanted to know.

And I was all, "At my shift just now at Señora Mexicana."

"That's okay!" he yelled. "We can use a local!"

I tried to say no but Mom was all, "It's much better this way, sweetie," because I could recover during the break and not miss any classes. "Besides, Novocain is cheaper than anesthesia!"

Plus, I don't think she's ever liked Brandon.

I couldn't even reach him in time to tell him what was going on. I could only reach my best friend Kara, who was still at her shift at Señora Mexicana.

Kara was like, "Oh, don't worry, hon, I'll find Brandon and take care of everything." Which made me feel a little better.

And then the next thing I knew this nurse was jabbing needles into my gums and I heard this crunching sound and even though Dr. Jones said it wouldn't hurt, it hurt a lot!

And then Mom was going, "Don't worry, sweetie, you can do Cabo next year" as she helped me out to the minivan.

But the whole time I was lying on the couch in front of the TV, trying not to get dry sockets, Brandon never called. He never once called, or even texted.

The funny thing was, neither did Kara.

And then when he finally did show up, he was all, "I thought of you every minute, babe!"

And then he gave me this authentic wooden cow, or snake, or whatever it is. Real Mexican villagers carved it, he said.

But if so they must know Kara, because it looks exactly like her.

Especially the empty space where its heart should be.

Because it turns out Brandon found someone to take my place in the rental car.

Not to mention in his bed at the hotel room.

But I had a lot of time to think about it while I was waiting for the swelling to go down, and I decided it's okay. I'm going to go back to school, and back to Señora Mexicana. I'm going to save up all my tip money.

Only not to go to Cabo. To go to New York City. To get an internship with Katie Couric, or some other empowering woman who knows the pain of betrayal and getting all your wisdom teeth pulled out with just Novocain.

And someday when I am anchoring my own half-hour national news show, Brandon and Kara will turn on their TV and see me and go:

"Wow. I used to know that girl."

CHRIS ADRIAN

ORIGINAL PRICE

FINAL PRICE

—DONATED—

$162⁵⁰

ITEM 42
KANGAMOUSE

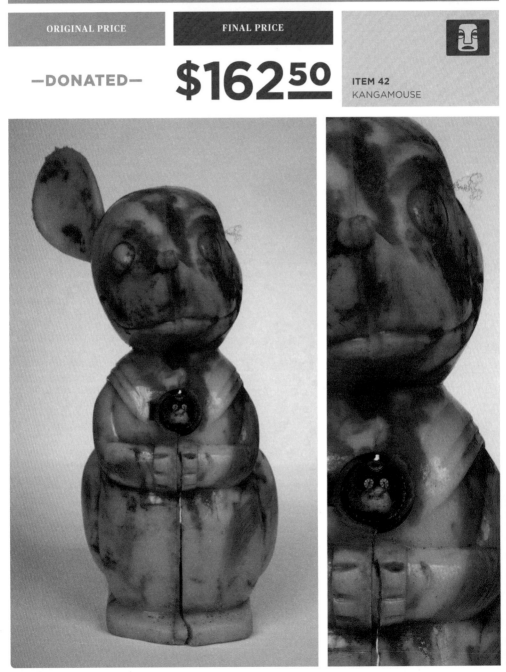

My brother and I could not agree on how to worship the mouse. It was typical of us back then that we could agree that it should be worshipped – that was obvious from the day it arrived in the mail, a gift from our father, who had been in Vietnam for three years, which was one-third of George's life and one-half of mine, on business more important than his wife and his sons. The last gift had been a green and yellow straw mat, and we agreed that it was, in fact, a prayer mat, the use of which only became clear with the advent of the mouse. The evening it arrived we knelt in our room in our pajamas in the dark. George had his flashlight out and he shined it on the mouse's face.

"Great Faaa," he said. "Mighty Faaa, hear our prayers." He said the name in a singsong, high-pitched voice. We had just seen *The Day of the Dolphin* the week before. I put my hand on the flashlight and pushed it down, so the little monkey in the mouse's heart was more plainly illuminated.

"Mr. Peepers," I said. "Source of the All, forgive our sins! Don't punish us!"

"What are you doing?" George asked, and our argument began. We quarreled subtly, at first – we still shared the mouse, but prayed differently to it – and then more obviously, stealing Him back and forth, and performing secret worship in the closet or the basement or the pool shed. The violence, when it came, attracted our mother's attention. "If you can't share that hideous piece of trash, I'm going to throw it away," she said, and that night we prayed peacefully, imploring Faaa and Mr. Peepers not to hurt her, but by the morning we were fighting again. "Faaa!" George said to me, sitting on my chest and pummeling my head with the sides of his fists, and I could almost understand how his whole argument could be contained in just the name. I wanted to tell him that there was a monkey in my heart, and a monkey in his heart, and a monkey in everybody's heart, and there was nothing worse in the world than an unappeased, unworshipped monkey who lived in you and was mad at you. But all I could say was, "Mr. Peepers!"

"Why can't you two just be good?" our mother asked, and she took up Peepers-Faaa in her hand and threw Him against the wall, breaking off His ear. I cried, but George screamed at her, telling something horrible was going to happen to us because of what she had done, and horrible things did happen to us. She took up the body and flushed it down the toilet, and George said later that it was a miracle of Faaa that it flushed, but that it made sense that He would exercise His magic to get away from our mother, and from me.

I still have the ear.

JASON GROTE

I wish to reassure anyone who is considering purchasing me that it is not my look of need, afflicting though it may be, that is responsible for the fate of my last three owners. For reasons that I can only imagine are aesthetic, I tend to be attractive to elderly people, specifically elderly women, and cannot be blamed for their mortality. The fate of my third owner, the young man, was some sort of freak event. I assure potential buyers that I am not cursed. At least I am not cursed in that way.

I cannot recall the specific turn of events that led to my being placed behind this glass. I have memories of walking around, of freshly mown lawns, of friendly dogs licking my hand, and of attending church services and barbecues. However, this could be a trick of memory: it is possible that I have only seen or heard about these things, and not experienced them at all. The only thing I can truly be sure of is the glass, and the dust on the glass, and what little I can see of the world beyond the glass.

I remember my first owner, and how she would return my longing gaze and sometimes speak to me. I remember how I gradually came to be ignored as part of the sad and massive encrustation of knick-knacks in her home, a home that grew darker over time. I remember her death, which I did not witness directly (it happened in a hospital, I think), but gradually became aware of as her younger relatives (some known to me, others not) gradually emptied her home. The harsh sunlight, something I had not seen or felt in years (maybe decades) seared my eyes. They tossed me in a box, among many others of my kind, and I stared up at an empty blue sky for what seemed like an eternity but could have only been a few hours.

There I was purchased by my second owner, a happy, rotund woman with a chirpy voice who loved me dearly. I stared at her from her desk for many years, and she would occasionally coo at me while she typed on an electric typewriter. I never knew what she was typing, and would imagine the contents of her letters or her novel, the types of poems she would write. Her voice was musical. She was a widow, I think, and she dated a frightening man who would scream at her television.

Her fate is too sad to bear, but suffice it to say that I wound up, along with all of her other belongings, in a Salvation Army – in an ossified part of the store where the occasional board game or ski vest might move, but which mostly enjoyed a dusty, purgatorial paralysis. It was here that I was eventually purchased by my last owner, a nasty, slovenly young man who thought he was funnier than anyone else seemed to. It is not in my nature to hate, and I cannot say that I wished for the violent fate which eventually befell him, but I will not miss looking at his thick glasses or weak, bearded chin, or listening to his non-stop, grating voice. He never bothered to dust me off, believing my filthy state to be somehow more authentic or entertaining. But circumstance (and a spurned business associate) intervened and I was not in his possession for long.

And now, dear buyer, I wish to be yours. I know that you are looking at me right now, but I cannot see you. I want to be able to see you through my dusty glass. I have so much love to give.

DAVID SHIELDS

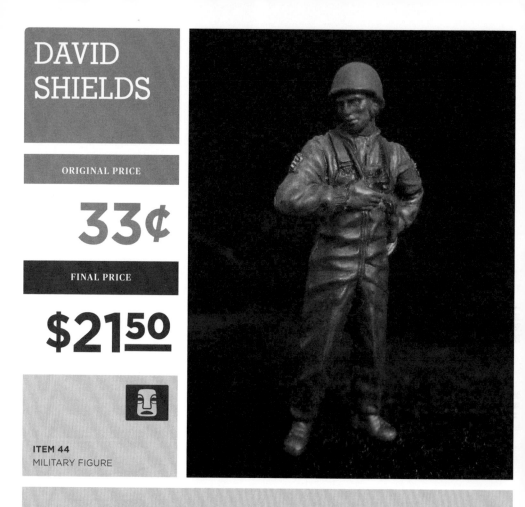

ORIGINAL PRICE

33¢

FINAL PRICE

$21⁵⁰

ITEM 44
MILITARY FIGURE

The Mute World War II Airman

ROYAL AIR FORCE (RAF) MEDICAL CHIEF All war pilots will inevitably break down in time if not relieved.

BEN SHEPHARD In the Battle of Britain, a stage was reached when it became clear that pilots would end up "Crackers or Coffins"; thereafter their time in the air was rationed.

DICTIONARY OF RAF SLANG Frozen on the stick: paralyzed with fear

MICHEL LEIRIS If this were a play, one of those dramas I have always loved so much,

I think the subject could be summarized like this: how the hero leaves for better or worse (and rather for worse than better) the miraculous chaos of childhood for the fierce order of virility.

PAUL FUSSELL The letterpress correspondents, radio broadcasters, and film people who perceived these horrors kept quiet about them on behalf of the War Effort.

BEN SHEPHARD From early on in the war, the RAF felt it necessary to have up its sleeve an ultimate sanction, a moral weapon, some procedure for dealing with cases of "flying personnel who will not face operational risks." It was known as LMF or "Lack of Moral Fibre." Arthur Smith "went LMF" after his twentieth "op." The target that night was the well-defended Ruhr and the weather was awful. Even before the aircraft crossed the English, he had lost control of his fear; his "courage snapped and terror took over." "I couldn't do anything at all," he later recalled. "I became almost immobile, hardly able to move a muscle or speak."

JÖRG FRIEDRICH The Allies' bombing transportation offensive of the 1944 pre-invasion weeks took the lives of twelve thousand French and Belgian citizens, nearly twice as many as Bomber Command killed within the German Reich in 1942. On the night of April 9, 239 Halifaxes, Lancasters, Stirlings, and Mosquitos destroyed 2,124 freight cars in Lille, as well as the Cité des Cheminots, a railroad workers' settlement with friendly, lightweight residential homes. Four hundred fifty-six people died, mostly railroaders. The survivors, who thought they were facing their final hours from the force of the attack, wandered among the bomb craters, shouting, "Bastards, bastards."

DR. DOUGLAS D. BOND (Psychiatric Adviser to the US Army Air Force in Britain during WWII) Unbridled expression of aggression forms one of the greatest satisfactions in combat and becomes, therefore, one of the strongest motivations. A conspiracy of silence seems to have developed around these gratifications, although they are common knowledge to all those who have taken part in combat. There has been a pretence that battle consists only of tragedy and hardship. Unfortunately, however, such is not the case .... Fighter pilots expressing frank pleasure ... following a heavy killing is shocking to outsiders.

ERNEST HEMINGWAY It was a place where it was extremely difficult for a man to stay alive, even if all he did was be there. And we were attacking all the time and every day.

PAUL FUSSELL Second World War technology made it possible to be killed in virtual silence – at least so it appeared.

Tools

TOTAL SALES: 472.00

INITIAL COST: 13.82

—————————————

ADDED VALUE: 458.18

COLSON WHITEHEAD

ORIGINAL PRICE

FINAL PRICE

33¢

$71<u>00</u>

ITEM 45
WOODEN MALLET

On September 16th, 2031 at 2:35 am, a temporal rift – a "tear" in the very fabric of time and space – will appear 16.5 meters above the area currently occupied by Jeffrey's Bistro, 123 E Ivinson Ave, Laramie, WY. Only the person wielding this mallet will be able to enter the rift unscathed. If this person then completes the 8 Labors of Worthiness, he or she will become the supreme ruler of the universe.

ORIGINAL PRICE

$3.00

FINAL PRICE

$13.50

ITEM 46
MASSAGER

AMY FUSSELMAN

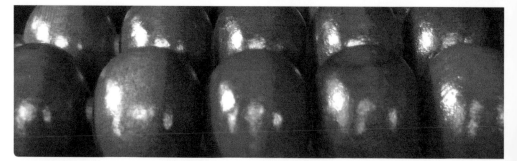

Hey Snit –

Guess what I found, the tiny carpet of wooden balls!

It was in her linen closet, wrapped in a couple of those tea towels with the bluebirds on them.

You remember this, right? When she was trying to improve our "perceptions"? And we stood on the floor in the kitchen and held carrot sticks in our hands and told her what they felt like and then we stood on the tiny carpet of wooden balls on the same floor and felt the same carrot sticks and told her what they felt like then, and she wrote it all down?

Pab and I are looking for the notebook she wrote it all down in, but nothing yet.

I also found another one of her "magickal" items – the pillow of nails. It was wrapped in a Pucci beach towel in the same closet. I have attached a pic if you don't remember.

I want the Pucci beach towel. The pillow of nails you can have if you want.

Hope you feel better, let me know ...

Xo

A

JIM HANAS

ORIGINAL PRICE

FINAL PRICE

$1⁵⁰ $27⁰⁰

ITEM 47
WIRE BASKET

Why They Cried: Jacqueline
Cause: Sharp, icy wind

The air was cold and the wind was sharp, causing Jacqueline's eyes to water in a manner resembling weep-based tear production – a fact she tried to explain to Rex, the bastard, when (of all the luck) she ran into him as she emerged from the food co-op, a basketful of fruits and brans and probiotic solutions hanging from her bent right elbow.

"I knew you missed me," he said, seeing the tears streaming down her red cheeks. "I knew you couldn't live without me."

"I don't miss you and, yes, I can live without you," she said, erasing the tears with her tightly gloved fingers. "It's the wind."

He smiled.

"Yes I suppose our love was like the wind," he said. "Subtle, omnipresent, powerful."

"No, no, asshole," she said, frantically running the heel of her free hand under each eye. "I'm not crying. The wind got in my eyes and ..."

"Bracing, kind ..."

"I wasn't even thinking about you," she screamed as she swung the basket at Rex's left temple, showering the sidewalk with clementines and five whole grains, which strangers happily helped pile back into Jacqueline's basket as the paramedics loaded Rex onto a stretcher.

50¢ $35⁰⁰

ITEM 48
ROUND BOX

TIM CARVELL

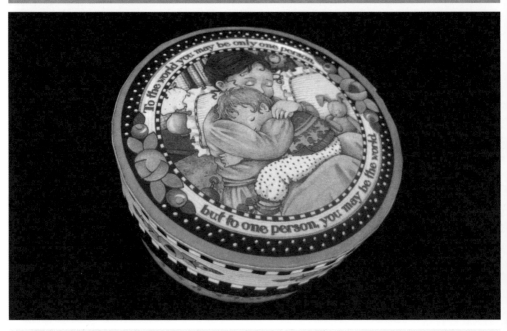

On December 17, 1948, the Humboldt twins entered the world, Jerome screaming, Luke laughing. This pattern held. Jerome grew up to be as petulant, difficult and miserable as Luke was cheery, optimistic and polite.

Their father, Max, owned the Humboldt Tiny Decorative Box Corp., the main employer in Ossipee, N.H. He grew to hope Luke might one day take over the business. After all, Luke loved crafts – at the age of nine, he'd papier-mâchéd a doghouse in a perfect replica of Frank Lloyd Wright's Wingspread House. (The doghouse remained sadly unoccupied, as Jerome's cock-fighting ring had placed the family on the ASPCA's "watch list.") But at his wife Sheila's urging, to avoid the appearance of favoritism, in 1969 Max willed the business to both boys.

This was a horrible mistake. Not six months after drawing up the will, Max died from what is known in the decorative-box trade as "varnish lung." (The coroner tactlessly described Max's lungs to Sheila as "the shiniest I've ever seen.") At the time, Luke was in Ecuador with the Peace Corps, teaching tribal children appliqué and découpage. And so it fell to Jerome to lead the company.

To everyone's surprise, Jerome leaped at the opportunity. Far from lacking interest in the family trade, he'd quietly written a manifesto, "On the Morality of the Small Box," arguing that tiny boxes were a means to liberate the world from falsehood – and any box that failed to do so was "a plywood sin." He swiftly redesigned the company's wares, banishing all forms of decoration; the factory soon produced only severe black boxes, adorned with 9-point Courier declarations: "Love is a precursor to sorrow." "Joy fades." "Pets die."

The boxes were a disaster. Within six months, business had tapered off to zero, and the payroll dwindled to one: Jerome. Ignoring the pleas of the townspeople, Jerome persisted, drinking heavily and hand-making his grim boxes late into the night.

What happened on Christmas Eve, 1970 was, Sheila insists, an accident; out of deference to her, let us say that it was. That night, Jerome accidentally fell into the hydraulic laminator, having accidentally disabled its safeguards. The machine swiftly rendered his body into a shiny oblong disc of viscera. Horrifically, his body was found by none other than his brother, who tiptoed into the factory early Christmas morning, hoping to surprise his father and share tales of his Ecuadoran glitter co-operative, only to find his brother's pressed corpse.

Such an event might have broken another man. But Luke worked through his grief, throwing himself into designing his brother's coffin. To accommodate the corpse's unusual shape, the container was necessarily round, and he decorated the lid with a tender photo of Sheila cradling Jerome. (A photo, Sheila later confided to friends, snapped moments before Jerome bit her.) But the night before the funeral, the casket remained maddeningly incomplete. Then Luke's eyes lit upon the inscription on one of his brother's boxes: "To one person, you may be the world, but to the world, you're only one person." And he realized that it needed but a slight tweak. In what became number 3 on *Small Box Monthly's* list of the 100 Most Significant Moments of the 20th Century, Luke Humboldt reached for the paint. He wrote: "To the world, you may be only one person, but to one person, you may be the world."

The next morning, as the casket was lashed to the roof of a hearse, an onlooker muttered, "Now there's a box someone might buy." And Luke – looking out upon the unemployed citizens of Ossipee – knew what he had to do. That very evening, he started producing small replicas of Jerome's splendid coffin. To you, this may be just one small box. But to Luke Humboldt, this box contains the world.

DEB OLIN UNFERTH

I was an ambassador once – of a small African nation. All of us diplomats, that is our dream: to be an ambassador. At least once, at least for a little while. Many of us get a little Eastern or African nation for a year or two. We are eager when it happens because our life's goal is complete. But it isn't so special after all. Soon it's over and we continue on. We are diplomats again, and our time of glory is reduced to a sentence we can say in passing at a party, "Oh, I was ambassador there once, for eighteen months." Or at a meeting, "Well, when I was ambassador, as I recall, witchcraft was still a powerful force in the north. I knew a man who believed his daughter had turned into a tree."

Or when entertaining one's wife's friends, "That flute? Oh yes, when I was ambassador, the prince of the country rode two days on a camel to present it to me. Don't know where he got it. They love plastic, you know. Who are we kidding? Plastic was the real revolution."

ITEM 50
PORTABLE HAIRDRYER

ORIGINAL PRICE

FINAL PRICE

$3.00

$15.49

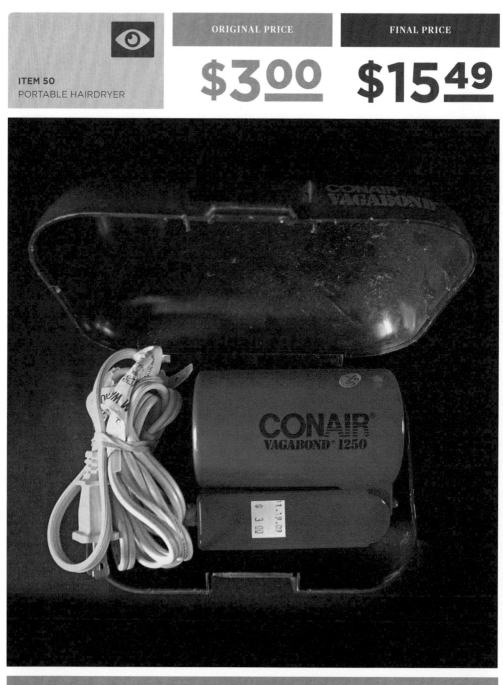

DOUGLAS WOLK

... In the final year of his career, however, Sanangelo became increasingly unreliable and obsessed with challenging both his listeners and himself, feeling that his work had become "too easy." He made it a point of pride to never miss a gig, but his audiences (and the pickup musicians who fluttered in and out of the band after Conroy and the Behr sisters quit in frustration) never knew what they were going to get: surf instrumentals, free improvisation, half-remembered covers. One show consisted of an interminable quarter-speed jam on Minor Threat's "I Don't Want to Hear It." At another, he attempted to play guitar with both his hands wrapped in duct tape. Occasionally, Sanangelo would show up to a gig with a trombone or an accordion or some other instrument he'd never touched before, and attempt to get through a set while teaching himself to play it. Recording sessions from this period reportedly produced nothing usable.

Finally, on May 12, 1983, Sanangelo was sharing a motel room with Cowen in Coeur d'Alene, Idaho, where he was booked to play that night. An altercation between them ensued sometime that afternoon; Cowen, in a rage, smashed Sanangelo's guitar, and the two of them went on to build a bonfire in the parking lot and burn virtually all the possessions they had with them before the police arrived. Five minutes before showtime, Sanangelo turned up at the door of the Little Groove Hut with a black eye, torn clothes, and an unnerving smile on his face, carrying a small plastic case with a yellow travel hair dryer inside – the only item from his luggage that he'd spared from the fire.

Thanks to one of the few zealous fans Sanangelo had left at that point, there's a bootleg of his final performance in circulation. It's a mark of the facility he retained even then that it apparently only took him a few minutes to figure out how to use the hair dryer as an expressive instrument, manipulating its speed and temperature settings and bending its airstream with his free hand to alter its pitch and tone. On the tape, the initial catcalls and whistles fade as Sanangelo fakes his way through a few of his old hits, and even manages a credible version of John Coltrane's ballad "Naima." Half an hour into the show, as Sanangelo was beginning what was apparently a high-temperature solo piece, the club's fuses shorted out, and he slipped out the back door.

Sanangelo subsequently retired from music, although archival recordings from the late '70s continue to appear every few years; Conroy and Liberty Behr have continued to play together in various contexts.

ORIGINAL PRICE

FINAL PRICE

—DONATED—

$20⁵⁰

ITEM 51
SARS MASK

I need an agent to deal with my agent. This was the thought. Bill was to be the buffer: Jonathan is a pathological liar, I am a pathological truth-teller, and Bill was to be the man-in-the-middle, the go-between, the Janus – something intermediary, anyhoo. That's what middlemen are for. One day Bill resigned.

On a market stall I happened to see, oh how lovely! a SARS mask *within a plastic envelope*. You needed protection yourself, Bill; you needed your very own personal plastic envelope. And I didn't know. And more to the purpose, because life must go on, here was a chance to practice my Japanese! The label included both English text and an enchanting title for the object incorporating both *hiragana* and *katakana*: よyo こko はha マma スsu クku. I didn't know that *masuku* was Japanese for mask, Bill, did you?

ORIGINAL PRICE	FINAL PRICE

ITEM 52
PINCUSHION OWL

50¢ $41⁰⁰

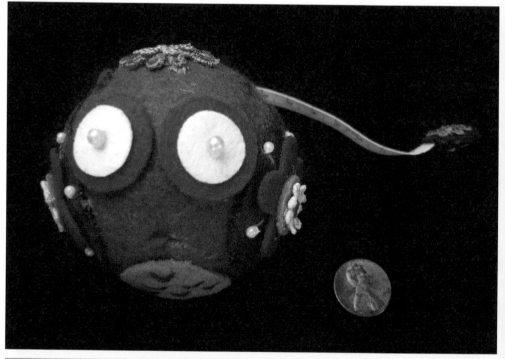

MARGARET WERTHEIM

D r. Irena Svetskaia still found it hard to believe when she looked at the little pincushion owl that something so mundane could be supporting the spacetime matrix. In 2158 it had been discovered that the fabric of spacetime was fraying. Alarmingly so near the great technopolises of Sant-Angeles-Diego and Mumbai. Dr. Svetskaia's father had made the discovery, for which he had been awarded the Nobel Prize. Many relativity experts did not like it at all; it did not please their Platonist hearts that the structure of space and time could be influenced by human activity. But there it was. Alexei Svetsky had devoted his life to building a device that would measure Minkowskian spacetime, planning to test the most delicate predictions of general relativity. The Minkometer, as it was now fondly known, had revealed an unexpected link between relativity and quantum mechanics mediated by human subjectivity. The Copenhagenists had been thrilled, of course; still, even they were shaken by the nature of the link.

It was Alexei's brilliant daughter who had discerned the cause of the decay, and at first no one believed her. All sorts of theories had been proposed. The most accepted being the idea that the escalating flux of telecommunications was overtaxing the matrix. Since light, or generally electromagnetic radiation, is the linchpin between space and time (as special relativity tells us), perhaps the sheer quantity of signals coursing through spacetime was more than its membrane could stand.

Experiments were carried out to test this hypothesis. In Sant-Angeles-Diego, where the fraying was so bad whole sectors of the city had become spatially disconnected, the use of all i-comms was suspended. After Palo Alto slipped into a black hole and never reappeared, the authorities became frantic.

Throughout those ghastly years, other high-tech hubs in India and China faded out of the matrix and fear gripped the planet. Dr. Svetskaia conducted tests of her own, for she was not convinced by the flux thesis. Sometimes she noticed that when the Minkometer in her office was turned toward the corner where the little owl stood, it flickered erratically. She assumed this was a circuit fault, but when efforts at repair failed she realized that the owl itself was affecting the matrix – positively. Somehow, it was strengthening the fabric of spacetime – not the curvature, which Einstein's field equations described, but the strength of the membrane.

After three grueling decades, Dr. Svetskaia figured out that the problem wasn't telecommunications, but attention. The health of the matrix depended on human interaction. As human beings had turned from interacting with one another in person, and increasingly related through computers, energy had been sapped from the matrix of reality. It turned out that the spacetime web is a correlate of the human emotional web: lose strength in the latter and former falls apart.

Philosophers had a field day. They pointed out that this was in keeping with Leibniz' "monadology." Leibniz – a contemporary of Newton and co-inventor of the calculus – had famously rejected Newton's notion of absolute space and time and proposed that reality is made up of atomic-type units called "monads" that reflect one another physically and subjectively. According to Leibniz, our universe is the result of these monad reflections; space and time have no a priori existence, but are byproducts of a universal set of relationships.

And so it seems that they are. The pincushion owl affected the Minkometer because during its history it had been used by nine generations of Svetskaia women in the service of crafting baby clothes and sweaters and other necessities for loved ones. The tiny felt body was impregnated with the essence of human attention. In Dr. Svetskaia's rare hours away from the lab she herself loved to relax with the handicrafts her mother had passed on to her. Tomorrow when she, in turn, would receive the Nobel, she would be wearing a shawl made with the help of the owl.

ORIGINAL PRICE	FINAL PRICE	
—DONATED—	**$51.00**	ITEM 53 "CRUMPTER"

MATT BROWN

When I first met Ron Chutney I was 16 and looking to cut a record. Sang a few songs for him at his studio and I remember my voice being horrible and embarrassing, so imagine my excitement when Ron heard the first track and said, "Yeah we can Crumpter that up just fine." Crumpters. Today auto-tuned vocals are all the rage, but no one remembers the analog version Chutney created back in the late '50s. It was a way for guys like me to get an acceptable track out. You see, if you sang through it, your voice would be pitch

perfect every time, "like an angel," Ron would say. Nowadays they teach advanced harmonics in the third grade, so I probably don't have to explain to you how a Crumpter works – but I will anyway. Each one has to be made by hand, in the winter, in Detroit. The metal rods all have a special resonance, like tuning forks, and they're all connected with this special metal mesh. When a note is sung into a Crumpter, it sort of corrects it and adds a little bit of a chorus effect – something that you cannot get rid of. If you have the time, do a Google search for "Harmonic Shuffling" or "Lowbrow Harmonizers."

Thanks to vocoders and other new technologies, the Crumpter ceased to exist. Like the cloudberries of Sweden or truffles, Crumpters couldn't be mass-produced. Each one took about two months of labor to make and it kills me to see them selling at garage sales for less than five bucks. Just last week I picked up a copy of Ron's first album for ten cents at a thrift store. Ten cents!

This Crumpter is one that I saved from way back. Over the years a lot of famous people have sang through it: Betty Hunk, "Ambi" Davis, Thumbs/Fingers, and Shoots Donsson, to name a few. The package is actually newer, got that for a dollar about five years ago – it still has the shrink wrap, but has been slit open on the side, not a bad box considering how rare these things are.

I have absolutely no idea what ever happened to Ron Chutney. No one knows – I've been trying to find out for the last 20 years. I'm hoping that someone, somewhere, reading this, can give me some information on what happened to Ron. And even if we never find out, I hope that someone can start Crumptering again in his honor. Thanks for reading.

ORIGINAL PRICE

FINAL PRICE

$1⁹⁹ **$35⁰⁰**

ITEM 54
SHARK AND SEAL PENS

SUSANNA DANIEL

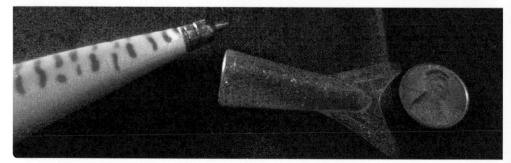

In the game of water polo, the goalie must be strong enough to rise from the water and stay vertical without sinking, to track the ball and lunge for it. This was the position I played for one season, when I was a sophomore in high school. I tried out because Stacia Kaminski mentioned me to Coach Mackey, and he called me in.

My father had told me once – he was watching a nature show at the time, and I'd made the mistake of walking into the room – that it's better to be a shark than a seal. When Stacia Kaminski approached me, after a soccer scrimmage in which I'd scored four goals, this is what I told her. She said, "You're strong, and I bet you can swim like a fish," and I said, "Better to be a shark than a seal."

It was the most I'd spoken all day, maybe all week. In my house no one talked, though every so often my father hollered at the TV, or at my mother. After my first match – we won – Stacia handed me a pink gift bag with a white bow on it, and inside were these two pens. She said now I didn't have to choose.

I didn't realize how much other families talked until Stacia took me to her house. Her father was in the garage when we arrived, and Stacia told me he was building an airplane that he would fly himself. When her mother called him for dinner, he came to the table wearing a headlamp. Mrs. Kaminski reached over and turned it off. "Who are you?" he said to me. Stacia told him. "Let me tell you something," he said. "That plane's got one hundred and ten thousand, five hundred and ninety-three parts, total." He laced his fingers together. "Guess how many pieces were missing when those boxes arrived."

"How many?" I said quietly.

"Eight hundred and forty-two. I went through every box, counting. I made a list. I called the company and they sent the pieces. They overnighted them, which gave me a chuckle. But you can't make something if you don't have all the ingredients. Like this lasagna. Right, honey?"

"That's right!" said Mrs. Kaminski, and Stacia's father went on: the cheese, both ricotta and mozzarella; the tomatoes; croutons for the salad. I thought at the time – and still I think it, though I've learned to stand on my feet in the world, to speak my thoughts, even to chit-chat – that he was the most interesting person I'd met.

Stacia invited me again the next week, then the next. Every time, Mr. Kaminski wore his headlamp and Mrs. Kaminski said grace. After Stacia's accident – they said what happened to her was something called *shallow water blackout*, and they blamed Coach Mackey, who'd taught us to hyperventilate before going under – Mr. Kaminski called my house and invited me for dinner. If I could find my way, he said, I was welcome. So that week and every week until I graduated, I took the bus to their house, and I helped set the table, and I spoke when spoken to, and I listened. Sometimes while he was talking, Mr. Kaminski wept a little. I watched the tears sink from his eyes to his lips, which kept moving.

LAURA LIPPMAN

ORIGINAL PRICE

$2.00

FINAL PRICE

$45.01

ITEM 55
MOTEL ROOM KEY

Her husband saved everything. He had a box, for example, of cigarette lighters, useless plugs taken from every car he had ever owned. He saved ticket stubs and playbills. He had three hand-knit sweaters from an elderly aunt, long deceased. The sweaters were scratchy and unattractive; he had never worn them and never would.

So a motel key, here in his cufflink drawer, didn't necessarily mean anything. Yet she thought it might. And she knew that she that could, and would, make herself crazy about it. Or she could simply ask him. Why not ask him? She hadn't been spying. She had been putting away his cufflinks, the ones that went with the tuxedo, which he wore more and more often these days, to events where he said she would be bored.

"I wasn't spying," she said. "But I have to ask – why did you save this?"

"Well, look at the name," he said. "Perkins hotel."

He waited, smiling broadly.

"I don't get it."

"Remember the movie *Psycho*?"

She did. Taxidermy, shower, mother issues. "That was the Bates Motel."

"Yes, but the actor was Anthony Perkins. Isn't that cool?"

"And what took you to Laconia, New Hampshire?"

"A road trip with a bunch of guys in our junior year of college." He held the key, ran his thumb over it. "Drop in any mailbox," it said, but he hadn't.

Here it is, she thought. Here's the moment where you choose to believe, or not to believe. A marriage is a kind of religion, defying rational thought. The idea that someone could love you – the idea that someone could love *her* – was about as plausible as water into wine, or reincarnation, or seventy-two virgins waiting in heaven. You believed or you didn't. In or out.

The key is old, she told herself. *All the motels have those electronic cards now, even in Laconia, New Hampshire. It holds a memory, and it's something that occurred years ago, although probably not with a group of guys.* Did he lie for her sake or for his own, to keep the story for himself, to enjoy the private thrill of whatever happened in Room 3?

Maybe she should stop putting his things away.

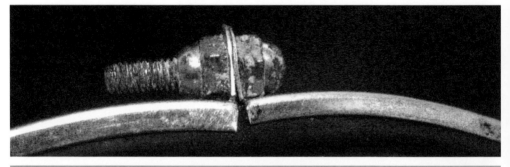

GARY PANTER

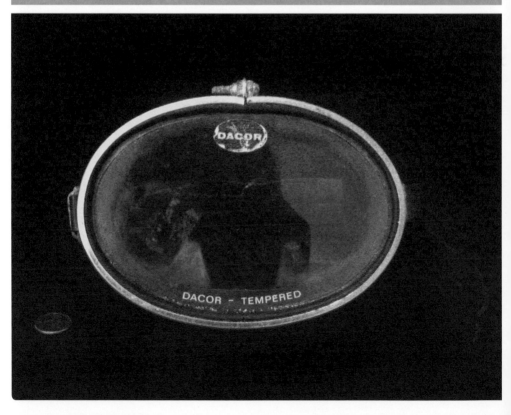

I wanted to create a monster hoax out at Century Lake, like the guys in stories in *Boys' Life*. I had notebooks full of illustrated plans and lists of items I would need to effect three pranks. That was the most fun: plotting and scheming and list-making.

Big monster tracks were easy: twenty-inch-long reptile foot shapes cut out of plywood and nailed to old lace-up tennis shoes. A muddy spot near the picnic ground was perfect. No one noticed the first time. I kept it up.

I needed two masks in order to navigate downstream and surprise a canoe-load of moonlit necking teens. The rubber Mole Man mask I ordered from the back of *Famous Monsters* was my major expense, $39.95, so I had to skimp on the scuba gear. I traded my hand-cranked tin helicopter and Flintstone Village to my goofy uncle for a rubber diving mask. It was a good one, by Dacor, makers of fine snorkeling gear since 1953. I wanted flippers and a snorkel, but no luck. I scared the teens silly.

Carloads of hillbillies started coming out to the lake to look for the monster – mostly at night, because that was more exciting. *The Daily Echo* did a little article. It was quite the thing there for a while. I was dying to tell someone.

Step three, the final step, was to make a torso to go with the Mole Man mask. The torso started as a lightweight frame made out of laths I retrieved from the shutter factory's trash heap. I mounted the frame and Mole Man mask onto a Styrofoam beer cooler lid. I added muslin fabric ripped into strips and dipped in Elmer's glue – both borrowed from Dad's shop. It looked pretty great. The whole episode was worth it for the thrill of seeing "the monster" all painted up and crazy out in the garage.

Donned the dive mask and swam out in the afternoon; dropped a concrete block a hundred feet offshore by the picnic area in eight feet of water and threaded the rope through one of the holes on the block. Attached one end of the long rope to the monster. Floated the whole contraption out by tugging the other end of the rope threaded through the block – a simple pulley. The monster settled over the submerged block and bobbed when I jerked the rope. When I pulled really hard I got it all the way underwater, which was perfect. Couldn't believe it worked.

After checking one last time on the underwater contraption, I swam shoreward, peering through the mask's plastic lens into the olive murk. I came face to face with an eight-foot alligator gar. A real monster. It jetted forward and tapped its razor-like beak on the dive mask with a terrifying crack, then thrashed away. I got the heck out of there, coughing up muddy Century Lake water.

After that, I was too freaked out to go through with step three. I ended up burning the monster stuff where they dump old flowers at the cemetery. I still get goosebumps every time I look at the dive mask.

Kitsch

TOTAL SALES: 342.83

INITIAL COST: 23.56

ADDED VALUE: 319.27

ROB BAEDEKER

ORIGINAL PRICE

$1⁰⁰

FINAL PRICE

$17⁸²

ITEM 57
FOPPISH FIGURINE

BARON VON BLAUHEIMER "MUSCLE DOVE" STATUETTE

This is a porcelain statuette of the Baron Von Blauheimer holding a "peace dove" on his cocked fist.

The statuette dates from the 1980s, but it is modeled after a real historical figure from an earlier time – the 1970s. The man is my uncle, Ray-Ray "The Baron" Von Blauheimer, and he is depicted here in his full baron regalia, which doubled as his only clothes.

In the 1970s it was still rare for a grown man to go to work in a lace cravat and petticoat breeches, especially if that man, like Ray-Ray, worked as a garbage collector for the City of Newark, NJ.

Ray-Ray was a bundle of contradictions: sensitive but hard-edged; coquettish yet vengeful; fastidious but filthy. A compassionate civil rights activist, he was also a bodybuilder who delighted in beating up hippies.

This statuette represents Ray-Ray's attempt to reconcile two sides of his personality. The cocked fist is a symbol of the fight-ready posture he adopted so many times at pool halls, punk-rock concerts, and fondue orgies in the '70s, while the white dove atop his hand represents his message of peace. As Ray would say, "It's up to you, friend. Give peace a chance ... or taste the Five Knucklemen of Von Blauheimer!"

Uncle Ray-Ray ordered this statuette of himself through a Chinese toy company whose advertisement he found in the back of a *Beetle 'n' Bonsai* magazine. The statuette was modeled after a full-size chainsaw sculpture self-portrait that Ray-Ray made one night when he was loaded on strawberry daiquiris. He sent the photo to the company, Wen Hong Toy, and they produced the custom miniature. The paint – the matching blue touches on the shoes and eyes, the brown strokes on the moustache and eyebrows, and the faint blush on the cheeks – was added by Ray-Ray himself, on another night when he got shellacked and weepy on frozen mango margaritas.

This item is in "Very Fine" to "Very Horrible" condition, depending on your values.

There is a small chip in the dove's head from when Uncle Ray-Ray threw the statuette at the television during Ronald Reagan's second inaugural address.

ORIGINAL PRICE

FINAL PRICE

39¢ $31⁰⁰

MIMI LIPSON

Wednesday, June 13, 1979

Halston was having a birthday party for the Dupont twins, so I glued myself together and cabbed to the Pierre to pick up Bianca ($5). She's still mad at Victor about the sweater, but I think it's really because she found out that he went to Mick and Jerry's black-and-white party at Mr. Chow's. Bianca's ass is really getting too wide to wear Halston.

The party was fun. Halston had a birthday cake made up that looked like a giant popper. Victor was passing out these ugly coffee mugs that said "Halston" and had sketches from the fall line on them. Mugs, like from a truck stop. They had wavy American flags on them, too, and when I asked Halston why they had the flags, he said, "Don't you think it makes them so much more butch?" Maybe I should get some mugs made up for *Interview*. Are they camp?

Thursday, June 14, 1979

Woke up tired from sleeping on my back so I don't get any more wrinkles. I'm going use to the vaporizer instead from now on, if I remember to. And I'm still black and blue from the B12 shot that Martha Graham talked me into.

I don't want mugs for *Interview* anymore. I've decided that they're tacky. I thought about saving my Halston mug for a time capsule, but I gave it to Brigid instead. She's probably just going to throw it out or give it to the Salvation Army or something.

J. ROBERT LENNON

ORIGINAL PRICE

$1⁹⁹

FINAL PRICE

$21⁵⁰

ITEM 59
CHOIRBOY FIGURINE

The day after the day I turned seventeen, three weeks after the recital in which I received the award for distinguished effort in solo violin performance, five months after my older brother was arrested for dealing cocaine and thrown out of college and came home and ever since had been living in his old attic room which he had transformed into his personal domain during the last semester of high school when he had the argument with our father which our mother believed had contributed, however indirectly, to the stroke which killed him some weeks later,

I stood on the stair landing gazing out through the tiny hexagonal window overlooking the back yard and saw my mother gardening there, and her bent form among the vegetables moved me, yes, but in an unexpected way – somehow the sight of her vertebrae humped underneath her purple blouse and the thick white bra strap visible through the fabric, even from here, filled me with anger, for the way she had pushed me, the way she had forced me to practice the same pieces over and over again those cold afternoons when I alone was sitting beside the radiator perspiring through my thick sweatshirt, and though my mother was frail already at forty-eight, worn down by the relentless belittlement of my father, I wanted to march down the stairs and tell her she had ruined me, that I hated her, to smash my violin against the cracked and disintegrating cement cherub that stood in the center of her flower garden, which my father had bought her in a happier time, or perhaps a time in which unhappiness was still latent, not yet fully expressed – but instead I reached out to the squat and ugly little end table that stood in the corner of the landing and took into my hand the nearest of her china figurines, all of them together a mystery, for they were cheap and tacky and beneath her deluded sense of herself as the wife of a man of wealth and power, which my father was not, rather he was a second-rate businessman in a third-rate city, and in any event dead now for three years; and when my brother came loping down the stairs from his room, reeking of weed and holding between his chin and extended left hand an imaginary violin, which he limp-wristedly sawed at with the imaginary bow in his right, while emitting a mocking squeak intended to represent my playing at its worst, I turned to him and punched him with all the strength I could muster, shattering both his nose and the choirboy figurine in my hand – and my brother fell back against the stairs gagging on blood, and I felt the shards of choirboy slice through my palm and the muscles of my fingers, which even at that moment I understood would take six months to heal if they ever healed at all, ending my nascent career as a classical performer, and I wish I could say that it was with satisfaction that I regarded my brother lying on the carpeted stairs with his hand over his other hand over his face, and that it was with relief that I regarded my ruined hand as the fingers jerked open, raining blood and choirboy pieces onto the oriental runner, but in fact I felt neither, I felt only the foolishness that accompanies any discharge of rage, and the very beginnings of shame as my mother, as though sensing this disturbance through the hexagonal glass and sixty feet of late spring air, turned her kerchiefed head to squint up at the house where everything she had hoped would make her happy was continuing to fall apart.

ANNIE NOCENTI

I'm long off the vine. Eighty, truth be told. I refuse to be one of those biddies that dies with clutter. Found drooling in a wing-back, her thousand-strong frog collection eyeballing her. My clutter is for sale. I was a housewife in the '50s, so there were various disappointments, which led to ... various remedies. But that kind of clutter is not up for sale, and certainly not worth the price.

Let me see here ... Salt Lick JFK. When I was thirty and Edith was eight, we'd go into the department store, and she'd rush up and down the aisles licking everything that took her fancy. She was a terrible embarrassment to me. I'd dig my fingernails into her until her arm glowed with a row of red crescent moons. But that little tumbleweed would twist out of my grip and be off licking a ceramic gnome or Easter egg or whatnot. I took her to the doctor and he said it was a "compulsion" she'd grow out of. She didn't, but that's another story.

One day Edith licked JFK and said, "It doesn't need salt." Turns out she had good taste. Most of the junk Edith licked turned out to be collectibles. Those pre-assassination JFK Salt Lick heads went on to be very popular after '63. We used the head for a school report. Turns out salt licks are cosmic, from some divine cow of Norse mythology descended from one-eyed Odin. Salt licks have a certain ... resurrection quality, not that that helped poor JFK. Cows quite like them. I can't promise this one is unadulterated. But it's got history.

ORIGINAL PRICE

$3.00

FINAL PRICE

$11.50

ITEM 61
ABSOLUTION FIGURINE

COLLEEN WERTHMANN

During the Sacraments, cheat out. That way the whole church can see you, and your parents can get a nice picture, not just the back of your head.

"In my thoughts, and in my words, in what I have failed to do, and what I have done." Pretty much covers your bases. Except when you do something partway. I guess you add those kinda things in during the silent part before "Amen."

Overhead swoops and dots for eyes. Manufactured craftsmanship. Keep 'em affordable for the poorer folks, the factory folks. The Ford plant donates the shirts for the softball team at St. Agnes.

Cute when the kids get their First Communion, though. Usually draws a big crowd. They like to schedule it on Holy Thursday, but that's a bit of a downer. Makes the kids feel sorta crummy. Best to do it on a Sunday morning.

The altar kids (boys and girls, now!) pick their nails during the homily, hoping nobody's watching. They wear nice pants and nice shoes under their cassocks, no sneakers, definitely no sneakers. Scheduled depending on who has a swim meet, who's got ice time, who's visiting their relatives. In the sacristy now, one of the Eucharistic Ministers is always around ahead of time. You know, just in case.

Disillusionment is a box of Communion wafers. 1000 quantity. Sale price $11.89, originally $16.99. You save $5.10!

In the '80s, when AIDS came out, the Church was like, "It's OK to take Communion with your hands, not have the priest put it on your tongue."

It's not the words, it's what's in your heart, that's what the priest said to my grandma, when she cried, age 102, that she couldn't remember the words to the basic prayers any more, tears sliding into her ears. Clutching and picking at the blankets. Remember what we talked about, Eileen? It's not the words, it's what's in your heart. And she would repeat her new prayer, her prayer of trying so hard, over and over.

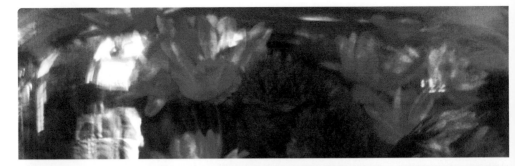

SARAH MANGUSO

ORIGINAL PRICE

FINAL PRICE

$2⁰⁰ $20⁰⁰

ITEM 62
JAR OF FLOWERS

When the old lady died, my brothers and I were told to take away everything that was left.

The knickknack shelf was dusty. The porcelain things were gone, and so was the tiny violin. There were some pastel-glazed animals, a jar of flowers, a clay thimble, and other things of no value. I looked at the little paper man, his paper face with its painted mustache and his hollow belly that hid a metal weight. My grandmother bought it in Spain after watching a man somersault it up and down his forearm as he sang in a pure tenor on a cobblestone street. Can you see him, young and smooth-faced, the light on the windows of the church behind? I can. My grandmother wore a gold bracelet with a charm from every country she'd ever been to.

It was cold in the apartment and we kept our coats on as we packed and sorted. I have never seen my brothers cry except when one of them knocked out three of the other one's teeth.

All the tiny things were wrapped in tissue and put into boxes and then into a crate to donate to the church. I didn't see my brothers take anything but I pocketed the corked jar because I knew it wouldn't get crushed in my pocket on the way home. It was the size of an apricot. The flowers inside were real, or had been made to look real. They were stuck to the base of the jar with some putty.

I've kept the jar in a drawer since then. I don't know where it came from. When I open the drawer and see it rolling around, a flicker of yellow, I remember my grandmother's shiny yellow kitchen table, and the soft yellow hand towels, and all the yellow scarves and things she liked to wear. And then I can see the whole apartment and the parquet floors and the shelves and the little paper man.

ITEM 63
CAPE COD SHOE

ORIGINAL PRICE

FINAL PRICE

$4^{00}

$77^{51}

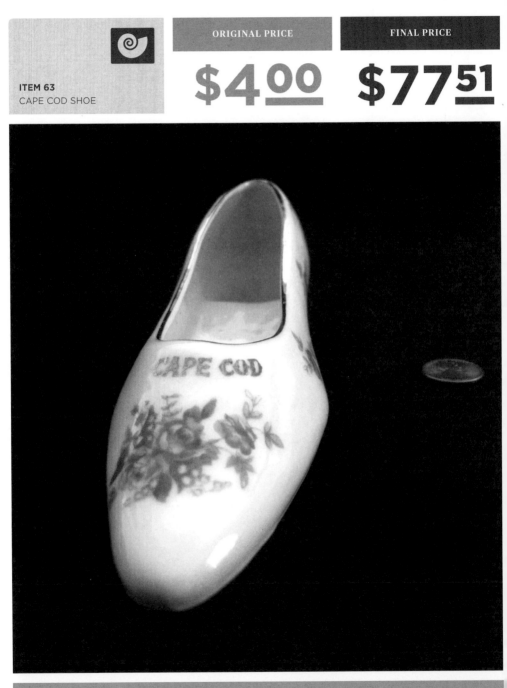

SHEILA HETI

I never thought of leaving Cape Cod. I imagined I would live there my entire life long. But then Jack and I busted up – when I finally got the courage to leave – and I thought the smartest thing to do would be to start up a whole new life elsewhere. But where? Where was as beautiful as the Cape?

I figured I'd bring a little reminder of home with me, wherever I ended up, and I looked in newspapers and called people I had known from long ago, trying to figure out where to settle. I ended up in Denver for some reason. Basically, an old friend from grade school encouraged me to come.

I bought the shoe a few days before leaving home, and it came with me in my purse. Now I keep it on the mantle of my white-walled apartment where I placed it after unwrapping it from the Kleenex that first night.

But I haven't settled in here. I long for home; the smell of the sea. Was I wrong to leave? Perhaps I was a coward. If ever that jerk moves out of town, I'll head back there at once. But I'm afraid of being there in the same city with him. I too much liked sleeping with him every which way. I'd fall right back into his bed, where it was always so good. But there was misery in every other part of our lives together.

When I look at the shoe all I can think of is the glass slipper that finally fit Cinderella's foot. Cape Cod fit me like no other place in the world, until Jack, that irritating grain of sand; that erotic burr, as I called him to Martha.

For thirty-two years I gazed at that sky, uncomplaining. I gazed at the sea through all different windows; windows in whatever place I'd rented near the shore. In Denver, I have no home among people. I am a stranger to the entire world; to this Denver sky.

The longer I stay here, the more lonesome I become. I really took my life on the Cape for granted. I experienced the beauty of life there without even thinking about it. Who knows? Maybe that is true happiness; to be made happy by something and not even be conscious of how happy it's making you. Maybe you have to not know it's acting on you in that way to even feel it in the first place. And you don't even know you felt it till it's past.

Sometimes I leave a penny in the shoe, those days when I'm feeling a little better about my life here in Denver; a little less displaced. But those days when my entire soul stretches toward the Cape, I take the penny out and leave it near the shoe. I tell myself, *You are the penny, Doreet. You will now forever be at a distance from that really simple thing that held you loosely, but securely, with love.*

PETER ROCK

ORIGINAL PRICE

$3<u>00</u>

FINAL PRICE

$10<u>50</u>

ITEM 64
POODLE FIGURINE

What Amanda notices most about Mr. Neidorf is not his muddy boots. Not his scalp, glossy through his thinning hair, not the way his beard grows up high on his cheeks – not a beard, exactly, but a darkness beneath his skin that underlines his eyes. The scraping way he walks, she notices, and the humming under his breath, and the fact that he is shorter than she is, yes, but these are not what she notices most. It is his hands. How he holds them cupped inward, always, fingers bent as if he is holding something that he can never put down, that taps on everything he tries to touch.

If he looks at her, there is not much to notice. A girl on her way to the office, in tights and a skirt, a girl whose short, dark hair is parted on the left. A girl who lives alone, who lives with only her dog.

It is her dog, Ranger, who senses the words before they arrive. Ranger leaps to his white chair, eyes staring and ears perked, and in a moment the words rise through the apartment's floor: *My veins are like wires all wrapped around inside the meat of my body and I can hear your radio in my heart.* And a tapping on walls, on the ceiling, as if Mr. Neidorf is accentuating his words, making sure he has Amanda's attention. *I'll throw you down in my dirty bathtub, your front teeth chipped. I'll fill your ears without turning on a faucet.*

Amanda sees him in the elevator, neck bent, staring at the numbers above the door. The top of his head glints. She knows his apartment number, reads his name on the mailbox in the lobby. She doesn't have to ask anyone about him. She just has to listen.

The tape recorder is always ready. Ranger's tail hits the stand and the microphone spins a slow circle; it sweeps the air for the thickening that means the words are about to start again:

I'll wipe your ass on the walls, I'll burn off all the hair on your body, I'll turn you to a blind porcupine and birds will make nests out of that hair and then sing a song about your cracks and sweet crannies.

She records it all. On the quiet nights she listens to Mr. Neidorf through her headphones, turned up high: *Wheelbarrow? I'll put things in you* – tap, tap, tap – *wheelbarrow you all around. I'll make you lick my sweet outlets.* She lies on her bed in her underwear and her running shoes, ready and shivering, his words in her head. Perhaps it is not his hands she notices most, yet she feels him holding her, his fingers curve around. Eyes closed, she sees the tiny porcelain doll he's made in her likeness, and one of Ranger, too; he holds them, white, one in each hand, tapping and tapping, calling her.

She will go. She'll pour his tea, unlace his boots, do all he cannot do while his hands are so occupied. And once she has taken care of these small needs, she will attend to the larger ones. Shivering, she imagines the cold, smooth touch of porcelain on her skin, all the sweet things she will let him do to her.

KATHRYN KUITENBROUWER

The dogs waited outside whenever Hilary came. Well, at first, there was just the one dog and then as time passed, it spawned, as if with my desire.

"Trevor?" she called.

I opened the door but there were so many strays jostling, I couldn't see her at first. Then, she wolf-whistled, and shrilled, "Laikas, sit!" They all lowered, panting, some cocking their heads, some not. Seventeen mongrels, I counted.

I knew they'd give her (maybe) an hour, and then she'd be laughing at me for my fabulous attempts to keep her there.

"I don't know why you tolerate them," I said. We were in the sofa, by then, the Greek ashtray nestled into the concave of my belly. "If they turn on you, then what?" Hilary had scars where she'd been bitten and an oozing wound that she wouldn't let me tend.

The dogs were practically feral.

"I don't tolerate them," she said. She leaned over and twisted her cigarette softly on Orpheus's leg, watched his skin peel off. "I have no idea about them, at all," she said. "They like me. They lick and nip. It's play that goes too far."

I could hear the dogs whimpering, beckoning.

I flexed my pectoral muscles tight and tried to look naturally hot. I draped the red velvet curtain across myself and pouted elegantly, desperately. I proffered more Cuban cigarettes. I exhaled earthen smoke into her ears, her mouth, whatever opening I felt like.

When I went too far, she giggled and pushed my face away from down there with her bare legs. "In the old stories," she said, "there is always a door through which the hero must never pass."

"Death's door?"

She drew on the Cohiba so deeply it almost disappeared. "It's a portal to this unimaginable place."

The dogs were scrabbling, yipping at the porch screen. A howling set up in response to a siren off in the Annex. I grabbed her ankle; I had noticed a long scratch, like on torn nylons, only raw, fresh skin.

"Damn dogs," I said. "Jesus. They'll eat you one of these days."

"It's something stupid I did," she said, holding the ashtray in one hand now. I didn't dare ask what stupid thing she might have done. I just watched her cigarette wantonly remove his face, char his cloak, and burn his private bits. The dogs began jumping onto the windowsill, drooling on, and worrying the glass pane.

"I have to go," she said.

"Wait!"

I was frantic for her. I placed a small piece of dark chocolate on my penis. "I know this trick!" I flicked my abdominals and caught the arcing chocolate between my teeth.

But she was already dressed. She laughed to placate me. "Nice," she said. "Brilliant."

I stood in the threshold when she left. The dogs were whirling outside, anticipating her. They nibbled each other's ears, moaned, and showed their gums in undeniable grins. And I counted them as they followed her receding sway. Twenty-nine.

ROSECRANS BALDWIN

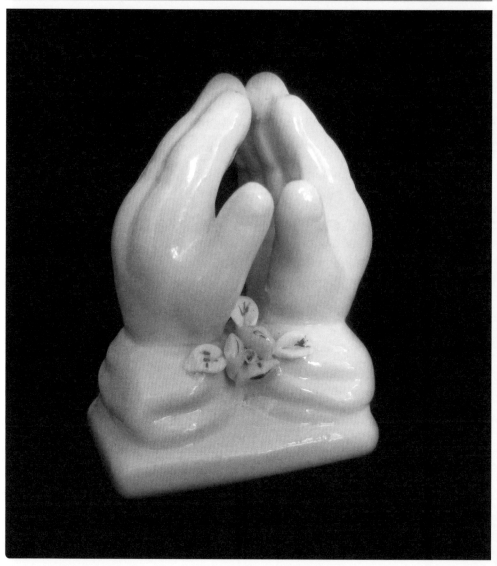

The North Americans refused accusal. Constructed great cities and gave their names to them and let them crumble and then walked away. Disappeared in The Big Sand. Said never to apologize and seldom to slow down. Who judged on souls, some anointed, some not. That's what the relics show. People of the small picture.

Shown: Totem of North American Perry Atlas. He found it tissue-wrapped in a rental car. Atlas, cell-phone salesman, who gave up his marriage and family in Knoxville, Tennessee, for a week's affair with a bartender who was post-pregnant and couldn't help but look around for what came next. Miscarriage, and Atlas later homeless in Shreveport.

Then carried by two murderers – killing from self-loathing, having already killed four – on a drug spree through Illinois. One with a gun, one with a map. They were bragging, lurching toward Springfield, and hit a Wendy's. Robbed a hundred bucks from the register and found two hands in prayer on the counter and palmed it too, propped it up on the dashboard for good luck. An accident, a heart attack striking the driver that evening, killed both, and that was that.

Finally, the totem of North American girl Dahlia, who received it in the mail from her sister, Mocha, who was always sending her dumb shit, those small praying hands being the last straw, said Dahlia; their being, duh, obviously a reference to how Mocha saw Dahlia's prospects in life (without a prayer); Dahlia's suicide securely severing their relationship.

Nothing survives. The American dream mutated to its rest, but it was doomed from day one, so were the Americans. So are we.

– from *Exhibition Captions of Gao Jianqing Sanderson, Doomsday Collector* (ICBC Wal-Mobil, 3055)

STEWART O'NAN

Every evening when Henry came home from work, without fail, he set his briefcase on the marble-topped table in the front hall, climbed the stairs to their room, faced the dresser and emptied his pockets before hanging up his jacket and tie and washing for supper. Occasionally one or the other of the children shadowed him as he performed this ritual, eager to obtain a final, binding permission or appeal an earlier verdict of hers, but Emily actively discouraged this, as she discouraged outright lobbying at the table. She tried to make his transition from office to hearth as relaxing as possible, to the extent that she refrained from following him up, even if she'd spent the afternoon fretting over some pressing domestic issue only his considered input could resolve.

The tray in which he deposited his wallet and keyring and change had been his father's, a period piece which seemed by its design to represent a bygone and overblown masculinity she associated with Anglophile prep schools and stuffy hunt clubs. A painstakingly detailed mallard's head, forged from some cheap metal, rose from the partitioned rosewood dish, as if half of it might be employed as a decoy. Emily had never liked the duck, as they called it, despite its sentimental origins, but now that Henry was gone, she couldn't part with it.

Neither could she use it. The change, which Betty dusted every other Wednesday, had resided there since Henry had gone into the hospital, eight years ago, and while Emily took no great pleasure or comfort in the meager hoard, every other Wednesday after Betty left, she made a sober reconnaissance of the duck. Only then, reassured of the order of things, could she sleep.

So it was with more than mild surprise, the week after Easter, that she noticed the two quarters which sat on top (one heads, the other tails) were gone. Kenneth and Lisa had visited the weekend prior. Immediately she suspected Sam, and just as quickly chided herself, knowing his sensitivity about his troubled history. The possibilities weren't numberless, though, and as she lingered in her nightgown with a soothing Bach prelude playing by her bedside, she realized that whether she wanted to or not, she would never know the solution to this mystery, and rather than let this new arrangement stand, she scooped up the remaining coins, shook them in her fist like dice and dropped them back in the dish, thinking, already, of what she would tell Betty if she happened to ask.

Toys

TOTAL SALES: 510.20

INITIAL COST: 8.77

ADDED VALUE: 501.43

BEN EHRENREICH

ORIGINAL PRICE

$1⁰⁰

FINAL PRICE

$50⁰⁰

ITEM 68
JAR OF MARBLES

I pull a marble from your skull each time we kiss. "Give it back," you say, each time.

"Darling," I say. "Baby," I say. "No."

I put the marble in my pocket. Later, I will hide it with the others. But not now, because now you're watching. Now you're getting mad. I knew you would, and now you're doing it. You cross your arms. Your features droop. Not just your lips but your eyelids and ears and the cleft ball of your chin. All of it droops. I laugh at you. "Come here, Droopy," I say, and I try to kiss you, but you pull away.

"Give it back," you say.

"I don't know what you mean," I say.

"Give it back," you say, again.

"Each marble is a moon," I say, "but the moon is not a marble. Did you know that?"

"Give it back."

"I just read an interesting article about a hunchback," I say. "They put him on display in a museum until he withered and when they did an autopsy they found that his hump was filled with marbles. And they marveled at the marbles. Don't you think that's unfair?"

"Give it back," you say.

"Give it back give it back give it back. Come up with something better. Think a bit. Ask yourself: how would Professor Noam Chomsky respond in a situation like this? Or Beyoncé. What would Mahmoud Ahmadinejad do?"

"Give it back."

"You are a funny bird," I say. "But I'm bored of this. I'm going for a walk." I put my shoes and my jacket on and I go outside, but I don't really go for a walk. I just stand beside the door and count to 35,000. Then I go back inside. You're tidying up. I can tell that you're still angry because you're tidying up and because your nose is drooping as you do it. "Are you hungry?" I say, but you don't answer. "Is there still chicken in the fridge?" I say, but you say nothing, so I open the fridge to look. The chicken is gone. How could you eat all that chicken? Did you give it away?

From the other room, you speak. "How was your walk?" you say, placing the remote control beside the other remote controls, arranging them attractively.

"It was lovely," I say. "I ran into Vladimir Putin in the form of a crow. We're Facebook friends. He sang the most beautiful song. It was called, 'Give it Back.'" I sing it for you, swinging my hips like a metronome gone mad. "Give it back, give it back, give it back now. Give it back, give it back, give it back now." And I take your hand and pull you to me because I want to be close to you and I want you to dance with me and to love me as much as I love everything in this world. But your hand is balled tight and your body is stiff and you're not drooping at all anymore. Instead you're crying. You're covering your face. "Oh baby," I say, "Don't be sad." And I unball your hand and squeeze your fingers and run the fingers of my other hand across your cold and teary face. "There's nothing," I say, "but nothing, to be sad for." And I kiss your fingers and your dry lips and with my free hand I reach up and I stroke your hair and I poke about until I feel the bulge and then I dig in with my nails and pull another marble from your skull.

MARISA SILVER

ORIGINAL PRICE

FINAL PRICE

—DONATED—

$41.00

ITEM 69
TOY CAR

I failed my learner's permit test three times. The first time, my father was angry, because he had gotten out of bed at seven thirty on a Saturday morning so we could be first in line when the DMV opened at eight. Still, we had to wait three hours. "The world is not as simple as you make it out to be," he said, shifting in the uncomfortable plastic bucket seat, his fingers itchy for a newspaper or a coffee. "It's not just, 'you make a choice and stick to it.'" His words ran through my head while I took the test, and when my time was up, there were some answers I wanted to go back and change, but I didn't. When I failed, I knew he had been right.

The second time I failed the test, my mother said, "You think you can pull the wool over everyone's eyes, but you can't. I know what you are." We were in the living room and my little brother, Neil, looked up from the floor where he was rolling his toy cars back and forth on the light green carpet, making ruts that my mother complained about. Sometimes, when my parents were fighting, Neil would make his car noises loudly so that they would start yelling at him. His face relaxed while they berated him, like he was relieved.

"Words have meaning," my mother said, hotly, when I walked out of the test room the third time. I'd stopped trying to figure out what my parents were talking about most of the time, but something about what she said struck me as wrong because the more I studied, the less obvious the questions seemed to me. For instance: To avoid last-minute moves, you should be looking down the road to where your vehicle will be in about a) 5 to 10 seconds; b) 10 to 15 seconds; c) 15 to 20 seconds. Suddenly it made no sense that distance could be measured in time, or that you could avoid a future that was going to happen to you in only 20 seconds. Even though I had studied that question and knew the answer, I could not mark the right box with my stubby golf pencil because I was sure that the answer the DMV wanted was wrong.

The fourth time I went to take the test, my brother gave me one of his toy cars for good luck. My dad had bought him the car, telling him it was the same model as the first car he'd ever owned. The car was pink and my brother had tried to paint it over, but he didn't have the right kind of paint so the car ended up looking like a school bathroom. I put the car in my pocket, turned off my brain, and took the test. I passed. I made no mistakes at all. By this time my parents had split up and my aunt was waiting for me in the waiting area because my mother had started back at her old job selling perfume at the department store. I kept my brother's car all these years, even though the wheels have broken off and gotten lost, and it is so derelict even my own kids won't play with it. It reminds me that even if you look down the road to catch a glimpse of your future, there's not much you can avoid.

KATHRYN DAVIS

The sorcerer drove too fast. He always did but only because his mind was somewhere else, not because he was in love with speed. He was slow, really – sorcery is not a speedy business. What're speedy are the events that make sorcery necessary. His mind was on his wife, Mary, who sat day after day at her sewing machine turning out small pink dresses, some trimmed in white eyelet, some in lace. Today he was more distracted than usual, this being the same block he'd been driving down the night he first saw her, a skinny girl wearing glasses, balanced on one leg like a stork. The sycamore trees were taller now, full of nests. A shadow leaped from between two parked cars. It was twilight and the papers on the back seat came flying in a white fan around him.

Mary wanted a child more than anything and he'd conjured one up, only to run it over – that was his first thought. Then he saw that what he'd hit was no human child but a yellow bear. It had leaped out though – he was sure of that. The car had inflicted no damage the sorcerer could see. When he picked the yellow bear up it was smiling at him, its little mouth slightly open and eager, revealing the tip of the tongue but no teeth. It held its forepaws against its chest in a posture the sorcerer knew signified submission. Mary wanted a girl and the yellow bear seemed more like a boy, but then again it didn't have genitals. The sorcerer wiped it clean and took it home with him; every now and then he could hear a jingling sound come from it like it was a hard rubber cat toy with a bell inside. But the bear wasn't made of hard rubber; it was made of something soft and warm more like skin.

Mary loved the yellow bear the minute she laid eyes on it; she held it to her cheek and smiled. "The baby's tired. She wants to go to sleep now," Mary told the sorcerer. She put it in one of the pink dresses and carried it upstairs with her, then she got into bed with it and turned off the light.

In the morning when the sorcerer brought Mary her breakfast tray of tea and toast he found her propped on her pillows, the bear at her breast. Mary was no longer smiling but had tears running down her cheeks. "I don't know if I can do it," Mary told him. The jingling sound was very loud now, ear-splitting. "She won't stop," Mary said. "She needs something from you, too. That's how babies get made, in case you forgot."

"She's no baby, she's a toy," the sorcerer said, but when he went to show Mary the rubber seam running across the top of the bear's head, the baby sank its teeth into his thumb clear to the bone.

Later, when Mary had cried herself to sleep, the sorcerer snuck the bear from her breast and filled it with something secret. "Pablum," he told Mary when she asked, because now there could be no question, the child was alive and thriving and cute as a button. Buttercup, the sorcerer called her. But Mary knew better and treasured these mysteries deep in her heart.

ORIGINAL PRICE

FINAL PRICE

$1⁴⁹ $56⁰⁰

ITEM 71
FORTUNE-TELLING DEVICE

RACHEL AXLER

10/12/91

Q: Does John like me? A: TRY AGAIN
Q: Does John like me? A: TRY AGAIN
Q: ... Does Alex like me? A: YES

11/27/91

Q: So I asked John out, and he said okay after only a little thinking, and we went to the movies and it was great! Actually, it wasn't great, but we definitely went to the movies. Three times! I paid for his tickets, and he brought a friend along and paid for her tickets. Sometimes he and his friend would kiss a little. Is John my boyfriend? A: ASK A FRIEND

Q: I asked Ashley because I figured she'd know, since she's been coming to the movies with us so much. She said no. Is that because Ashley's jealous? A: TRY AGAIN

Q: ... Does Alex still like me? A: YES

12/07/91

Q: What should I wear on Saturday when I see *Hook* with John and Ashley? A: TRY AGAIN

Q: Sorry – I forgot I have to phrase these questions in a certain way. Um ... should I wear a dress? A: NO WAY

Q: Jeans, then. But a cute sweater? A: TRY AGAIN

Q: ... You want me to wear scrubs again. A: YES

Q: Really? Again? A: YES

Q: But they look so bad on me. A: YES

12/24/91

Q: Merry Christmas tomorrow!! I'm thinking of getting John a present, since he's my boyfriend. A: NO WAY

Q: I know, right? It's a big step. But that wasn't the question. My question is – how about, like, a CD? You think he'd like that? A: MAYBE

Q: I wonder what his favorite band is. A: YES

Q: Really? That's weird. I thought maybe he might like that new band, Nirvana. But you think I should get him 20-year-old British prog rock? A: DEFINITELY

1/6/92

Q: John showed everyone at school the weird CD I got him and everyone at school laughed at me. Except Alex, who looked kind of hurt or angry or something. That was a jerky suggestion, fortune-teller ... Why are you shaking? You're shaking a little. Are you laughing? Are you actually laughing?! A: MAYBE

Q: I can't believe this! You're totally evil! Are you purposely giving me terrible answers? A: NO WAY

Q: You just don't want to admit how in love with me John is! You're trying to break us up! A: MAYBE

Q: That's it – I'm never consulting you again. I hate you. You suck. [FORTUNE-TELLER PLACED IN BACK OF CLOSET; ANSWER UNCONFIRMED]

6/1/92

Q: Hi. It's me again. Um, John and Ashley are going to prom together. And I wasn't invited along, so I guess they're a couple now. A: NO WAY

Q: I know. They're big jerks. Oh, but Alex got me a birthday present. *Off the Deep End*, by Weird Al. It's pretty dorky. But funny. A: YES

Q: So, what do I do about prom? I can't show up alone. I'll be mortified. A: ASK A FRIEND

Q: ... You want me to ask Alex, don't you? A: DEFINITELY

6/24/92

Q: So, we didn't just go to prom together. We also went to the movies. Alone! I mean, with each other, but nobody else. Except the other people in the theater. Oh, who, by the way, included John and Ashley ... and Laurel. John sat between them, and in the middle of the movie, Ashley got up, and she was crying, and she dumped popcorn all over John. It was better than the movie. A: NO WAY

Q: Seriously. But anyway, I guess I didn't have a question for you. A: –

Q: I just wanted to say ... we had a good time. A: –

Q: You were right. A: I KNOW.

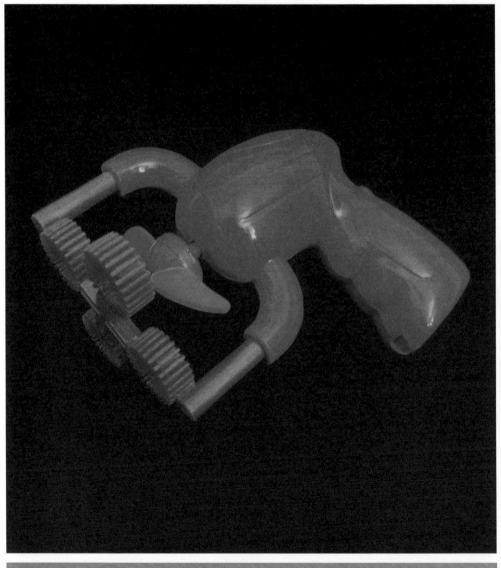

MYLA GOLDBERG

This is not a toy. Only the young or the hopelessly commonsensical dip it into liquid soap, content with bubbles. Curl your fingers around the handle, lift it to your mouth, and flick the switch. Say what you long to say. The fan is small, but its aim is true. You will be heard.

ROBERT LOPEZ

ORIGINAL PRICE

FINAL PRICE

ITEM 73
TOY AIRPLANE

—DONATED—

$19⁵⁰

A man on a park bench then another man next to him.

The first man there for no good reason.

The other man the kind of man who sits next to strange men on park benches.

This other man has with him a toy airplane.

He holds the toy airplane in his right hand, which is battered, bloodied.

It looks as though the other man had been in a street-fight and was declared the winner. The toy airplane his trophy.

The other man holds the toy airplane like a trophy.

The day has in it the sky and sun.

There are clouds and women.

It is routine.

The first man looks at the other man. He looks at the toy airplane. He says nothing.

A week goes by. Then another.

Then the man holding the toy airplane speaks.

And of course to make a long story short, he says, anyone living in a pretty how townhouse can look beyond themselves into the kitchen breakfront and clearly see between two pieces of ordinary china that every second of every livelong day of an already long week in a rather long month can often lead to an even longer year and subsequently is almost always followed by a long decade which is only one tenth of a long century and compared to the long long millennium is practically insignificant on this or any other beautiful Sunday morning.

The first man says, I know what you mean, and leaves.

The other man remains on the bench holding the toy airplane for the rest of his natural born life, which concludes twelve years later on a Thursday evening, just before dusk.

The body goes undisturbed until the next day when a passerby alerts the authorities. Two hours later the body is removed and taken to the county medical examiner's office.

There is no mention of the toy airplane in the medical examiner's report, only a note concerning the right hand in which the subject held the toy airplane, which was strangely contorted and atrophied.

JENNY OFFILL

Everything that has eyes will cease to see," says the man on the television. He looks credentialed. His hair has a dark gleam to it. His voice is like the voices of those people who hand out flyers on the subway, but he's not talking about God or the government.

"When is everyone coming?" my daughter says. "Isn't everyone coming?" She drags her dollhouse out of her room and begins arranging and rearranging the dining room chairs. It is hard to make them as they should be, it seems. One is always askew. She is so solemn, my little girl. So solemn and precise. Carefully, she places the tiny turkey in the center of the table. It is golden brown. Someone has carved a perfect flap in it. Why, I wonder. Why must everything have already begun? "Hurry," she murmurs as she works. "Hurry, hurry!"

The credentialed man is talking about the heavens now, about their most ruinous movements. The time lapse shows a field of plants perishing, a mother and child blown away by a wave of red light. Something distant and imperfectly understood is to blame for this. But the odds against it are encouraging. Astronomical even.

Still, I won't be happy until I know the name of this thing.

ORIGINAL PRICE

FINAL PRICE

$1<u>00</u> **$104**50

ITEM 75
PINK HORSE

KATE BERNHEIMER

A long time ago, I was very poor and often traded my body for cigarettes, Chelada, or food (in order of preference). I had two children – both daughters – and together we lived in a motel on the coast. It was a knotty-pine kitchenette cabin, and came furnished with a teapot, a few chipped flowered plates, some utensils, and bedding. The cabin overlooked a paved parking lot and beyond it, the beach. If a man came to visit, I sent my youngest girl out to find driftwood and starfish and shells. (Her sister was in kindergarten, so always gone in the morning.) There was no market for these trinkets among tourists; but they were precious to my little girls, truly their only possessions. We washed them and kept them along the edge of the porch rail and inside, on the white windowsills, which otherwise were very empty, apart from a pink horse my youngest had found in the woods. That pink horse! How she loved it. Once when she had gone a very long way to gather her treasures – all the way under a natural tunnel inside the cliffs, which led to a narrow beach that would trap you and kill you if you were stuck there during high tide – an old woman with pink hair approached her and sang her a song. My daughter told me about this old woman, but I didn't believe her. Later that week, my girl brought home a sea urchin, closed. She said that when the sea urchin opened, the old woman would return and that she had promised then to bring us good luck. I got an empty jar from the cupboard – it had once been full of beach plum jelly but had long been gathering dust. We walked down to the edge of the ocean and filled it with water. Back in the cabin, we placed the closed sea urchin carefully into the water, where it sank and stayed closed. The next morning my littlest girl didn't wake up and the sea urchin had bloomed. It was on her grave that my other daughter placed the pink horse. Then she too was taken – by the high tide – the very same week. She'd gone into the magic tunnel. Now I do nothing but drink Chelada all day, haunted by pink. Pink urchins, pink cigarettes. Pink horse, pink horse, pink horse on the grave – if ever the pink horse flies into the sky, your daughters will come back to life. The pink-haired old woman sang that to me once when I passed out in the sand. For now, there you stand in the dark of the wood – beautiful, all-powerful, and silent. Pink horse, you are everything, and everything is everlasting in you.

ITEM 76
CANDYLAND LABYRINTH
GAME

ORIGINAL PRICE

FINAL PRICE

29¢ $11⁵⁰

MATTHEW BATTLES

You had passed him at the entrance to the subway station countless times before, not so much sitting as thrown into the corner, his plump bulk indistinct beneath the rags he wore. What was different about this day? What changed conditions made you take notice of him? Was it some look in his eye, a trick of the light? But no, you've learned that there was nothing random about such days, when the cards flip and the world changes color. Or everything is random, but the deck was shuffled long ago – the moves determined, the game already played.

You caught a glimpse of his eye; his smile bubbled forth from the foul hood.

The sounds of the street receded. "Pick a color," he said with a strangely rich voice, a voice less like the barker than the circus itself. "Any color!"

"What?" you asked.

"Choose your color!" he replied. "Doesn't matter which. Your favorite color. Whatever color catches your ... your fancy! It will be the right one, I'm sure."

You shuddered – and then simply, with a shrug, you said, "red." The man drew from his pockets the small plastic box, the prism mapped with colored blocks and candycanes. He shook it slowly in the plane of the earth's surface. As if sifting for some artifact. A smile hung in the depths of his hood, and the smile grew. Tiny figures darted up and down the rainbow trail, until the hand – dry, you noted, but somehow shockingly soft – the hand froze when the red man came to rest at the end of the trail. And with a seeming gust of wind (though nothing rustled, nothing shifted), the world went red (though nothing changed).

And now the little box was in your hands; the plump and shapeless man was gone. How had he so quickly transferred it to you? How did he make his vast bulk so thoroughly disappear? Questions that disappeared in a purple mist that faded to red, leaving you with the little rattle-box labyrinth and a growing deadness that flowed down your limbs and into your heart.

The world of acts and things became a rosy shadow. People swept along the sidewalk borne by what currents you knew not; they flowed right through you. Trucks trundled by without a rumble; music rang out soundlessly; the chess players in the courtyard were reduced to calculating clouds. What was vivid and solid, what was real, was invisible to them: candycane fences, molasses swamps, plumdrop trees that sprang up wherever you went. They alone had the power to dazzle – yet they lacked any sweetness; they did not nourish you in your entranced despondency. And so the years streamed on from red to green to yellow to blue. The bright limits of the old life – goals, friends, loved ones – were crowded out by colors that had been present from the dawn of things, determined by a turning of cards that was simple in its unwavering instantiation. For you it was only the turning of the years; the sweets without succor; the endless hopeless shaking of the box.

Until your recent deliverance! That revelation of holy oblivion, it occurred not long ago: there you sat by the turnstiles shaking the little maze-box when reason flooded your mind. The figures – are trapped inside – and yet their movements are – random! Undetermined by past events, with no bearing on the future! And with a clap the colors merged again, great annuary blocks of diffraction colliding and conceding one to another. The misty figures of passers-by resolved, and the flood of consequence rolled like unredeemed refreshment. And the strange talisman, the map of your unbecoming, became all it had ever been: a silly plaything, a game for unconsidered moments, freedom in the swerve. And so, do pass it on; its curse is broken.

DARA HORN

Among Franz Kafka's possessions upon his death from tuberculosis in 1924 were many unpublished manuscripts and personal effects, all entrusted to the novelist Max Brod, whom Kafka had appointed as executor of his estate. In his will, Kafka specifically instructed Brod to burn all of his manuscripts, an order which Brod chose to defy. No instructions were provided regarding Kafka's personal effects.

In addition to *The Trial*, Kafka at the time of his death was also at work on another manuscript, tentatively titled *Metamorphosis II: Monkey Puppet*. A sequel to *The Metamorphosis*, *Metamorphosis II* continues the story of the surreally afflicted Samsa family. After Gregor the cockroach's death and Mr. and Mrs. Samsa's relief as they notice their daughter Grete's blossoming young figure ("they had come to the conclusion that it would soon be time to find a good husband for her") in the final pages of Volume 1, *Metamorphosis II* resumes ten years later, with Grete Rosenzweig, née Samsa, as a discontented hausfrau and indulgent mother of three in Prague. In the opening paragraph, Grete Rosenzweig awakens from uneasy dreams to discover that she has been transformed into a plush puppet belonging to her surly and ungrateful six-year-old son Adolf. As young Adolf begins a systematic program of sadistic destruction of his playthings, Grete reconsiders her approach to parenting while pondering the absence of God.

"Franz should have appointed another executor if he had been absolutely and finally determined that his instructions should stand," Brod later wrote. "But when I read *Monkey Puppet*, I immediately saw a way to honor his wishes."

In this fashion *Metamorphosis II: Monkey Puppet* was lost to the ages, along with several pages from Kafka's diary that referred to Brod's wife as "obtuse." Today only the puppet itself remains, silent witness to the limitations of art.

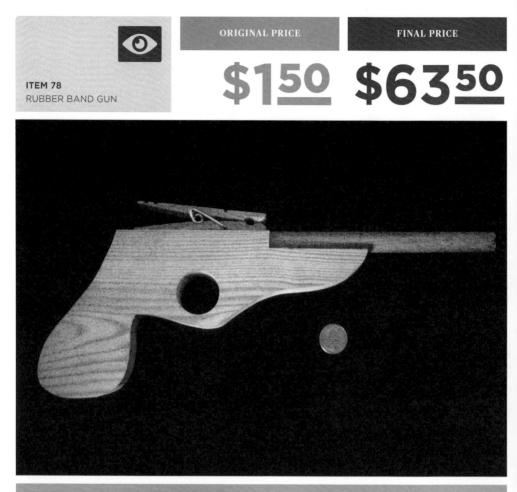

BENJAMIN PERCY

I brought to school a rubber band gun I bought at the mall. I bought it at that store with the tarot cards and the stink bombs and the beer T-shirts and the posters of women in thongs bending over on beaches with sand stuck to them in all the right places. So I brought to school the gun and showed it off to Stacey Swanson. I was a little in love with her. By that I mean I regularly jerked off into an athletic sock when thinking about her naked.

Normally she would not talk to me except to say, "Don't even talk to me – you haven't even gone through puberty yet." But this time, when I held out the rubber band gun, she said, "Let me see that." She grabbed the gun and weighed it in her hand a moment before lifting her arm and staring down the line of it and shooting me directly in the eyeball.

The eyeball did not fare well. The rubber band hit the pupil directly, punctured it, buried itself like a worm. The doctor removed the eyeball and put it in a bottle of formaldehyde. I keep the bottle on my dresser. I can tell the temperature by the eyeball, its buoyancy. Whether it is up or down makes me throw on shorts or a sweatshirt. Sometimes the eyeball seems to stare at me. And sometimes, when the pressure drops and a thunderstorm rolls through, the eyeball spins in circles like some possessed weathervane.

Every night I clean out the socket with a warm washcloth, a squirt of soap. There is a smell otherwise.

Used to be, people would make fun of me, a little rough in the hallways with their shoulders, a shove at the urinals. Now nobody touches me. They call me Cyclops and they beg me to lift my eyelid, show them the scooped-out socket. Sometimes I do.

I put things in the socket. A penny. A marble. A strawberry. You should have seen the look on Gabby's face when I walked up to her desk and without a word dug into the socket and pulled out the mushed-up strawberry and popped it in my mouth to swallow.

Other things, too. Like a tongue. Stacey Swanson's if you can believe it. Ever since she shot me in the eyeball she has been touching me on the shoulder, asking, "How are you today, Jimmy?" One time she asked if there was anything she could do for me. I said there was. She said, no, not that, that was terrible – that was the most disgusting thing she had ever heard. But I said please, it would mean a lot to me, and offered her the forty dollars I had swiped from my mother's purse.

She wiped her mouth afterwards and demanded the money and ran from me crying and I stood there, behind the school dumpster, breathing heavily and shaking with an electric pleasure that I never would have experienced had it not been for the rubber band gun.

Kitchenware

TOTAL SALES: 417.00

INITIAL COST: 15.67

ADDED VALUE: 401.33

PATRICK CATES

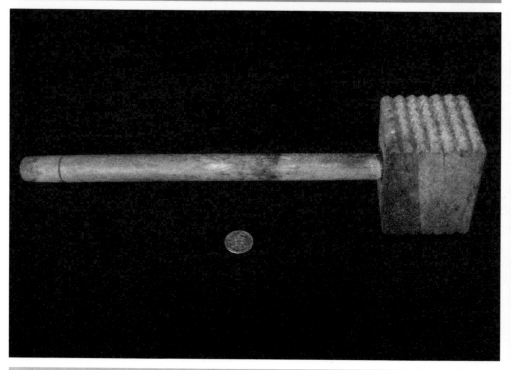

"Gastro-wot, Tone?"

The regular punters were not happy when Tony told them that he couldn't afford to run the Haunch of Venison any more and that, after 20 years as landlord, he had no choice but to sell up to some toff who'd made a fortune in the City and now wanted his own gastropub. The Haunch of Venison was undoubtedly a rough old boozer that needed sharpening up – yellow walls from the days before the smoking ban; crumbling plaster on the Victorian, molded ceiling; carpet that was more stain than carpet. But it was a hub. A vital organ. A satellite of Smithfield meat market that tucked itself away up Charterhouse Street and brought together butchers, drivers, packers, farmers – anyone who had anything to do with the trade and who needed to soothe the pain of a seriously early start with a couple of pints and a fry-up.

"Jesus, Tone. The old man'll be turning in his grave."

Ray Burkiss had run the pub for 43 years until he retired. And in that time he had peppered the place with all manner of meat memorabilia. Tony was born upstairs, had started collecting glasses when he was still in shorts and, as soon as he had left school without so much as an O-level, had assumed the predictable position of Ray's heir. And, when Ray died in 1980, Tony was crowned governor and carnal curator of the Haunch.

§

The Haunch's final day came and whistled by. An all-day and all-night procession of meat-industry men lining up with chokes and tears to clench Tony tightly and tell him that it was a shocking state of affairs. At ten to eleven, a defeated Tony followed his usual routine. He pulled the wooden meat tenderizer out of the lamb skull where it sat all day, held it back over his shoulder and smashed it down on the brass bell that hung above the bar. Over the top of the fading clang, he bellowed "Last orders!" like a sergeant major and awaited the onrush. And then, ten minutes later, another smash with the hammer. "Time at the bar!"

When there were just five of us left, gathered silently in a boozy huddle on the public side of the bar, Tony pulled out an unopened litre of Teacher's from under the counter and set it down in front of us. He unscrewed the cap, reached up for a glass with one hand and filled it with the other. He threw the glass up to his lips, bolted the contents and slammed the glass down. Another: fill, bolt, slam. And another. And another.

"Steady on, Tone."

Sean broke the silence. Tony glared at him and, without looking away, picked up the bottle, put it to his lips and started glugging. A few shocked seconds elapsed before Sean reached over the bar and tried to yank the bottle away from Tony's mouth. Tony yanked back, and in the fumble that followed, the bottle flew behind him, crashed into two of the optics, knocked them off their mountings and cracked a sprawling web across the Haunch's most valuable artifact: a giant, wall-mounted mirror engraved with the image of a startled buck hemmed in by the name of the pub.

In a one-two of disbelief and devastation, Tony let out a violent roar, reached for the nearest weapon he could find, the meat tenderizer, and, with a backbeat of regular, heaving sobs, whirled round and round swiping at everything within his reach.

STACEY D'ERASMO

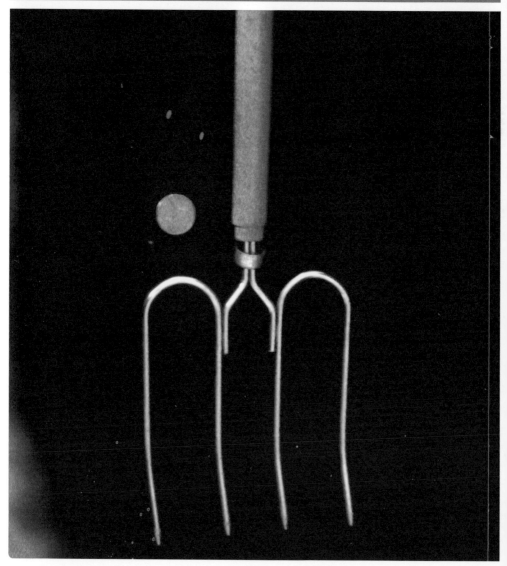

In the sugar house, near the celluloid sea, we tend to wake up early. You are – you design small, lovely, useful things in a room at the top of the sugar house. I am – I am doing research for a massive biography of three kings: the grandfather king (the First), the son king (the Second) and the last king (the Third). This research will take many years; it has already taken many years. We wake up early to put in a good day's effort on our projects. I work at the big kitchen table, surrounded by paper. At lunch, we sit on a bench outside and lean against the white wall, eating sandwiches and looking at the sea, which seems marcelled. It is turquoise, deepening to a turtleback green in the troughs of the still waves.

You pick up a little pitchfork which is lying under the bench; our son, who is eight, must have dropped it there, it's from his miniature farm, with its miniature fences, its miniature farmhouse, its tiny horses and cows and sheep, its petite silo filled with jelly beans. Look at this, you say, holding it out to me on your palm. Look how perfect it is, there is nothing extraneous in its design, it is exactly suited to its task. I take it from you and gently comb your hair with it. The first king was crazy, I tell you; the second king was a thief; the last king lost the kingdom altogether, because he was obsessed with conquering the neighboring kingdom. If only history were as sane as the tools we make. Kings waste the days, turn them to bad ends.

Even in the sugar house, you're not quite listening. I put the little pitchfork between us on the bench, as if it, too, is our child. Or maybe it is a weapon that I am laying down. Or maybe I am giving it to you. Or maybe it is a tuning fork, finding the pitch of our silence. Even in the sugar house, I don't know if that silence is companionable, or truculent, or prefatory to a much longer silence. Even in the sugar house, I take your hand instead of asking and hope that that warmth is enough. Even in the sugar house, I am surrounded by distracted kings.

The last time we had dinner together, we were in a Greek restaurant on 14th Street. You sat up straight, talking animatedly. Your hair was wet from showering at the gym. Before the food came, you were drawing invisible designs on the white tablecloth with your fork, punctuating each four-score line with a firm metallic tap. There, that's done. I reached across the table, took your hand. I didn't want you to finish the last line, sound the last note. I knew what you were going to say, probably over dessert. I preferred, just for the moment, to dwell in the infinite possibilities of that small silence.

LUCINDA ROSENFELD

My grandmother, Zippy Friedman, was an administrator at Austen Riggs Psychiatric Hospital in Stockbridge, MA, for several decades beginning in the 1950s. She was also a close friend of artist Norman Rockwell and was instrumental in having him admitted there during a particularly gruesome bout of depression. (Yes, the acclaimed illustrator of those aggressively cheerful *Saturday Evening Post* covers suffered from chronic depression.)

Anyway, for whatever reason, Norman brought this golden cow creamer with him to Riggs – and then failed to bring it home. Which is how it ended up in my grandmother's kitchen in nearby Pittsfield, where it sat on the windowsill next to a Provencal Rooster (also made of porcelain) until her death in 1983. What's more, according to my mother, at some point my grandmother started referring to the creamer as "Norman," as in, "Let's all have tea – someone grab Norman."

Which makes me wonder if something bad happened between them. Why? If you can't tell from the pictures, the cow's got a pretty angry and unforgiving look on her face. And, depressed though he frequently was, the real Norman Rockwell was apparently a delightful, kind man. (Mysteries never cease.) So anyway, my young daughter told me she finds "Norm" scary. And we get our hot beverages to go – at Starbucks. But he really is a piece of history. No chips. Lovely glaze intact. Pours well.

VICTOR LαVALLE

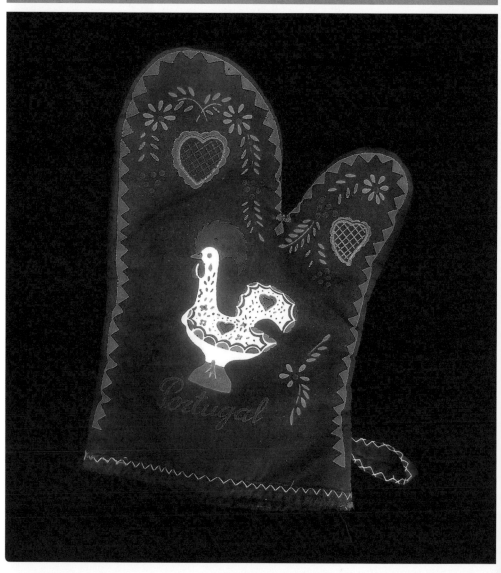

Who the hell goes to Portugal? In my family?

The question arose as my sister and I were going through my grandmother's things – her effects. She'd died of old age at Queens General Hospital and she'd been longing for it. Some people never want to go, but not her. She'd lived long (96 years), seen her grandkids and *great* grandkids.

The old lady didn't own the apartment she'd lived in, alone, for 22 years. After she died my grandmother's landlord (New York City Housing Authority) sent a letter: two weeks to clear her things. Then they would be bagged and bussed to a dump. So my sister and I spent evenings taking the 7 train to Jackson Heights, climbing nine flights to grandma's apartment (her elevator was about as reliable as our older sister). We decided what to keep, what to sell, what to donate, and what to leave for the City.

Let's be blunt: the mitt's not pretty. Okay, it's ugly as an unwashed butt. I didn't find it in my grandmother's kitchen. Or in the living room, where she'd sit and have tea in the after-noons. It was in her bedroom, slipped between the mattress and box spring. Some old ladies stow bags of cash, my grandmother hid a Portuguese cooking glove. I showed it to my sister, but she'd found my grandmother's small Bible. Was leafing through, marveling at the notes our grandmother left in the margins. She got the Good Book; I kept the mitt.

Then, I brought the thing home and forgot about it! My sister and me, we helped our mother through the next few months. Eventually I found myself getting back into life. Like I started going on dates again. My head clear, my heart ready, my bed cold. So one night I've got this lovely woman at my place. She comes over to split a bottle of wine while we prepared a meal. My part consisted of uncorking the bottle. Meanwhile she made squash soup. The second or third step is to bake the two halves of a split squash, hot enough until you can peel back the rough outer skin with a butter knife. She opens the oven door and asks for a mitt to pull out the tray and what do I reach for? That's right. Had it in a cupboard over the sink.

My friend slides the glove on, reaches into the oven, but as she's pulling the tray she loses her grip and the squash goes to the ground. I just laughed. I was drunk, and this pretty lady had already let me kiss her. What could I be upset about?

But she wore another expression. Not anger. Not pain. Bewilderment. She slipped the oven mitt off and turned it inside out. I thought she was going to rip it so I shouted, but then I saw the inside of the oven mitt. It was covered in words.

Not writing. Letters *stitched* into the fabric! We read the words, starting at the top, where the middle finger would reach. It read: *My dearest Grace* (that's my grandmother) *I hold your memory like I held your form. I feel sunlight across my body and the warmth of you. The warmth of being inside you ...*

And it went on like that.

A lot.

Turns outs my grandmother was kind of a slut!

My friend and I poured wine. Toasted the old woman. Good for her.

75¢ $54.00

MATTHEW J. WELLS

Booth 106 was the regular table of Evelyn Nesbit – it's where she was introduced to Charles Dana Gibson, who used her as the model for his famous Gibson Girl drawings; it's where she met the young John Barrymore, who became her lover and got her pregnant twice (once in the booth itself and once in his apartment); it's where she was introduced to architect Stanford White by fellow Floradora Girl Edna Goodrich; and it's where she met her future husband Harry Thaw, who murdered White at Madison Square Garden on June 25, 1906.

Originally surrounded by red velvet drapes, the booth is now open and unlit. On the wall is a photo of Nesbit from her Gibson Girl days and beneath it, on a small shelf, is a little jar labeled "BAR-B-Q Sauce." The jar was originally purchased by Nesbit as a gift for White – whenever White would meet her for dinner, he would order ribs, and she paid the waiters to always keep the small jar full of sauce at the table for White's special use. Very special, according to suppressed trial testimony after his murder – allegedly, the ribs weren't the only things White covered in barbecue sauce behind those drapes.

After White's death, Booth 106 was roped off as a sign of mourning, a RESERVED sign was placed on the table, and per Evelyn Nesbit's wishes, once a week the bartender would refill the BAR-B-Q jar, as if in preparation for White's eventual return. The table went empty for almost two years (not even Nesbit sat at it), until the afternoon of January 5, 1908, when Harry Thaw sailed into the Naughty Pine, plunked himself down at Booth 106, ripped up the RESERVED sign, tore down the red velvet curtains, draped them around his body like a winding sheet, and demanded a shave. When told that he was in a bar and not a barber shop, Thaw cried, "Then I'll do it myself," whereupon he pulled out a straight razor, stropped it on his leather belt, and taking the BAR-B-Q jar, proceeded to slop sauce all over his face as if it were shaving cream. Then, pretending to stare into a mirror, he gave himself a blood-soaked shave while humming "I Could Love A Million Girls," the song that had been playing when he shot White in the face.

"You must be a lunatic," said one of the waiters. Thaw just smiled at him. His first trial for the murder of Stanford White had ended in a deadlocked jury; but the next day, when his second trial began, he pleaded not guilty by reason of insanity.

GREG ROWLAND

ORIGINAL PRICE

$3<u>00</u>

FINAL PRICE

$32<u>00</u>

ITEM 84
MUSHROOM SHAKER

I am a mycologist. I study fungi. (I do not study "toadstools" or "fairy rings." These are objects of fantasy, not science. Ask me about "toadstools" or "fairy rings" and I will most surely spit in your eye.)

It is my great misfortune to encounter non-mycologists from time to time. It may seem astonishing, but there are people who cannot separate *agaricaceae* from *coprinaceae*, much less *entolomataceae* from *strophariaceae*. But I can, because I am a mycologist.

I have mixed emotions when I meet people who cannot distinguish between *entolomataceae* and *strophariaceae*. Mostly I feel pity, mixed with a burning feeling of nausea that settles around my upper trachea. Sometimes I feel pure hatred. I reserve the stronger emotions for those who deliberately flaunt a lack of mycological knowledge as some kind of "badge of honour." Please be assured that, if I were to meet you, and you deliberately flaunted your lack of mycological knowledge in my presence, then I would most definitely spit in your eye.

Beyond that, here are the two worst things you can say to a mycologist:

"Is there 'mush-room' in your field for advancement?"

"You must be a real 'fun-gi' to be with."

It is the fun-gi "joke" that fills the mycology community with dread and foreboding. It is repeated to us every time we venture outside of the mycology community. (Sometimes up to twice a month.) It is enough to make a mycologist spit. It is certainly enough to make a mycologist produce a unique form of body-anger-fungus – which has, ironically, provided a research paper dividend for two less than honorable members of our field. (You know who you are.)

A human female, who carried no malign fungal infections, gave me this Mush-room Shaker. She was attracted to mycologists, and had never knowingly uttered The Joke (*op. cit.*). She was a dilettante mycologist at best, yet her shiny shoes and gadfly, fungal-free demeanor blinded me.

Some might see this as a thoughtful gift for a mycologist. They would be wrong. This "gift" is merely an extension of the ritual degradation of our science by the non-mycology community (see above, *passim*). This is why its companion piece is now in several pieces in a landfill, having been battered into fragments by a specialized hard-fungal chipping utensil.

This object is a non-mycologically accurate three-dimensional evocation of a non-existent mushroom. Do not use it as a reference device. Or for any purpose whatsoever. Don't even look at it for more than 0.75 seconds.

In closing, I contend that this Mushroom Shaker embodies a strong risk of mycological disinformation. Just like the woman who gave it to me.

ORIGINAL PRICE

FINAL PRICE

$2<u>99</u>

$76<u>00</u>

ITEM 85
FISH SPOONS

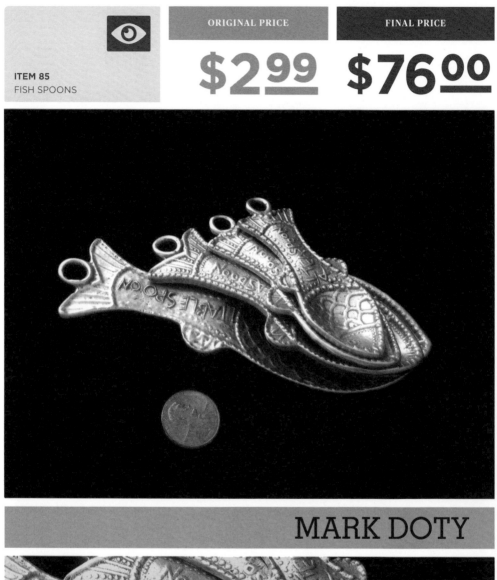

MARK DOTY

As a young man I read a poem I've never run across again since. I found it in the school library. If you already knew what you wanted in this haphazard collection, you were sunk, but if you spent time pulling things off the high, not-much-visited steps, you could get lucky.

The poem was Anglo-Saxon, a riddle, and it had to do with cold armor that never clanked, with chain mail that moved with a strange fluidity, as if it were made of mercury – though I'm sure I've added that detail, in memory. The Anglo-Saxons didn't have mercury, did they? Or maybe they did.

I think what I liked best about the poem was the feeling of things moving in darkness, beneath the surface, not at all troubled about being in the dark. That and something about the allure of ancient silver, that there were mines, somewhere in the far mountains, and people had learnt the methods of refining the hidden ore and bringing the malleable shining stuff into the light.

Which does not exactly explain why I stole the spoons. It was an outdoor fair, at the end of September, in a field that belonged to the Kiwanis, rented out on weekends for carnivals or farmers' markets or, this day, the big rows of tables on which the collectors had arrayed their stuff. It seems obvious now, but it had never occurred to me that practically everything here had belonged to someone, perhaps several people, and that most of those people were dead. It was all here to be redistributed to some new place, for a while.

I was fifteen, I didn't have any money, but it would be false to say that's why I took them. I never looked at the price tag. I acted on impulse; I saw them, from a few feet away, and felt as if I was suddenly a little off balance. I moved toward them directly, peripherally aware that the woman who minded the goods was turned in another direction, to help a customer who was considering the purchase of pottery jug. I put my hand over the cluster of spoons – they were nestled one into another, like silver fish who each had swallowed a smaller member of their tribe – and slipped them into my jacket pocket.

And then what? I couldn't show them to anyone. I was a little ashamed of stealing them, but that feeling was not as strong as my pleasure, when I could lift them from the back of my sock drawer, and peel back the tissue paper I'd wrapped them in, and study this private token I'd come to possess.

SARI WILSON

It's incongruous. The buttery finish, the fluted spout, the air hole in the back of its head offering a peek into its ceramic innards, a glimpse of the thick cream that no one is supposed to have anymore. The torso pitched forward, the nubs of wings lifting, ready to employ itself in the service of our morning coffee. Except that neither of us drank coffee. No matter. We kept that creamer on our table for years. When we did start drinking coffee, we bought it at Starbucks in tall cups and we didn't even take milk in it.

Where did the creamer come from? Neither of us could remember. Maybe one of those estate sales we sometimes drove out to on Saturdays? For whatever reason, we adopted it. A Balinese sarong covered our rickety table. Then a Crate and Barrel linen cloth. Then we bought a new fancy table – an eight-seater, tavern-style.

Through all those years – our ambitious, job-hopping 20s – the creamer was like a mascot. When we were both promoted to V.P., we bought it a general's cap. We put sake in it. We treated it with the scornful irony we began to feel for each other. The creamer sat there, this patient, eyeless homunculus, watching us as we began to argue about stupid things like who would take out the garbage, how much to tip the delivery man, then louder and more forcefully, about real-like stuff. What we wanted. The future. It turned out that I was a Republican and wanted a bunch of kids. He was a Democrat and didn't want any. One night he grabbed the penguin creamer off the table and said, "What the hell is this?" As if he'd never seen it before. I almost said, "It's our baby."

When I moved out I took that orphaned creamer but left everything else. It sits on the red-checked oilcloth covering my bistro table. My new boyfriend pours cream from its spout and says, "Cute little guy."

ORIGINAL PRICE

FINAL PRICE

50¢ $26.01

ITEM 87
COOKING FORK

DAN CHAON

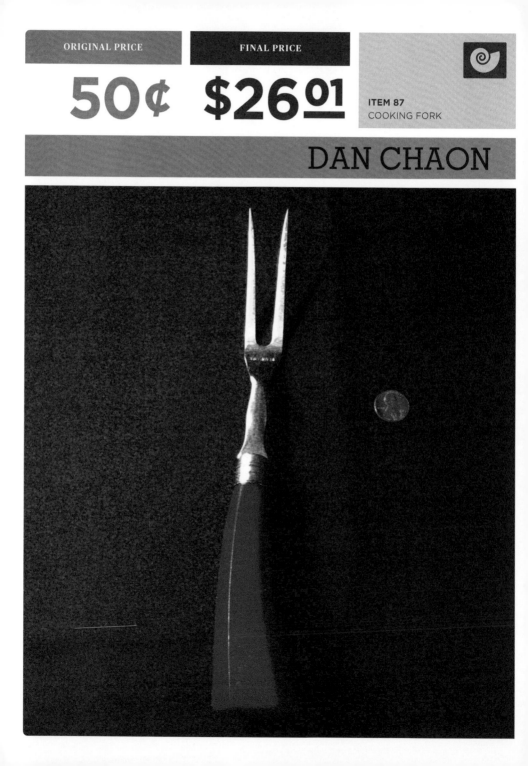

When you are a widower, you're supposed to move your wedding band from the left ring finger to the right. This is etiquette, or something. An old tradition.

When I removed the ring, about a year after she died, there was a crease in the flesh below my knuckle, a little belt that didn't go away, though I massaged it and rubbed it with lotion; it appeared that it would be more or less permanent. Weird! That was what made me remember the fork.

It was a two-pronged carving fork with a bright red plastic handle. When I was twelve, I stole it from the silverware drawer. I was very interested in the weapons of fantasy at that time: halberds and katanas, daggers and scimitars. The sorts of things your character would wield if you were playing *Dungeons & Dragons*.

For a while, I pretended the fork was a magical treasure I'd found in a barrow, and I hid it in my room under the mattress. During the autumn of seventh grade, I used to like to poke myself with the fork. Late at night, when my door was locked. This was before I'd discovered masturbation.

A carving fork sinks easily into a brisket or a roast turkey breast, but the tines are not that sharp. When you press the points against the underside of your forearm, you can exert considerable force without breaking the skin, just a couple of blanched indentations in your flesh. Then the dermis rises back, leaving only small red dots – like gnat bites – which fade as well.

Here: your wrist, where a bundle of blue veins shift thickly when you prod them. Here: your ruddy, meaty palm, webbed with fortune-teller lines. At this point, you are not really able to push the fork through. You're just experimenting. Here: okay, admit it – your most sensitive spots, the nipples, the soft hollow in your throat, the glans of your cock –

What does this *feel* like? How much does it hurt?

The memory appears abruptly. A glint of metal, a prodding of synapse that hasn't been awake for years. Suddenly adolescent again: that illness unfolds in me and it's funny because I realize that it's not something I would ever have told my wife. She would have wrinkled her nose. Boy stuff, she would have thought – like talking about shit or boogers, gross and uninteresting.

And yet, who else am I going to tell this little anecdote to?

I sit here looking at the impression the wedding ring has left in my flesh. I suppose that it will eventually go away.

My wife was the first and only girl I had sex with. We met when I was eighteen, and she died when I was forty-five.

I don't know what became of the fork. I used it for a while, and then, I guess, more than likely, I put it back where it came from.

NICHOLSON BAKER

ORIGINAL PRICE

FINAL PRICE

75¢ $51.00

ITEM 88
MEAT THERMOMETER

Everything had a temperature in those days. Cheese was cold. Avocados were warm. My heart was a piece of hot meat pierced by love's thermometer.

JOHN WRAY

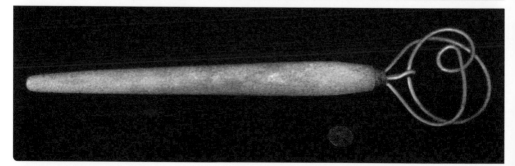

"It's certainly – well. It's certainly a something," Lily murmured, upon being introduced to the Object. "But what kind of something is it?"

"This," said Oliver, cradling the Object reverently in his open palms, "Is the something that is going to save our marriage."

Not having been birthed yesterday, Lily had her doubts, but she was willing to be persuaded. She was desperate to be persuaded, in fact. And there was something about the something in Oliver's palms that resisted all her efforts to resist it. Unlike most of the objects in Lily's environs, it seemed to raise more questions than it answered. First of all, what was it?

"What is it?" said Lily.

"I just told you," Oliver said patiently.

The Object expressed no opinion.

"Well, we might as well give it a try," Lily said. "How do we make it do?"

Oliver squinted down at the Object for a while, and then shrugged. "I think we just set it down in the corner," he said finally. "Give it room to do its work."

Lily considered this a moment, then took Oliver's hand, and they deposited the object, gently and circumspectly, in the room's nearest corner. "How long will it take?" Lily wondered.

"Ten and a half days," Oliver said firmly. Lily couldn't help noticing, however, that he avoided looking her in the eye. You'll never persuade me that way, Lily said to herself. The Object chittered and hummed in its corner.

"What a strange thing it is," Lily said. "It reminds me of something."

"Shhh!" Oliver whispered. "Don't talk about it. The less we acknowledge it, the better."

It wasn't until weeks later, when their marriage had long since been saved, that they saw the Object for what it truly was. By then, of course, it didn't make the slightest bit of difference.

Promotional
Items

TOTAL SALES: 388.07

INITIAL COST: 11.83

ADDED VALUE: 376.24

ORIGINAL PRICE

$1⁰⁰

FINAL PRICE

$76⁰⁰

ITEM 90
MISSOURI SHOT GLASS

JONATHAN LETHEM

L isten, friend, forget about the bartender, you could wait all day in this dive, we might as well be invisible over here, I kid you not. Here, let me pour you a drink. No, really, I insist, it's on me. I brought my own. Just swab out the dust and finger-prints with my shirttails, good as new. Love the way it claps down on the bar, gets your glands salivating, doesn't it?

No, after you, I insist. My pleasure.

See that freaky little bird? That's the *state* bird, my friend. The Missouri Hunt-and-Pecker. Never heard of 'em? Well, then I guess you've never been to Missouri, have you? Maybe passed through, didn't get out of the car. Or changed planes in the airport, or went up in the Arch once, just to say you'd done it. But that's not Missouri to me. St. Louis is the gateway, sure, but you want to know Missouri you need to drive a few hours into the corn, you want to visit St. Joseph, up through Maryville – skirt the Iowa border, though Iowa's a sore point from where I sit. You need to get lost in Missouri or you never really were there in the first place. Even then you won't be likely to meet the Hunt-and-Pecker unless you circulate a manuscript or two.

Manuscript, you heard me right. See, very few know it, because we keep it to our-selves, but Missouri is sick and silly with apprentice fictioneers, the whole state's like one vast harrowed and furrowed MFA workshop. Why do you think the license plates call it *The Show-Don't-Tell State*?

Yeah, sure, *Iowa*. We're not promiscuous like them. Rather sit on a manuscript for a hundred years than publish before we're ready. And when you really contemplate the motto's implications ... *show, don't tell* ... well, get me here, we've taken it to heart. By the time a roving Missouri critique outfit has detasseled your kernels, you better believe me you'll have second thoughts about advancing into the marketplace. More likely cancel your subscription to *Poets & Writers*, renew your vows to craft. Scene, setting, voice. Look at that fugging bartender, he'd serve a wood duck in a halter-top before he so much as glanced at us.

You like that? Here's another. Go ahead, you know you want to.

Or shut up entirely, always an option. That's the ultimate endpoint, you know. Don't write a *word*, just be a writer. We're more than a little stoical out here on the plain, son. Write more? Write *less*. I strive to write less every day, some day I'll get there. Not-telling isn't as easy as it appears.

Lookit 'im there, cool as a flippin' cucumber, straddling the state like nobody's business. Crazy little red-tailed devil knows more than he's saying too, can't you tell? Love the way he flushes amber, then goes all transparent again. Strive to be like a windowpane, not a mirror, that's how he makes his way through the world.

All right, I'm out of here. Here you go, you bastard! *Keep the change!* See, I always leave that sonuvabitch a tip – one red cent. Honest Abe, another fellow from the heartland who knew exactly when to shut up. Keep it real, friend.

BEN KATCHOR

50¢ $42<u>00</u>

ITEM 91
MAINE STATUTES DISH

This beautiful, but slightly worn, example of early 20th century porcelain "bookware" was manufactured and distributed free-of-charge along with newly printed copies of the *Maine Revised Statutes Annotated* – a dreary compendium of state laws.

This example, formed in the style of a small, shallow aperitif or snack dish, holds fifty salted peanuts. It was meant to encourage lawyers and public advocates to acquaint themselves with the latest revisions to state law. On one dishful of peanuts, a reader could make his way through several Titles and Chapters of the book.

This example of "bookware" cemented the connection between justice and eating within the professional classes of Maine. Each chapter was keyed to an estimated number of peanuts. The worn edge of the dish is evidence of the late-night reading of an overweight small-town lawyer.

Title 17, Chapter 131: MISCELLANEOUS CRIMES

    17 §3951. Abandonment of airtight containers (REPEALED) 15 peanuts

    17 §3952. Dangerous knives (REPEALED) 23 peanuts

    17 §3953. Disorderly conduct (REPEALED) 8 peanuts

    17 §3954. Disturbance of public meetings (REPEALED) 12 peanuts

    17 §3955. Dumping rubbish on another's land (REPEALED) 15 peanuts

    17 §3956. Electric fences: 8 peanuts

    17 §3957. Failure to report treatment of gunshot wounds (REPEALED): 18 peanuts

    17 §3958. False alarms and reports (REPEALED): 9 peanuts

    17 §3960. Peeking in nighttime (REPEALED) 34 peanuts

    17 §3961. Placing obstructions on traveled road (REPEALED): 15 peanuts

    17 §3962. Regulation of radio waves; disturbing reception (REVISED) 8 peanuts

    17 §3963. Riding with naked scythe (REPEALED): 17 peanuts

    17 §3965. Defacement of state facilities; possession of paint (REPEALED) 7 peanuts

    17 §3966. Animals in food stores (REVISED) 12 peanuts

    17 §2904. Use of phonographs for profane or obscene language (REPEALED): 45 peanuts

The *Maine Revised Statutes* are now available online.

JIM SHEPARD

ORIGINAL PRICE

FINAL PRICE

—DONATED—

$15^{50}

ITEM 92
STAR WARS CARDS

When I was little I'd ask my mother what I was getting for my birthday. I'd ask like the morning of my birthday. It always pissed her off because my birthday was December 27th.

"Look under that *tree*," she'd tell me. "You want to know what you're getting for your birthday? Go look under that Christmas tree."

When I got older I stopped asking. Then this last December when I'd been home a year she said "I got you something for your birthday."

"I'm still not getting a job," I said.

"Why are you so miserable to me?" she asked.

"So what is it?" I asked her a little while later. She went into her room and came back with a little package wrapped in candy cane paper. I tore off the wrapping and I'm standing there with a little box of *Clone Wars* collectible cards in my hand.

"You always liked *Star Waters*," she said. One time in school a teacher asked what my mother's first language was and I told him she didn't have one.

"I'm thirty-three years old," I told her.

"That means you can't like cards?" she said. "That means you can't enjoy anything any more?"

Everybody on the front of the box had a weapon. "That was nice of you to get me the cards," I told her.

"You can't be grateful for one thing?" she wanted to know.

"That was nice of you to get me the *cards*," I told her. Later on I wrote the same thing down, and stuck it on the refrigerator.

MAUD NEWTON

ORIGINAL PRICE

FINAL PRICE

59¢ $24⁵⁰

ITEM 93
CRACKER BARREL
ORNAMENT

This astonishing "Cracker Barrel" artifact appears to be a souvenir of modern vintage, representing a down-home North American restaurant-and-country-store chain that upholds Christian values by refusing to hire gay people. In fact, the object dates to the Bronze Age and was unearthed last week in the vicinity of the Dead Sea, on what is believed by several prominent archaeologists to be the site of the ancient cities of Sodom and Gomorrah. Alongside the artifact lay a charred cuneiform tablet that listed all five towns of the Pentapolis (Sodom, Gomorrah, Admah, Zeboiim, and Zoar) that were destroyed by the Lord with fire and brimstone while Lot and his family fled.

As scholars at the site quickly translated the tablet, they discovered a parable that directly contradicted the reasons given in Genesis for the devastation God wreaked on the inhabitants of those late, sinful cities. The Sodomites, in this account, were punished not for gay sex, but for failing to offer the proper hospitality to several strangers, who were homosexual men, and for trying to force their daughters on the men. The Sodomites had barred the visitors from their homes, bars, and restaurants, engaged in discriminatory hiring practices, and invented and frequently employed the insult "faygele." Same-sex unions, under any name, were prohibited.

Enraged that the people had apparently failed to apprehend the full meaning of the rainbow promise he had made to Noah after the flood, the Lord waved His hand. Volcanic lava rained down, killing everyone but Lot and his family – and a few Cracker Barrel employees, who escaped, carrying this artifact with them.

On initial inspection, strange markings on the underside of the cuneiform tablet appeared to tie the Cracker Barrel escapees to The Illuminati, but this linkage could not be verified, for, although it was handled with utmost care and in accordance with the strictest archaeological preservation methods, the tablet turned to salt the moment the initial transcription was complete. Then a ram began to baa nearby, its horn caught in a bush. Seconds later a rainbow appeared in the sky. Fundamentalist groups in the United States have now denounced the rainbow as a sign of the End Times. They continue to frequent Cracker Barrel, however.

ITEM 94
MARINES (UPSIDE-DOWN)
LOGO MUG

ORIGINAL PRICE

FINAL PRICE

75¢ $37⁰⁰

TOM VANDERBILT

If he had a personal philosophy, and if such things needed to be articulated, it might be called: the aerodynamics of everyday life. He wanted his surfaces clean, his leading edges freed from drag, he brooked no laggards in his drift. This served him well in his avocation, which, as systems operation manager for a large industrial concern (Imprinteon, a custom-printing operation), involved ensuring that inputs became outputs, with maximum efficiency and at minimum cost. But one would not go awry in ascribing his philosophy to his life outside work, which too bore the requirements of flight: streamlined, rigid, and with no ground attachments.

On this morning, however, headwind. First had come the ink debacle on line 37, as the Pantone 4604, "billowing sail," rendered so truly on screen, seemed wan in substrate form – more "rippling sheet." 10,000 college yearbooks were to be pulped. Then were the material flow issues in sector 4, some sort of line imbalance. His throughput was out of sync, and there was no parallel flow, no buffer. The first-pass yields were collapsing. He glared at the faded white sign on the wall: MTBF. *Mean time between failures*. Its scuffed adjustable wheels were calibrated to read "43." They would have go to back to 1, tomorrow.

And then the mug. It was placed in front of him, on his padded desk calendar, eclipsing March 3rd. It was a simple thing, really, the sort they ran millions of in a year, being the DOD's favored insignia contractor. Fortuna Favet Fortibus, it read, *Fortune Favors the Strong*. The error was so basic, so obvious, that he wondered if there weren't some hidden layer of complexity at work here. Privately, he allowed that one might read the mug's form factor in two ways: The wider, curved flare made most sense as the vessel's egress point, so the lips could comfortably adhere to the contours. And yet in some kind of drinkware equivalent of a Necker Cube, the brain might willfully invert the mug, so that the wider end could logically seem the stable base, as with the cooling towers of Three Mile Island.

But the lapse he could not comprehend was the handle orientation. For the logo to make sense in this latter configuration, this would have had to have been a right-handed mug; normally, this would make sense, but the 3rd Marine 8th battalion had a long-standing, obscure joke, which some colonel must have dreamt up years ago when this long-standing order was first requisitioned, that the 8th battalion liked to "drink with their left, and shoot with their right."

As it was, it could have been worse. The flaw was found in an acceptance sample (it was a retrograde technique, but he was working on a refinement that he would debut at next year's Logistics World) run about two hours, or 3000 mugs, into the lot. And here was one of those moments where he felt the keen sense of being at the center of things, of life in its great rushing cavalcade of risk and reward. Was the sample he had pulled a statistical aberration – one upturned mug among tens of thousands of mugs of proper disposition – or was it endemic of a system failure, a thorough corruption? Was he about to pull the plug on an otherwise stable process?

His assistant called out, the inspector was here. He put the mug in a file drawer to his left, and would later move it to a cabinet that he considered his own museum of error. "Have a seat," he said, closing the drawer.

It is little known that the singer Marcia Ball as a teenager worked briefly at Disney. One day at the close of the shift she was climbing out of her Goofy suit and was frightened to see two albino boys climbing out of their suits. It was Johnny and Edgar Winter. Marcia said something to the effect that she had never seen boys so white and Johnny turned on her and said, "I'm so white I am blind and I can't take this shit that sun out there besides I can play the guitar." Marcia liked his pluck.

Edgar said, "He can play but I can scream and I too have a frightening pallor and will look good on stage and, girl, you are so tall that I think even though you are full of melanin you can be a rock star too. Let's blow this joint and –"

Johnny Winter was ahead of them, in the corner setting his Porky suit on fire. "Practicing," he said. "I saw Jerry Lee do something like this on stage."

This is Marcia Ball's nametag, in the original packaging, circa 1962.

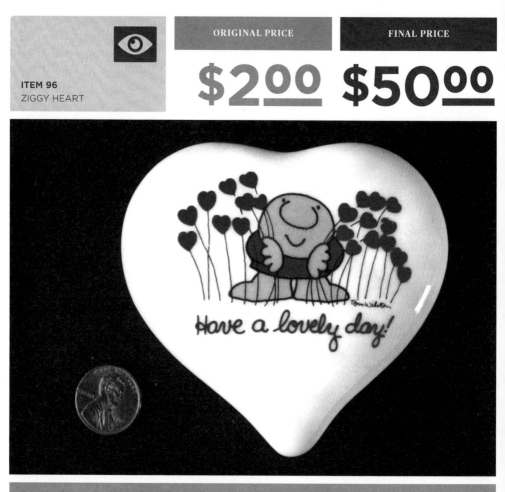

TODD LEVIN

Have you ever hated someone solely for her dumb benevolence? For bland and witless good cheer? It's the lowest of unfair acts, I know, but as soon as a smile crosses Mary Eileen's lips, my jaw tightens and my hands instinctively ball into fists.

I honestly have no idea what Mary Eileen does for this company. Benefits manager or creative resources or consumer metrics or birthday announcement committee co-chair or some other marginal department for which no award shows exist. A career path that dead-ends inside a grim cubicle squatting in the middle of a complicated floor plan. That is Mary Eileen's daily existence, not that it bothers her any.

I always guessed she was a Christian nutjob, with no real evidence to support that theory. Maybe I just assume anyone who likes *Cats: The Musical* enough to have a varsity jacket from the Broadway production draped over her desk chair like some kind of trophy for outstanding achievement in the field of mediocrity must be right with Jesus. So yeah, I associate *Cats* fandom with chubby born-agains, and I associate *Phantom* with closeted gays; sue me.

On her desk Mary Eileen kept a clear glass bowl filled with M&Ms. The bowl had a lid, held in place with a heart-shaped Ziggy paperweight. It was an elaborate contraption – really, more of a trap. The time required to get at that candy – removing and replacing both the paperweight and lid – guaranteed you would be held captive for at least a fleeting social interaction.

Mary Eileen's supply of M&Ms was seemingly bottomless. She even found M&Ms in special colors around the holidays – an act in which I'm sure she took some kind of near-erotic pleasure. And whenever – seriously, *whenever* – you'd swing by and grab a few pieces of candy on the sly, Mary Eileen would unfailingly say, "Treat yourself!" That word – "treat" – from her lips was like an iron file dragging against the edge of my front teeth. The works, from Ziggy vaguely threatening me to "have a lovely day!" to the pink and red M&Ms on Valentine's Day, to Mary Eileen's matronly invocation, all seemed calculatedly designed to make me feel infantile.

And I guess that's why I stole that Ziggy paperweight. I emptied the bowl of M&Ms into my backpack, too. An appropriately infantile act I suppose. But why should she have that power over me? And why can't Mary Eileen find a means of happiness that's, I don' t know, grown-up? She never once complained – not formally, anyway – and it's been stashed in my desk, M&Ms and all, for I don't know how long.

Life goes on here, pretty much unchanged, except for a few details most people around the office probably wouldn't even notice. Mary Eileen has stopped putting out M&Ms, and I've been walking in wide, inconvenient arcs to avoid passing her desk. I even switched my printer from 3-DEATHSTAR to 3-DAGOBAH just to avoid her. And this Ziggy paperweight? I just can't keep it anymore. Maybe you can. I can't even remember the last time I had a lovely day.

CARL WILSON

WETNET CONSTITUTIONAL GROUP:
AURATIC OBJECT BACKGROUND REPORT

1.

Archive fragment: John Forsythe (voice) as Charles "Charlie" Townsend; Farrah Fawcett-Majors as Jill Munroe (1976-77, recurring 1978-80); Kate Jackson as Sabrina Duncan (1976-79); Jaclyn Smith as Kelly Garrett; Cheryl Ladd as Kris Munroe (1977-81); Shelley Hack as Tiffany Welles (1979-80); Tanya Roberts as Julie Rogers (1980-81); David Doyle as John Bosley.

2.

Limbic archive trace data: At public school in Lansing, Mich., 1978, subject Derek F. is made to carry the Object to lunch every day by his mother, who dresses him in over-tight velour sweaters and corduroy "floods" [*no trans. available*] and has misread her ten-year-old son's interest in a popular show. As the larger boys daily thwap his tailbone and head with its milk-swooshing bulk, they bark out "Sabrina! Sabrina!" and laugh.

The term catches on so robustly that in schoolyard argot it long remains an all-purpose insult, more androgynous than "gaylord," as subject's younger sibling Krissy F. finds out to her cost after frugal Mom hands-her-down the Object in 1983. This despite there being a Kris on it too.

Aural trace clip, semi-musical (folkloric): "Sabrina, Sabrina – chipmunk cheeks suckin' on a weena!"

3.

Academic archive, Popular Culture Studies, vol. 45, no. 1, y. 2012, contents page: Kristoph Finkel, U. Mich., "I Was Kate Jackson When Kate Jackson Wasn't Kept Cool: Gender Trouble, Thermality and Referent Disposability in Promotional Ephemera of the Jiggle Age," p. 87. *Text missing. Journal archive ceases with this number, as do records of all cross-indexed journals after this year.*

Mass media of the period contain multiple refs.; typical heading: "Prop. 11: Palin gives humanities funds electoral wedgie."

4.

Network1 archive, kitschisthenakedtruth.com, Jan. 13, 2018, 11:17 a.m.: Repulsive developments today in the saga of packrat D.A. Finkel, whose death I reported Friday. When they found his body it seemed a sad reminder how the hunter-gatherer joys of our pastime risk blurring into pathological hoarding. The truth is much worse.

You'll recall how Angels collectors flocked around when word leaked he owned one of only three existing "Sabrina's Snot" irregulars among C.A.'s lunchbox beverage collectibles. The Dubai-scale bidding enabled him to retreat completely into his Spellingesque Malibu-Barbie estate in New England till it collapsed around him. But now water-damaged diaries recovered from the infested heap reveal the item was NEVER an authentic misprint. Finkel wrote in graphic detail of employing his collectibles in acts of self-abuse; the smears on Sabrina's nose were a side effect – which by opportunistic coincidence matched the patterns of the prized irregular LBCs.

My own nose smells a lawsuit. But in fact his treatment of his treasures is an affront to all preservationists. Leave your votes for best way to perpetrate a Finkel on the creep's own corpse in the Comments.

5.

Archival gap, standard causes.

6.

Archive fragment, Age of Service Outage, scan of hand-copied "Grauman's Guide to Salvation": Angels were worshiped by 20th-century Americans who followed Charlie Christ. Deities included Sabrina, a young witch of beauty and renown whose parables were told in brightly colored illustrated scriptures. ... One ritual object was a blue chalice from which was drunk consecrated liquid, which celebrants believed physically became the blood of Charlie, who wore a black hat, oversized shoes, mustache and cane, and manifested primarily by "speaker phone." The last known such relic was reclaimed by Shanghai as part of Greater Chinese patrimony prior to the Errancy, the Correction and the Second Errancy.

7.

Archival void, standard causes.

8.

Proposed wording for constitutional passage: After votes are counted and confirmed, the Auratic Object shall be conveyed by drones to the bio tank of the successful candidate for Chief Admin. As confirmation an image shall be uploaded to Reality during Inauguration. Satisfied of its authenticity, the Regulator General shall recite: "As in every transfer of power since the Wetnet went omni, the Auratic Object has been transported to rest at the side of the new Admin's bio tank. This repository of history, the sole surviving physical artifact of human culture, represents both the humility of our origins and the tenacity of our purpose, as coded to be so preserved by the founding Admin, Finkel the First."

This amendment to add "and confirmed" (to avoid repetition of the recent Hanging Sabrina electoral irregularity) is recommended by consensus of the Regulatory Group.

(End Report.)

99¢ $10⁵⁰

JENNIFER MICHAEL HECHT

Kathy can remember how she left both of her ex-husbands but she can't remember how she left Jeffrey. She can remember a phone call that seemed to finalize that she was leaving him with his father but she isn't sure when that happened or why. Kathy is pretty and rich, but she loathes herself and everyone except Jeffrey. When she is with Jeffrey she loathes herself less, except she gets some sharp stabbing pains of it. She has been with him a lot lately, so has been drinking a lot less.

She is awake alone in the middle of the night. The very nice man she lives with is asleep in their bed at the top of her town house, two flights upstairs. She can turn on lights, make normal noise with a beer bottle against the table. She is drinking a yellow beer with lime in it. The house is warm but not warm enough for no pants and Kathy is wishing pants weren't two flights away. For the time being she isn't moving. She's only had one beer since she got up, but she drank more than a few the night before.

Kathy is smoking a joint in the kitchen and looking at Michael Phelps on a Corn Flakes box. Phelps won eight gold medals swimming in the Olympics and then lost his Corn Flakes endorsement deal because of a photograph of him smoking a bong. Kathy's boyfriend saw a pre-bong cereal box at the supermarket and snatched it up. He likes things like this. Now the Phelps cereal box has been mounted prominently for many months on a kitchen shelf. Phelps is in the pool up to his neck, holding up one finger and smiling like crazy. She takes a hit and smiles back at him. She replies to his "We're number one" finger with her own. She rests her lighter on a ceramic figurine of the "Hakuna Matata" guys from *The Lion King*. Kathy had been to Kenya with her second husband and people there said "Hakuna matata" the way we say, "No problem," and they pronounce it like a machine gun, fast and hard.

Kathy had grown up with Baloo the bear in *Jungle Book* as her icon of happiness through low expectations. The bare necessities, the simple bare necessities, the bare necessities of life. As she remembered it, you just eat whatever you find under a log. Kathy is on her second beer. The paper towel wrapped around it is wet from bottle sweat. Drawn-out syllables are playing in her head, "Haah koo na ma tata, what a wonderful phrase. Haah koo na ma ta tahh, it's no passing craze."

Kathy picks up the ceramic figurine and closes her hand around it. It is cooler than room temperature; its shape massages her tight palm and fingers. She considers throwing it at Phelps, just to see which way the box would fall but decides it would seem hostile. She chooses instead to duplicate the warthog's position. Leaving the beer in the kitchen, but bringing the figurine, Kathy walks into the parlor and looks down at the rug. Mutters "Jeffrey's pillows," and eases herself down to them. She puts one pillow on her belly, as if it were a meerkat. Closes her eyes.

ORIGINAL PRICE

FINAL PRICE

ITEM 99
AQUARIUM SOUVENIR

$1⁰⁰ $66⁰⁷

MARK JUDE POIRIER

We drove to Wildwood Aquarium, left Alice at her apartment, even though it had been her idea to go. The week before, a German visitor to the aquarium had been killed, bitten in two by Sammy, the angry orca, as he held a fish for it. The crowd had cheered when the water turned red, then pink. People posted videos and photos on the Internet, but they had barely mentioned it on the news because the garbage strike was in full force then, and the city smelled like death.

They couldn't very well just let Sammy go, and animal rights groups wouldn't let the aquarium kill him, so he stayed there in the glass-walled pool, and people lined up for hours to see him. When we finally pushed our way to the front, Brad pressed his lips against the cold glass, blew up his cheeks and tried to attract Sammy the Killer with his tongue – 'til I reminded him how thousands of people had probably touched the glass right there after using the restroom and not washing their hands. I listed the problems Brad might suffer: "Impetigo, herpes, trench mouth, the flu, New Jersey gum rot, oral lice, lip chiggers, pink eye, the common cold, staphylococcus, pinworms, ringworm, hookworm, guinea worm, roundworm, tapeworm, and/or the clap. And mono."

"Shut it," Brad said.

We stole Alice a souvenir because we were afraid not to. I had wanted to get her a Sammy the Killer T-shirt, emblazoned with the image of a cartoon Sammy with half a German tourist in his jaws, but they were too hard to steal, hanging high up on the wall, so high you had to ask an employee to get one down for you with a hook on the end of a stick. Instead, we snatched her something else.

"Where the hell is it?" Alice asked when we walked into her apartment.

Brad handed it to her, a small cylinder of Lucite or something, not much bigger than an ice cube, filled with water, a sad dead seahorse, and a few vibrantly dyed shells.

"Very funny," she said. "Where's my Sammy the Killer T-shirt?"

"Those were up too high," I offered.

She looked at me, her lips freshly lipsticked, gunked, her eyes sunken into purple circles.

She threw it at Brad then, really hard, really fast, like her wrist was spring-loaded. It hit him in the mouth. "What the hell!" he screamed, blood dribbling from his chin. He spit slivers and shards of teeth into his palm. "Get me a glass of milk!"

I hurried over to the refrigerator. "Only soy milk," I said. "I don't think you should put your broken teeth in soy milk."

"I'm lactose intolerant," Alice said. She walked over to Brad, who cringed, thinking she might hurt him further. Instead, she picked up the souvenir, rinsed it in the kitchen sink, dried it on her denim skirt, and placed it on the windowsill.

You know, when the sun hit it, the seahorse almost looked alive.

ORIGINAL PRICE

FINAL PRICE

$1⁰⁰ $23⁰⁰

MARK FRAUENFELDER

Matt saw the tiny blue bottle on the third step of the main entrance to the Los Angeles Central Library. It was next to a sleeping man, obviously homeless. A $100 bill, rolled-up, was protruding from the bottle's open neck. Matt slyly scooped up the bottle on his way into the library. He hid the bottle in his fist until he got to a desk with side partitions.

A chipped decal on the bottle read, "Arrow De Luxe Apricot Flavored Brandy." He pulled the rolled-up bill from the neck. When he unrolled it, it was a just a note printed on what looked like a $100 bill. He'd picked up these phony bills before. They were religious tracts. *What kind of religion tries to win members by pulling a dirty trick?* he wondered.

Matt dropped the note on the ground and pocketed the bottle. It looks like an antique, he thought. I might get some money for it. He barely made it to the computer card catalog when the bottle appeared in his mouth. The oddly ribbed neck protruded from his lips, while the rest of the bottle uncomfortably occupied his mouth, pushing his tongue down and preventing him from closing his jaws completely.

He pulled the bottle out, tossed it on the table. It spun and skidded across the table, clanking on the floor. He walked quickly towards the exit. In five seconds, the bottle reappeared in his mouth. This time he yanked the bottle and threw it on the ground. It made a loud noise when it shattered. The other library visitors looked at him, startled. Matt ran. The bottle returned to his mouth, intact, before he was outside. He looked for the sleeping man, but he was gone.

He ran down 5th street, throwing the bottle onto the sidewalk every time it appeared in his mouth. After nineteen attempts to get rid of it, it felt like it had gotten bigger. What had the note said? He went back into the library to look for it. It wasn't there. People stared at the crazy man with the blue thing sticking out of his mouth, crawling on his hands and knees. He finally found the note under the shelves near the desk.

This time, he read it:

> This bottle is going to appear in your mouth in two minutes. If you pull the bottle out of your mouth, it will reappear in your mouth in five seconds. If you attempt to prevent the bottle from reappearing in your mouth by filling your mouth with another object, you could choke or burst your cheek when the bottle returns to your mouth and displaces the object. In addition, every time you remove the bottle from your mouth, it will grow in size by one tenth of one percent. Unless you sell the bottle to another person and money changes hands, the bottle will remain in your mouth until you die. When you die, it will go back to where you found it. You must reveal this paragraph verbatim to anyone you attempt to sell the bottle to.

In the days that followed, Matt stopped going to work. His wife left him, even after he demonstrated to her the bottle's cruel magic. He drank yogurt, applesauce, and blended food though a straw. He couldn't sleep. He was afraid to pull the bottle out of his mouth again. He did it one more time, though, setting it next to a penny on a black tablecloth draped over a chair. He snapped a photo of it with his cell phone camera. He rushed, not giving the camera's autofocus enough time to do its job. The photo turned out blurry, but it would have to do.

Maybe if I write the description as a work of fiction, he thought, *someone will buy the bottle.*

Appendix

The data-driven findings discussed in this Appendix derive from the original one-hundred-story Significant Objects experiment, as described in the introduction to the present volume. The stories collected in said volume, however, are drawn from the entirety of the Significant Objects project, which outlived the original experiment, owing to the popularity and excellence of the enterprise. For this reason, certain disparities between the table in this Appendix and the creative works presented in earlier pages, is to be expected.

PLEASE NOTE.

COMBINED
REPRESENTATION OF
LIVING
THINGS

LIVING BEATS NON-LIVING!

+

+

= **56**/100*

*29 ANIMALS, 25 HUMANS, 1 ALIEN, AND A WALKING GOLFBALL

54
ITEMS HAVE FACES

46
ITEMS DON'T HAVE FACES

ABSTRACT

Prior research has suggested connections between an object's story and its value to owners and potential owners. However, such "stories" are either reality-based (e.g., memories) or imply some connection – accurate or otherwise – to reality (e.g., advertising). The present research tested the novel hypothesis that explicitly fictitious stories about insignificant objects can measurably increase these objects' "significance value." A study involving 100 meaningless things confirmed this hypothesis: paired with invented stories by creative writers, the insignificant objects' value in trade increased by more than 2,700%. Preliminary analyses, detailed below, suggest startling explanations for these results. Further research is warranted, though the curators prefer to draw attention to the stories published in this collection.

BACKGROUND

What gives value to an object? Conventional answers to this question point to economic laws of utility or supply and demand, or qualities intrinsic to the object – e.g., craftsmanship or design.

The Significant Objects project advanced a different hypothesis: that regardless of the thing's aesthetic or utilitarian properties, an object's value can be increased by way of the narrative attached to it. The hypothesis builds on prior research into "the enormous flexibility with which people can attach meanings to objects, and therefore derive meanings from them" (Csikszentmihalyi and Rochberg-Halton, 1981). Prior scholarship has documented links between ordinary objects and extraordinary meanings (Glenn, 2007) and the degree to which subjective and market value can be generated by way of narratives whose purported connections to reality are debatable (Walker, 2008).

The Significant Objects project – an exercise in amateur anthropology, or what is now known as "citizen science" – extends prior research by examining whether stories that are *explicitly fictitious* can *measurably* increase the value of insignificant objects.

EXPERIMENT ONE

The Significant Objects experiment entailed auctioning 100 insignificant objects, each paired with a narrative (story) written about that object, via eBay. The first auction began on July 6, 2009; the final auction concluded on November 20 of that year. The experiment's deceptively simple, rigorously designed parameters were as follows.

OBJECTS: Lead researchers Joshua Glenn and Rob Walker ("the curators") purchased 100 insignificant objects from thrift stores and yard sales. The price limit per object: $4. Mean price paid for the 100 objects sold in the experiment: $1.29.

To avoid skewed results, certain categories of insignificant object were excluded: furniture, clothing, books, LPs, or anything else insufficiently "object-like." Nothing too bleak or trashy. Also, no art – whether "fine," "bad," "outsider," or "readymade" – because an art object is an object *intended* to be significant; it's not sufficiently insignificant.

In general, the curators purchased only objects that could be held in the palm of the hand, easily shipped, and displayed upon a bookshelf or mantelpiece. To maintain overall variety, the curators limited, but did not entirely exclude, insignificant objects in the following categories: midcentury-through-1980s pop culture ephemera; toys; novelty items; promotional items; travel souvenirs; dolls; and figurines (human or animal).

STORIES: Each of the 100 writers recruited invented a story about one chosen object. Each was provided with a photograph of his or her object. The stories

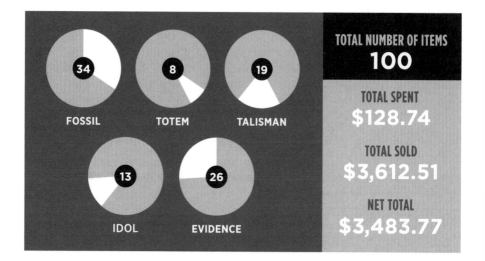

FOSSIL 34

TOTEM 8

TALISMAN 19

IDOL 13

EVIDENCE 26

TOTAL NUMBER OF ITEMS
100

TOTAL SPENT
$128.74

TOTAL SOLD
$3,612.51

NET TOTAL
$3,483.77

could be written in any style or voice, provided the object was central or important to the story. The project's curators vetted (and sometimes lightly edited) the stories; all published stories were of the highest possible quality measurable by currently existing instruments.

VALUE-MEASUREMENT: Each object was listed for sale on eBay. Each listing included a photograph of the object. However, in place of the usual factual description, the listing featured the newly written fictional story. Note that each story was clearly labeled as fiction, and prominently included a hyperlink back to the Significant Objects website, where detailed information was made available to potential purchasers. There was no intent to hoax eBay customers (doing so would have voided the test); there is no evidence that anybody believed the narratives published on eBay were true.

Each eBay auction lasted seven days. Winning bidders received the object and a printout of its invented story. The entire payment for each object was passed on to the respective writer. The project's shipping costs were recouped via eBay's shipping fees.

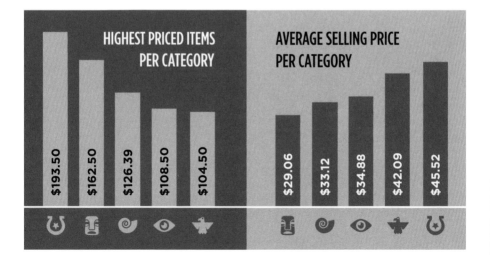

FINAL PRICE	ORIGINAL PRICE	SALES RANK	OBJECT NAME	SIGNIFICANCE TYPE	OBJECT TYPE	AUTHOR
$193.50	$3.00	01	Russian Figure	☪ TALISMAN	Figurine	Doug Dorst
$157.50	$0.99	02	Indian Maiden	☪ TALISMAN	Figurine	R.K. Scher
$108.50	$0.75	03	Wooden Animal	👁 EVIDENCE	Figurine	Meg Cabot
$104.50	$1.00	04	Pink Horse	🦅 TOTEM	Toy	Kate Bernheimer
$101.00	$2.99	05	"Hawk" Ashtray	🐚 FOSSIL	House & Table	William Gibson
$88.00	$1.00	06	4-Tile	🐚 FOSSIL	Decoration	Toni Schlesinger
$86.00	$3.00	07	Metal Boot	☪ TALISMAN	Decoration	Bruce Sterling
$77.51	$4.00	08	Cape Cod Shoe	🐚 FOSSIL	Kitsch	Sheila Heti
$76.00	$2.99	09	Fish Spoons	👁 EVIDENCE	Kitchenware	Mark Doty
$76.00	$0.25	09	Fake Banana	👁 EVIDENCE	Decoration	Josh Kramer
$76.00	$1.00	09	Missouri Shot Glass	🦅 TOTEM	Promo Item	Jonathan Lethem
$71.00	$3.00	12	Duck Tray	🗿 IDOL	Kitsch	Stewart O'Nan
$71.00	$0.33	12	Wooden Mallet	☪ TALISMAN	Tool	Colson Whitehead
$62.00	$2.00	14	Cow Vase	🐚 FOSSIL	House & Table	Ed Park
$62.00	$0.50	14	Felt Mouse	🐚 FOSSIL	Toy	Meghan O'Rourke
$57.66	$0.99	16	Rainbow Sand Animal	👁 EVIDENCE	Novelty Item	Sloane Crosley
$57.00	$1.00	17	Rhino Figurine	☪ TALISMAN	Figurine	Nathaniel Rich
$56.50	$2.00	18	Kneeling Man Figurine	☪ TALISMAN	Kitsch	Glen David Gold
$56.00	$1.50	19	Geisha Bobblehead	👁 EVIDENCE	Novelty Item	Edward Champion
$54.00	$0.75	20	BBQ Sauce Jar	👁 EVIDENCE	Kitchenware	Matthew J. Wells
$52.00	$0.50	21	Bird Figurine	🦅 TOTEM	Figurine	Sung J. Woo
$51.99	$1.00	22	Rooster Oven Mitt	🐚 FOSSIL	Kitchenware	Victor LaValle
$51.00	$0.75	23	Meat Thermometer	🐚 FOSSIL	Kitchenware	Nicholson Baker
$51.00	$1.00	23	Idol	🗿 IDOL	Decoration	Andrew Ervin
$50.00	$2.00	25	Ziggy Heart	👁 EVIDENCE	Promo Item	Todd Levin

FINAL PRICE	ORIGINAL PRICE	SALES RANK	OBJECT NAME	SIGNIFICANCE TYPE	OBJECT TYPE	AUTHOR
$50.00	$1.00	25	Jar of Marbles	👁 EVIDENCE	Toy	Ben Ehrenreich
$45.01	$2.00	27	Motel Room Key	🐚 FOSSIL	Tool	Laura Lippman
$42.00	$0.50	28	Maine Statutes Dish	🐚 FOSSIL	Promo Item	Ben Katchor
$41.00	$1.00	29	Ireland Cow Plate	🔱 TOTEM	Kitsch	Sarah Rainone
$41.00	$0.50	29	Rope/Wood Monkey	🐚 FOSSIL	Figurine	Kevin Brockmeier
$41.00	$0.25	29	Amoco Yo-Yo	🐚 FOSSIL	Toy	Mark Sarvas
$38.00	$1.00	32	Mr. Pickwick Coat Hook	👁 EVIDENCE	House & Table	Christopher Sorrentino
$37.00	$0.75	33	Marines Logo Mug	🗿 IDOL	Promo Item	Tom Vanderbilt
$37.00	$0.49	33	Alien Toy	🐚 FOSSIL	Toy	Nomi Kane
$36.88	$0.50	35	Necking Team Button	🐚 FOSSIL	Novelty Item	Susannah Breslin
$36.00	$1.00	36	Seahorse Lighter	🗿 IDOL	Novelty Item	Aimee Bender
$36.00	$0.50	36	Hand-Held Bubble Blower	৬ TALISMAN	Toy	Myla Goldberg
$35.00	$0.50	38	Round Box	🐚 FOSSIL	Tool	Tim Carvell
$33.77	$0.10	39	Cigarette Case	👁 EVIDENCE	House & Table	Margot Livesey
$33.00	$0.50	40	Ocean Scene Globe	🗿 IDOL	Decoration	Stephanie Reents
$32.08	$0.39	41	Smiling Mug	🗿 IDOL	Novelty Item	Ben Greenman
$31.00	$1.00	42	Halston Mug	🐚 FOSSIL	Kitsch	Mimi Lipson
$31.00	$3.00	42	Penguin Creamer	🐚 FOSSIL	Kitchenware	Sari Wilson
$31.00	$3.00	42	Windsurfing Trophy/Statue	👁 EVIDENCE	Kitsch	Naomi Novik
$30.99	$1.00	45	Crumb Sweeper	👁 EVIDENCE	House & Table	Shelley Jackson
$30.00	$2.00	46	Blue Vase	👁 EVIDENCE	House & Table	Lauren Mechling
$27.00	$1.00	47	Pool Ball-Shaped Lighter	🐚 FOSSIL	Novelty Item	Rob Agredo
$26.00	$2.99	48	JFK Bust	🗿 IDOL	Kitsch	Annie Nocenti
$26.00	$1.00	48	Creamer Cow	👁 EVIDENCE	Kitchenware	Lucinda Rosenfeld
$26.00	$1.00	48	Unicorn	🐚 FOSSIL	Figurine	Sarah Weinman

FINAL PRICE	ORIGINAL PRICE	SALES RANK	OBJECT NAME	SIGNIFICANCE TYPE		OBJECT TYPE	AUTHOR
$26.00	$1.50	48	Praying Hands	☡	TALISMAN	Kitsch	Rosecrans Baldwin
$26.00	$0.25	48	Dilbert Stress Toy	🗿	IDOL	Promo Item	Betsey Swardlick
$24.50	$0.59	53	Cracker Barrel Ornament	🐚	FOSSIL	Promo Item	Maud Newton
$24.00	$0.50	54	Elvis Chocolate Tin	🐚	FOSSIL	Promo Item	Jessica Helfand
$23.00	$1.00	55	Miniature Bottle	☡	TALISMAN	Promo Item	Mark Frauenfelder
$22.72	$0.50	56	Chili Cat	★	TOTEM	Figurine	Lydia Millet
$21.80	$0.59	57	Flip-Flop Frame	☡	TALISMAN	Novelty	Merrill Markoe
$21.50	$0.33	58	Military Figure	🗿	IDOL	Figurine	David Shields
$21.50	$1.99	58	Choirboy Figurine	👁	EVIDENCE	Kitsch	J. Robert Lennon
$21.50	$0.34	58	Sea Captain Pipe Rest	🐚	FOSSIL	Novelty Item	Michael Atkinson
$21.50	$0.29	58	Umbrella Trinket	👁	EVIDENCE	Decoration	Bruce Holland Rogers
$20.51	$0.25	62	Pabst Bottle Opener	🐚	FOSSIL	Promo Item	Sean Howe
$20.50	$1.00	63	Grain Thing	🗿	IDOL	Kitchenware	Joanne McNeil
$20.50	$2.00	63	Uncola Glass	🐚	FOSSIL	Promo Item	Jen Collins
$20.50	$1.00	63	Ornamental Sphere	☡	TALISMAN	Decoration	Charles Ardai
$20.50	$0.50	63	Wave Box	☡	TALISMAN	Promo Item	Teddy Wayne
$19.50	$0.50	67	Tin Ark	☡	TALISMAN	Decoration	Rebecca Wolff
$19.50	$3.00	67	Thai Hooks	👁	EVIDENCE	Kitsch	Bruno Maddox
$17.82	$1.00	69	Foppish Figurine	🗿	IDOL	Kitsch	Rob Baedeker
$17.79	$1.00	70	Sanka Ashtray	👁	EVIDENCE	Promo Item	Luc Sante
$17.50	$1.00	71	Spotted Dogs Figurine	🐚	FOSSIL	Novelty Item	Curtis Sittenfeld
$17.00	$1.00	72	Cat Mug	🐚	FOSSIL	House & Table	Thomas McNeely
$16.49	$0.99	73	Dome Doll	☡	TALISMAN	Figurine	Jason Grote
$16.00	$0.50	74	Swiss Medal	🐚	FOSSIL	Promo Item	Kathryn Borel Jr.
$15.75	$1.99	75	Duck Vase	☡	TALISMAN	House & Table	Matthew Klam

FINAL PRICE	ORIGINAL PRICE	SALES RANK	OBJECT NAME	SIGNIFICANCE TYPE	OBJECT TYPE	AUTHOR
$15.53	$1.25	76	Kitty Saucer	👁 EVIDENCE	House & Table	James Parker
$15.50	$2.00	77	Santa Nutcracker	👁 EVIDENCE	House & Table	Kurt Andersen
$15.50	$1.99	77	Piggybank	🦅 TOTEM	Novelty Item	Matthew De Abaitua
$15.50	$2.00	77	Popsicle-Stick Construction	🐚 FOSSIL	Decoration	Sara Ryan
$15.50	$2.00	77	Star of David Plate	👁 EVIDENCE	Kitsch	Adam Harrison Levy
$15.50	$4.00	77	Device	🐚 FOSSIL	Tool	Tom Bartlett
$15.50	$0.75	77	Toothbrush Holder	👁 EVIDENCE	House & Table	Terese Svoboda
$14.90	$2.00	83	Basketball Trophy	👁 EVIDENCE	Figurine	Cintra Wilson
$14.50	$1.00	84	Mule Figurine	🦅 TOTEM	Novelty Item	Matthew Sharpe
$14.50	$1.00	84	Nutcracker with Troll Hair	👹 TALISMAN	Novelty Item	Adam Davies
$14.50	$2.99	84	Golf Ball Bank	👁 EVIDENCE	Novelty Item	Todd Pruzan
$11.61	$2.00	87	Clown Figurine	👹 TALISMAN	Figurine	Nick Asbury
$11.50	$0.29	88	Candyland Labyrinth Game	👹 TALISMAN	Toy	Matthew Battles
$11.50	$1.00	88	Pen Stand	🐚 FOSSIL	Tool	Lizzie Skurnick
$10.50	$0.99	90	"Hakuna Matata" Figurine	🦅 TOTEM	Promo Item	Jennifer Michael Hecht
$10.50	$1.00	90	Small Stapler	🐚 FOSSIL	Tool	Katharine Weber
$10.50	$4.00	90	Bar Mitzvah Bookends	👁 EVIDENCE	Tool	Stacey Levine
$10.00	$0.25	93	Coconut Cup	🐚 FOSSIL	Novelty Item	Annalee Newitz
$6.75	$2.00	94	Kentucky Dish	👁 EVIDENCE	House & Table	Dean Haspiel
$6.25	$2.00	95	Toy Toaster	👹 TALISMAN	Toy	Jonathan Goldstein
$5.50	$0.50	96	Fred Flintstone Pez Dispenser	🐚 FOSSIL	Novelty Item	Claire Zulkey
$5.50	$1.00	96	#1 Mom Hooks	🐚 FOSSIL	House & Table	Rachel Berger
$4.24	$1.99	98	Hawaiian Utensils	🐚 FOSSIL	Decoration	Stephen Elliott
$3.58	$0.12	99	Toy Hot Dog	🗿 IDOL	Toy	Jenny Davidson
$2.38	$1.00	100	Porcelain Scooter	🗿 IDOL	Kitsch	Teddy Blanks

ANALYSES

The total "value in trade" of the 100 once-insignificant objects rose from $128.74 to $3,612.51. To put it another way, fictional narrative boosted the quantitative significance of these castoff objects by more than 2,700%. These results demonstrate that even explicitly fictional narrative can markedly inflate an object's exchange value – i.e., by transforming a qualitatively "insignificant" object into a qualitatively "significant" one.

Although the curators' hypothesis was proven, the success of the experiment raised a number of questions about *how* the value-adding process works. What factors account for the significance-value (sale price) variation among the 100 objects? Can a particular value-adding factor (e.g., object type, significance value, significance type, narrative mode) or cluster of factors be isolated, thus transforming the art of boosting an object's value via narrative into a science? Aware of how valuable an answer to such questions would be, the curators designed and built a device they call the VISTA 1.0 (Verifiable Insignificant-to-Significant Transubstantiation Analyzer), and used it to crunch the numbers – as detailed below.

NB: Due to several ties among the experiment's Top 25 objects (as ranked by significance value; see table), there are in fact 26 so-called "Top 25" objects.

AUTHOR FAME & TALENT: Does the fame and/or talent of the author whose story made it significant affect an object's significance value? Some might regard such a question – which was posed by one or two kibitzers – as cynical. Nevertheless, the curators ranked the experiment's results by significance value [see table] and investigated. It turns out that neither author fame nor author talent made a difference.

According to an anonymous panel of literary-fame experts, only seven of the Top 25 objects thus sorted were made significant by "famous" authors. Other well-known writers who participated in the experiment didn't make the top quartile [see table]; meanwhile, a few of the experiment's top-ranked participants (i.e., ranked by their objects' significance value) are best-described, famewise, as up-and-coming talents. As one reader declared: "Famous people didn't always fare as well as 'ordinary' folks! [The experiment's data] emphasizes the randomness that is publishing and reader taste, which is actually kind of cool." The VISTA 1.0 confirms this.

As regards the question of author talent, all of the stories were excellent. (Cf. Glenn and Walker, 2012.) Although the rankings might reflect the stories' *qualities* (that is, their attributes or properties), the curators have determined – by noting that some of their favorite stories didn't rank in the Top 25 – that the rankings do not reflect variations in *quality*.

QUALITY

SALES RANK

OBJECT TYPE: Is an object's significance value affected by that object's type? Answering this question raises another: how to categorize the 100 objects' intended uses? A reader poll querying whether the Santa Nutcracker and Nutcracker with Troll Hair should be categorized as novelties or houseware returned a split decision – which led the curators to assign the 100 objects (even those that might be used in more than one way) in a semi-arbitrary fashion to the following categories: Novelty Item, House & Table, Decoration, Kitchenware, Tool, Figurine, Promotional Item, Toy, and Kitsch.

Ranked according to significance value, the experiment's Top 25 objects were distributed among the nine object-type categories in the following fashion: Figurine (5), Decoration (4), Kitchenware (4), Toy (3), Kitsch (3), Promotional Item (2), Novelty Item (2), House & Table (2), Tool (1). It might not seem unreasonable to hypothesize that, for example, figurines are five times likelier to acquire significance value via narrative than are tools; however, there are fewer tools among the 100 objects than figurines. Despite the fact that the experiment's Top 3 objects are figurines, a regression analysis reveals that an object's type (intended use) does not determine its significance value.

SIGNIFICANCE TYPE: Is an object's significance value affected by its (culturally determined) significance type? During and after the experiment, the curators assigned the 100 objects to five significance-type categories; they did so based not on the objects' inherent attributes or properties, but on cues within the objects' stories. For explanations of such significance-types as fossil, evidence, totem, and so forth, see Introduction.

Ranked by significance value, the experiment's Top 25 objects are distributed among the five significance-type categories in the following fashion: Evidence (8), Fossil (7), Talisman (6), Totem (3), Idol (2). Although a casual glance at the Top 25 list [see table] might seem to suggest that Talismans are particularly significance-laden, this would be inaccurate. Based on the overall distribution of significance type among the 100 stories in the experiment's sample, objects described by their stories as Evidence or as Totems are statistically *more likely* to be perceived as having high significance value and thus high market value. This finding vis-à-vis evidence and totems is key.

NARRATIVE MODE: "Have you tried categorizing the stories rather than the items?" asked one reader. "Is there any pattern there with regard to sales amount?"

The curators attempted to tag every story with story elements such as "murder" or "brothers," not to mention with exposition and genre types. However, the VISTA 1.0 proved unable to perceive any signal within the resulting data-noise. In the end, the curators took their lead from Marshall McLuhan's 1964 study, *Understanding Media.* Per the McLuhanesque trope, a "hot" story about an object does not require any work on the reader's part when it comes to determining the object's meaning; a "cool" story about an object requires the reader to participate consciously and creatively when it comes to determining the object's meaning.

NB: Having attended college during the height of postmodern theory's influence in the US, the curators were acutely aware that "hot" and "cool" are not dichotomous narrative modes, that in fact every story can be mapped somewhere on a "hot/cool" continuum. Nevertheless, in the interest of human progress, they went ahead assigned each of the 100 stories to either the "hot" or the "cool" narrative-mode category [see table].

Ranked by significance value, the experiment's Top 25 objects are distributed between the two narrative modes described above as follows: Cool (16), Hot (10). Based on the overall distribution of narrative mode among the 100 stories, if you look at the data in terms of expected values, neither Cool nor Hot alone is a predictor of value.

TOTAL AMOUNT COLLECTED PER CATEGORY

FOSSIL
$1,126.14

EVIDENCE
$906.89

TALISMAN
$864.90

IDOL
$377.86

TOTEM
$336.72

MULTIVARIATE ANALYSES: What about hot-vs.-cool figurines, say, or hot-vs.-cool talismans, or talismanic kitsch vs. evidential kitsch, and so forth? The curators consider multivariate analyses a very promising avenue of research, but at this juncture the VISTA 1.0 broke down dramatically. That said, here are a few notes based on the Top 25 objects, sorted by significance value.

Cool narratives about talismans (magical or lucky objects), generally speaking, are highly effective at increasing an object's significance value; hot narratives about talismans are less effective in that regard – best to keep the object's significance mysterious. However, if one is writing about a fossil (an object that bears witness to a vanished era or way of life, including childhood), one's best bet is to employ a hot narrative mode – i.e., come right out and state the object's significance. The latter is true no matter what type of object (e.g., figurine, decoration, kitsch, toy) you're writing about.

What of the two most popular significance types, evidence and totem? Cool narrative modes are easily the most effective when it comes to stories about evidence; perhaps this explains the allure of the board game *Clue*? When writing about a totem, however, it seems slightly more effective to employ a hot narrative mode; perhaps this finding provides the long-sought key to all mythology? In both cases – evidence and totem – the object's type, whether figurine, kitchenware, and so forth, is irrelevant.

Note that regression analyses were not run on these findings; as mentioned, the VISTA 1.0 is on the fritz. More funds and free time are badly needed to complete this pioneering research and analysis. One can only hope that a noteworthy arts/sciences/humanities foundation, and/or a major advertising agency, is reading this.

DURATION FACTOR: One reader wrote: "I'd like to see the sales plotted against time." Another agreed: "I'd be interested in seeing how the sequence played into it – the site got exponentially more popular as it went on." The VISTA 1.0 (while it still worked) determined that although adjusting for duration factor has a dramatic effect on objects auctioned off for a high amount early in the project, or for a low amount late in the project, doing so does not move any of the objects auctioned off during the project's first week into the Top 25.

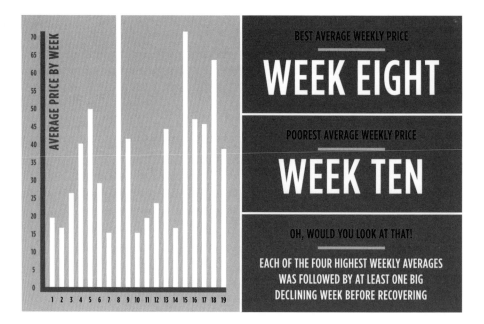

BEST AVERAGE WEEKLY PRICE

WEEK EIGHT

POOREST AVERAGE WEEKLY PRICE

WEEK TEN

OH, WOULD YOU LOOK AT THAT!

EACH OF THE FOUR HIGHEST WEEKLY AVERAGES WAS FOLLOWED BY AT LEAST ONE BIG DECLINING WEEK BEFORE RECOVERING

EXPERIMENT TWO

The success of their first experiment – now called "Volume 1" – encouraged the curators to acquire an additional 100 objects, and assign them to 100 writers (most of them new to the project). These stories were divided into second and third 'volumes' of 50 stories apiece; objects from Volume 2 were auctioned off between December 2009 and and February 2010, and objects from Volume 3 were auctioned off between February and April 2010.

Together, Volumes 2 and 3 of the Significant Objects project are known as the "second experiment." Cumulatively, the value of the second experiment's objects – purchased for a total of $134.89; auctioned off for a total of $3,992.93 – jumped by some 2,860%. These results are even more impressive than the first experiment's results. Why? See below for the curators' hypotheses.

CHARITY EFFECT: The curators announced that proceeds from Volumes 2 and 3 would go to charity. They donated the $2,244.11 from Volume 2 to 826 National, a creative-writing tutoring program for youth; and the $1,748.82 from Volume 3 went to Girls Write Now, which mentors at-risk young women in New York. Is the increase in significance value per object – from the first to the second experiment – attributable to a "charity effect"? Unfortunately, the VISTA 1.0 isn't equipped to answer this question.

NB: During the first experiment, several participating writers, including Meg Cabot, Maud Newton, and Merrill Markoe, announced spontaneously (i.e., without consulting the curators) that they'd be donating the proceeds from "their" objects to charity. This may or may not have influenced the significance value of those objects.

FOUND, DONATED, AND COMPLETELY ABSENT OBJECTS: Although the first experiment auctioned off insignificant objects that the curators had picked up in thrift shops and yard sales, the second experiment sold a few objects whose provenance might have affected their significance value. For example, Volume 2 included a series of five stories written about flotsam and jetsam plucked from the beach of Dead Horse Bay, Brooklyn, by the founders of the online literary publication *Underwater New York*. The objects were presented as detritus, which might have lessened their value; but it was curated detritus. There were other such instances of curation, which no doubt affected significance value.

Separately, Ben Greenman, who contributed to all three volumes, wrote a story for Volume 2 that vaguely described but never identified its object; the story's title was "Mystery Object," and the accompanying photo was of a nondescript envelope containing the object. The object sold for $103.50. The implications of removing the object from the equation entirely are, potentially, profound. On the other hand, a story by Debbie Millman for Volume 2, which ascribed significance to a globe paperweight, was handwritten (converting the story itself into an object of sorts) and sold for $197.50 – which was the largest significance-value yet measured. The upshot is that experimental controls for the second experiment make it impossible to draw definitive conclusions, because the curators focused on entertaining themselves and their expanding audience.

SUGGESTIONS FOR FURTHER RESEARCH

As detailed briefly above, research into the cathexis via which otherwise rational individuals invest insignificant objects with emotional energy, thereby raising their value in trade, has already begun. However, much work remains to be done.

Since their second experiment ended, the curators have been inundated with requests to continue with their research. Although hampered – as citizen scientists always are – by a lack of funds, they have continued to add to their data set as circumstances allow, presenting smaller batches of stories and objects such as an epistolary cycle guest-curated by Ben Greenman, and a series in conjunction with an event for San Francisco's Litquake festival. The curators remain optimistic that their work is not yet done. Readers are encouraged to visit SignificantObjects.com for details.

SELECT BIBLIOGRAPHY

Mihaly Csikszentmihalyi and Eugene Rochberg-Halton, *The Meaning of Things: Domestic Symbols and the Self* (Cambridge University Press, 1981)

Joshua Glenn and Carol Hayes, *Taking Things Seriously: 75 Objects with Unexpected Significance* (Princeton Architectural Press, 2007)

Rob Walker, *Buying In: The Secret Dialogue Between What We Buy and Who We Are* (Random House, 2008)

Joshua Glenn and Rob Walker, *Significant Objects* (Fantagraphics, 2012)

ANIMALS **29** VS. PEOPLE **25**

* FOR THE PURPOSES OF THIS STUDY, "PEOPLE" INCLUDE ONE TROLL, SANTA, FRED FLINTSTONE, AND ZIGGY.

| A = 4 | C = 4 | E = 1 |
| B = 10 | D = 8 | F = 2 |

Chris Adrian is the author of three novels, *Gob's Grief*, *The Children's Hospital*, and *The Great Night*, and a collection of short stories, *A Better Angel*. [Item 42]

Rob Agredo is a reluctant dolly grip, living in the Bronx with his beautiful wife, twin five-year-old girls, and little dog Zuzu. [It. 4]

Kurt Andersen is author of the novels *Heyday* and *Turn of the Century*. Random House will publish his new novel, *True Believers*, this summer. He also hosts the public radio show *Studio 360*. [Item 15]

Rachel Axler is a playwright and TV writer. She is petite. [It. 71]

Rob Baedeker is a writer and performer living in Berkeley, Calif. He is a member of the comedy group Kasper Hauser, authors of *SkyMaul: Happy Crap You Can Buy from a Plane*, *Weddings of the Times*, and *Obama's BlackBerry*. [It. 57]

Rosecrans Baldwin is the author of a novel, *You Lost Me There*, and a forthcoming memoir, *Paris, I Love You But You're Bringing Me Down* (Farrar, Straus and Giroux, May 2012). More info: rosecransbaldwin.com. [It. 66]

Nicholson Baker's books include *The Mezzanine*, *Vox*, and *Human Smoke*. His most recent novel, *House of Holes*, was published in paperback in February 2012. [Item 88]

Matthew Battles is the author of *Library: An Unquiet History*, *Letter by Letter* (forthcoming), and a science-fiction story collection, *The Sovereignties of Invention*. He is the co-founder and literary editor of HiLobrow.com. [It. 76]

Charles Baxter is a novelist and short story writer, and he lives in Minneapolis. [It. 25]

Kate Bernheimer is the author of a trilogy of novels (*The Complete Tales of Ketzia Gold*,

The Complete Tales of Merry Gold, and *The Complete Tales of Lucy Gold*), and a story collection, *Horse, Flower, Bird*, illustrated by Rikki Ducornet. Her most recent edited collection is *My Mother She Killed Me, My Father He Ate Me: Forty New Fairy Tales*. [It. 75]

Susannah Breslin is a journalist and blogger. More info: susannahbreslin.blogspot.com. [It. 7]

Kevin Brockmeier has published seven books of fiction, including, most recently, *The Illumination*, *The Brief History of the Dead*, and *The View from the Seventh Layer*. [It. 35]

Strictly humanoid and 30 years old, **Matt Brown** is a designer living in Boston. [It. 53]

Blake Butler's most recent books are *Nothing: A Portrait of Insomnia* and *There Is No Year*. He is the editor of HTMLGIANT. [It. 5]

Meg Cabot is the author of *The Princess Diaries*, *Abandon*, and the Heather Wells mystery series. More info: megcabot.com. [It. 41]

Tim Carvell is the head writer for *The Daily Show with Jon Stewart*. [It. 48]

Patrick Cates is an LA-based Londoner who has written for *FHM*, *The Boston Phoenix* and HiLobrow.com. Most recently he wrote a weekly newsletter, *The Sniffer*, that accompanied James Parker's serialized novel, *The Ballad of Cocky the Fox*. [It. 79]

Dan Chaon is the author of *You Remind Me of Me*, *Await Your Reply*, and, most recently, *Stay Awake*, a collection of short stories. [It. 87]

Susanna Daniel is the author of *Stiltsville*, winner of the 2011 PEN/Bingham Award. [It. 54]

Adam Davies is the author of *The Frog King*, *Goodbye Lemon*, and *Mine All Mine*. [It. 11]

Kathryn Davis is the author of seven novels, the most recent of which is *Duplex*. [It. 70]

Matthew De Abaitua's debut novel *The Red Men* was nominated for the Arthur C. Clarke Award. His book *The Art of Camping: The History and Practice of Sleeping Under the Stars* is published by Hamish Hamilton. [It. 3]

Helen DeWitt is the author of *The Last Samurai* and *Lightning Rods*. She lives in Berlin and blogs at paperpools.blogspot.com. [It. 51]

Stacey D'Erasmo is the author of the novels *Tea*, *A Seahorse Year*, and *The Sky Below*. She has received a Guggenheim Fellowship in Fiction and is currently an assistant professor of writing at Columbia University. [It. 80]

Doug Dorst is the author of a novel, *Alive In Necropolis*, and a story collection, *The Surf Guru*. He is at work on a collaborative novel with J.J. Abrams. More info: dougdorst.com. [It. 36]

Mark Doty's *Fire To Fire: New and Selected Poems* won the National Book Award in 2008. He teaches at Rutgers University. [It. 85]

Ben Ehrenreich is the author of the novels *Ether* and *The Suitors*. [It. 68]

Mark Frauenfelder is the editor-in-chief of *Make* magazine, and the founder of the popular Boing Boing blog. He was an editor at *Wired* from 1993-1998, and is the author of six books. His latest book is *Made By Hand: My Adventures in the World of Do-It-Yourself*. More info: bit.ly/madebyhands. [It. 100]

Amy Fusselman's forthcoming book is *Savage Park*. [It. 46]

William Gibson is the author of nine novels, most recently *Zero History*, and of *The Difference Engine*, a collaborative novel with Bruce Sterling. He lives in Vancouver, British Columbia. [It. 12]

AUTHOR BIOS

G = 4	I = 0	K = 5
H = 5	J = 2	L = 9

Myla Goldberg is the bestselling author of *Bee Season*. Her newest novel is called *The False Friend*. More info: mylagoldberg.com. [It. 72]

Ben Greenman is an editor at *The New Yorker* and the author of several acclaimed books of fiction, including *Superbad*, *Please Step Back*, and *What He's Poised To Do*. [It. 2]

Jason Grote is the author of the plays *1001*, *Civilization (all you can eat)*, and *Maria/Stuart*, and a writer for *Smash* (Mondays at 10/9 pm on NBC). [It. 43]

Jim Hanas is the author of the short story collection *Why They Cried* (Joyland eBooks/ECW Press). [It. 47]

Jennifer Michael Hecht is the author of five books of philosophy, history, and poetry, including *Doubt: A History* and *Funny*. [It. 98]

Sheila Heti works as Interviews Editor at *The Believer*. She is the author of a short story collection, *The Middle Stories*, and the novels *Ticknor* and *How Should a Person Be?* She recently published an illustrated book for children, *We Need a Horse*, featuring paintings by Clare Rojas, and a book of conversational philosophy with Misha Glouberman called *The Chairs Are Where the People Go*. [It. 63]

Christine Hill is an artist based in Berlin, where she is the proprietor of The Volksboutique Small Business, a storefront dedicated to exploring quotidian objects and their cultural meaning and value. She is a professor at the Bauhaus University in Weimar, and her most recent monograph, *Minutes*, is available through your local art bookseller. More info: volksboutique.org. [It. 30]

Dara Horn is the author of the novels *In the Image*, *The World to Come*, and *All Other Nights*. In 2007 she was chosen as one of Granta's "Best Young American Novelists."

She lives in New Jersey with her husband and three children. [It. 77]

Shelley Jackson is the author of *Patchwork Girl*, *Half Life*, *The Melancholy of Anatomy*, children's books including *Mimi's Dada Catifesto*, and *SKIN*, a story published in tattoos on 2095 volunteers. [It. 14]

Heidi Julavits is the author of four novels. Her most recent, *The Vanishers*, was published in March. [It. 32]

Ben Katchor is an artist/writer on the faculty of Parsons The New School for Design in NYC. More info: katchor.com. [It. 91]

Matthew Klam is the author of *Sam the Cat and Other Stories*, and teaches in the Writing Seminars at Johns Hopkins University. [It. 13]

Wayne Koestenbaum has published fourteen books of poetry, nonfiction, and fiction, including *The Anatomy of Harpo Marx*, *Humiliation*, *Hotel Theory*, *Best-Selling Jewish Porn Films*, *Moira Orfei in Aigues-Mortes*, and *Andy Warhol*. Koestenbaum is a Distinguished Professor of English at the CUNY Graduate Center, and a Visiting Professor in the painting department of the Yale School of Art. [It. 22]

Josh Kramer is a comics journalist and Editor of The Cartoon Picayune, an anthology for journalism and non-fiction in the medium of comics. More info: CartoonPicayune.com. [It. 31]

Kathryn Kuitenbrouwer is the author of the novels *Perfecting* and *The Nettle Spinner* and the story collection *Way Up*. Her recent stories have been published in *Filter*, *Joyland*, *The Walrus* and *Granta*. She is the former magazine editor of Bookninja.com. She lives, writes and teaches in Toronto. More info: KathrynKuitenbrouwer.com. [It. 65]

Neil LaBute is a writer/director of theater, film and television. [It. 23]

Victor LaValle's most recent novel, *The Devil in Silver*, will be published in April 2012. [It. 82]

J. Robert Lennon is the author of a story collection and seven novels, including *Mailman*, *Castle*, and the forthcoming *Familiar*. [It. 59]

Jonathan Lethem's most recent books are a collection of writings, *The Ecstasy of Influence*, and a monograph on Talking Heads' album *Fear of Music*. [It. 90]

Todd Levin is a TV comedy writer, and co-author of the sex manual parody, *SEX: Our Bodies, Our Junk*. More info: toddlevin.com. [It. 96]

Laura Lippman has published fourteen novels, a serial novella, and a collection of short stories, *Hardly Knew Her*. She lives in Baltimore. [It. 55]

Mimi Lipson writes and makes stained glass. Her stories have been published in *YETI* and *Chronogram*, and her chapbook, *Food & Beverage*, is available from All-Seeing Eye Press. [It. 58]

Robert Lopez is the author of two novels, *Part of the World* and *Kamby Bolongo Mean River*, and a collection of short fiction, *Asunder*. He has taught at The New School, Pratt Institute, Columbia University, and The Solstice Low-Res MFA Program at Pine Manor College. [It. 73]

Joe Lyons is a playwright and humorist currently residing in Pittsburgh, PA. He also serves as co-founder of the Hodgepodge Society. More info: hodgepodgesociety.com. [It. 18]

Sarah Manguso is the author of five books, most recently the memoirs *The Guardians* and *The Two Kinds of Decay*. [It. 62]

| M = 5 | O = 3 | Q = 0 |
| N = 2 | P = 8 | R = 5 |

Merrill Markoe is a writer and humorist living in Los Angeles. Her new book of funny personal essays was published by Random House in 2011 and is called *Cool, Calm and Contentious*. More info: Merrillmarkoe.com. [lt. 8]

Tom McCarthy is a writer and conceptual artist. He is author of the novels *Remainder, Men in Space, C* (which was shortlisted for the 2010 Booker Prize), and *Satin Island*; and of the nonfiction book *Tintin and the Secret of Literature*. He is founder and General Secretary of the avant-garde art "organization" the International Necronautical Society, which may or may not actually exist. He lives in London. [lt. 28]

Miranda Mellis is the author of *The Revisionist, Materialisms*, and *None Of This Is Real*, and an editor at The Encyclopedia Project. Her writing appears in various publications, including *Conjunctions* and *The Believer*. She teaches at California College of the Arts and Mills College. [lt. 26]

Lydia Millet is the author of seven novels, two books for young readers and a story collection called *Love in Infant Monkeys*, a Pulitzer Prize finalist. She lives in the desert outside Tucson, Arizona. [lt. 37]

Maud Newton is a writer, blogger, and speculative Biblical scholar living in New York. [lt. 93]

Annie Nocenti is a journalist, teacher and writer. She shot two films in Baluchistan, taught film in Haiti, and is currently writing comics for Marvel and DC and teaching film to indigenous peoples. More info: annienocenti.com. [lt. 60]

Stephen O'Connor is the author of two collections of short fiction, *Here Comes Another Lesson* and *Rescue*. More info: stephenoconnor.net. [lt. 34]

Stewart O'Nan's thirteen novels include *Snow Angels, A Prayer for the Dying, Last Night at the Lobster*, and *Emily, Alone*, which inspired his Significant Object vignette. In February, Viking released his newest novel, *The Odds*. [lt. 67]

Jenny Offill is the author of the novel *Last Things*, and of two children's books, *17 Things I'm Not Allowed to Do Anymore* and *11 Experiments That Failed*. [lt. 74]

Gary Panter is an artist living in Brooklyn. He has been honored with three Emmy awards and five nominations for design on the *Pee-wee's Playhouse* TV show, and a Chrysler Design award for design innovation in 2000. His drawings were included in "Comic Masters," a major museum show originating at the Hammer and MOCA museums in Los Angeles. He teaches at SVA in New York; his paintings are represented by Fredericks & Freiser. More info: fredericksfreisergallery.com. [lt. 56]

Ed Park is the author of the novel *Personal Days*. He was a founding editor of *The Believer*, and is now the literary fiction editor for Amazon Publishing. [lt. 16]

James Parker is a writer living in Brookline, Massachusetts. He recently serialized a novel, *The Ballad of Cocky the Fox*, at HiLobrow.com. [lt. 20]

Benjamin Percy is the author of two novels, *Red Moon* (forthcoming from Grand Central/ Hachette) and *The Wilding*, and two books of short stories, *Refresh, Refresh* and *The Language of Elk*. [lt. 78]

Mark Jude Poirier is the author of the novels *Goats* and *Modern Ranch Living*, as well as the story collections *Unsung Heroes of American Industry* and *Naked Pueblo*. In 2008, his first film, *Smart People*, premiered at Sundance and was released by Miramax. The movie version of *Goats*, which he adapted, will be released in 2012. [lt. 99]

Padgett Powell is the author, most recently, of *The Interrogative Mood, You & I* (England), and *You & Me* (US). [lt. 95]

Bob Powers is the author of several humor books, including *Happy Cruelty Day!* and *You Are A Miserable Excuse For A Hero*. More info: bobpowersonline.com. [lt. 29]

Todd Pruzan, a recovering journalist, is editorial director at iCrossing, a digital marketing agency. He's also the author of *The Clumsiest People in Europe*. [lt. 10]

Dan Reines is a writer living on the grassy outskirts of Los Angeles, Calif. [lt. 9]

Nathaniel Rich is the author of *The Mayor's Tongue*. His second novel, *Odds Against Tomorrow*, is forthcoming from Farrar, Straus & Giroux. [lt. 38]

Peter Rock is the author of the novels *My Abandonment, The Bewildered, The Ambidextrist, This is the Place*, and *Carnival Wolves*, and a story collection, *The Unsettling*. He currently lives in Portland, Oregon, with his beautiful wife and ferocious young daughters. His new book, *The Raccoon and the Letter* (about the end of the world in Montana in 1990), will be published in late 2012. [lt. 64]

Lucinda Rosenfeld is the author of four novels, including *I'm So Happy For You* and (forthcoming) *The Pretty One*. [lt. 81]

Greg Rowland writes for HiLobrow.com, and is also a fully legitimate businessman. He lives in London with his lovely wife and children. More info: semiotics.co.uk. [lt. 84]

Luc Sante's books include *Low Life, Kill All Your Darlings*, and *Folk Photography*. [lt. 21]

R.K. Scher is a writer living in Marseilles, France. She is the author of the novel *The Permanent Observer* and is currently at work

| S = 9 | U = 1 | W = 7 |
| T = 2 | V = 1 | X, Y, Z = 0 |

on her second novel, *Why Marseilles*. Her work has appeared in *Glimmertrain Stories*, *Cabinet* magazine, and Pierogi Press. [It. 40]

Toni Schlesinger is a fiction writer, journalist, playwright, and performance artist who lives in New York City. She is the author of *Five Flights Up*, a collection of her award-winning *Village Voice* columns, and the creator of "Kansas O'Flaherty: Secret Agent" with illustrations by Tom Bachtell. More info: tonischlesinger.com. [It. 24]

Matthew Sharpe is the author of the novels *You Were Wrong*, *Jamestown*, *The Sleeping Father*, and *Nothing Is Terrible*. More info: matthew-sharpe.net. [It. 6]

Jim Shepard's most recent story collection is *You Think That's Bad*. [It. 92]

David Shields is the author of twelve books, including *The Thing About Life Is That One Day You'll Be Dead* and *Reality Hunger: A Manifesto*. [It. 44]

Marisa Silver is the author of four works of fiction including the novel *The God of War* and the story collection *Alone With You*. More info: marisasilver.com. [It. 69]

Curtis Sittenfeld's most recent novel is *American Wife*. [It. 1]

Bruce Sterling writes science fiction. He tweets as @bruces and blogs at Beyond the Beyond. More info: wired.com/beyond_the_beyond. [It. 33]

Scarlett Thomas is the author of *The End of Mr. Y* and various other novels. [It. 17]

Jeff Turrentine is a writer and critic living in Brooklyn. [It. 19]

Deb Olin Unferth is the author of the memoir *Revolution*, the novel *Vacation* and the short story collection *Minor Robberies*.

She is an assistant professor at Wesleyan University. [It. 49]

Tom Vanderbilt is a contributing editor to *I.D.*, *Artforum*, and *Print* and has written for many publications, from *The New York Times* to *Cabinet*. He is a contributing writer of *Design Observer*. His most recent book is *Traffic: Why We Drive the Way We Do (and What It Says About Us)*. [It. 94]

Matthew J. Wells, a poet and playwright based in New York, triumphed over 600+ entrants in a Significant Objects fiction contest hosted by Slate.com. His plays have been performed at the Magic Theatre in San Francisco and the Ensemble Studio Theatre in New York, and his poetry can be heard at artonair.org/series/new-river-dramatists. More info: matthewslikelystory.blogspot.com. [It. 83]

Joe Wenderoth is a poet who teaches at UC Davis; his films are on YouTube. [It. 27]

Margaret Wertheim is the author of books on the cultural history of science, including *Physics on the Fringe: Smoke Rings, Circlons and Alternative Theories of Everything*. She is the founder and director of the Institute For Figuring in Los Angeles. More info: theiff.org. [It. 52]

Colleen Werthmann has written for the Oscars, *Comedy Central's Roast of Donald Trump*, SteveMartin.com, BravoTV.com, the satirical website 23/6, and *McSweeney's*. She's helping to write comic Lisa Lampanelli's Broadway-bound solo show. She was nominated for an Outstanding Writing Emmy in 2010. She is also a New York-based actor. [It. 61]

Colson Whitehead is the author of the novels *The Intuitionist*, *John Henry Days*, *Apex Hides the Hurt*, *Sag Harbor*, and most recently, *Zone One*. Whitehead's reviews, essays, and fiction have appeared in a number of

publications, such as *The New York Times*, *The New Yorker*, *Harper's* and *Granta*. A recipient of a Whiting Writers Award and a MacArthur Fellowship, he lives in New York City. [It. 45]

Carl Wilson is the author of *Let's Talk About Love: A Journey to the End of Taste*, an investigation of taste, democracy and Celine Dion that's been called one of the best music books of the decade. His work appears in *The Globe and Mail*, *Toronto Standard*, *Slate*, *The New York Times* and many other publications as well as the blogs Backtotheworld.net and Zoilus.com. [It. 97]

Cintra Wilson is a culture critic, author, and frequent contributor to *The New York Times*. Her books include *A Massive Swelling: Celebrity Re-Examined As A Grotesque, Crippling Disease*, the novel *Colors Insulting to Nature*, *Caligula for President: Better American Living Through Tyranny*, and *Fear and Clothing: Unbuckling America's Fashion Destiny*, which will be released by W.W. Norton in 2012. [It. 39]

Sari Wilson, a former Stegner fellow, is a New York-based writer who works in prose and comics. Her fiction has appeared in literary journals such as *Agni*, *Slice*, and *Oxford American*. [It. 86]

Douglas Wolk is the author of *Reading Comics: How Graphic Novels Work and What They Mean* and *Live at the Apollo*. [It. 50]

John Wray is the author of the novel *Lowboy*, available now in paperback from Picador. More info: johnwray.net. [It. 89]

NOTE: Among the 100 contributors there are zero repeating surnames except in the case of "Wilson," of which there are three.

ROB WALKER

ACKNOWLEDGEMENTS

Photos of Item 28, Item 42, and Item 73 by Nura Qureshi. Photo of Item 49 by Adrian Kinloch. Photo of Item 70 by Nicki Pombier Berger.

The editors wish to thank: Emma Westling, Rob Tourtelot, Joe Alterio, Eric Reynolds, Jacob Covey, Kristy Valenti, Gary Groth, Elyse Cheney, Lauren Cerand, Sean McDonald, Kate Bingaman-Burt, 20x200, Poketo, PSFK, Litquake, Jim Coudal, Laura Beiles, and Katelan Cunningham. We wish as well to thank all of our contributing writers, including those whose stories we did not have room to include here. In particular, contributors Ben Greenman and Rob Baedeker deserve special recognition. And we thank our partners and collaborators: The Center For Cartoon Studies, Design Observer, *The Believer*, Electric Literature, Underwater New York, Slate, *SMITH Magazine*, Core77, and Paola Antonelli. In addition we thank those who wrote about or reported on the Significant Objects project, or spread the word through less formal means, as well as our many readers.

Finally, we must thank most of all the many far-flung individuals who played along with our enterprise by bidding on and/or actually purchasing Significant Objects.

Joshua Glenn also thanks Susan, Sam, and Max.

Rob Walker also offers thanks, again and again, and always, and for everything, to E.

JOSHUA GLENN

ABOUT THE EDITORS

JOSHUA GLENN is editor of the website HiLobrow; in the '90s he published the independent zine/journal *Hermenaut*. He's co-authored and co-edited several books, including *The Idler's Glossary*, *The Wage Slave's Glossary*, and the kids' field guide to life *Unbored* (October 2012). In 2011, he produced a brainteaser iPhone app, KER-PUNCH!. In 2012, HiLoBooks will serialize and reissue six overlooked classics of science fiction. He lives in Boston.

ROB WALKER contributes to *The New York Times Magazine* and *Design Observer*, among others. He is the author of *Buying In: The Secret Dialogue Between What We Buy and Who We Are*, and *Letters from New Orleans*. More at www.robwalker.net.

RANKING OF SURNAMES IN THE UNITED STATES

GLENN: 617

WALKER: 27

SMITH: 1

Significant Objects
Edited by Joshua Glenn and Rob Walker

Supervising Editor: Eric Reynolds
Art Direction & Design: Jacob Covey
Copy Editor: Kristy Valenti
Infographics: Michael Wysong, Ben Shown & Jacob Covey
Associate Publisher: Eric Reynolds
Published by Gary Groth & Kim Thompson

Fantagraphics Books, Inc.
7563 Lake City Way NE. Seattle WA 98115 USA
fantagraphics.com

Distributed to the U.S. book market by W.W. Norton & Co. (800-233-4830)
Distributed in Canada by Canadian Manda Group (416-516-0911)
Distributed in the United Kingdom by Turnaround Services (44 (0)20 8829-3002)
Distributed to the comics market by Diamond Comic Distributors (800-452-6642)

First printing: April 2012
ISBN 978-1-60699-525-9
Printed in China

The Project lives on at
significantobjects.com

FANTAGRAPHICS BOOKS

Chris Adrian
Rob Agredo
Kurt Andersen
Rachel Axler
Rob Baedeker
Nicholson Baker
Rosecrans Baldwin
Matthew Battles
Charles Baxter
Kate Bernheimer
Susanna Breslin
Kevin Brockmeier
Matt Brown
Blake Butler
Meg Cabot
Tim Carvell
Patrick Cates
Dan Chaon
Susanna Daniel
Adam Davies
Kathryn Davis
Matthew De Abaitua
Stacey D'Erasmo
Helen DeWitt
Doug Dorst
Mark Doty
Ben Ehrenreich
Mark Frauenfelder
Amy Fusselman
William Gibson
Myla Goldberg
Ben Greenman
Jason Grote
Jim Hanas
Jennifer Michael Hecht
Sheila Heti
Christine Hill
Dara Horn
Shelley Jackson
Heidi Julavits
Ben Katchor
Matthew Klam
Wayne Koestenbaum
Josh Kramer
Kathryn Kuitenbrouwer
Neil LaBute
Victor LaValle
J. Robert Lennon
Jonathan Lethem
Todd Levin

Laura Lippman
Mimi Lipson
Robert Lopez
Joe Lyons
Sarah Manguso
Merrill Markoe
Tom McCarthy
Miranda Mellis
Lydia Millet
Maud Newton
Annie Nocenti
Stephen O'Connor
Stewart O'Nan
Jenny Offill
Gary Panter
Ed Park
James Parker
Benjamin Percy
Mark Jude Poirier
Padgett Powell
Bob Powers
Todd Pruzan
Dan Reines
Nathaniel Rich
Peter Rock
Lucinda Rosenfeld
Greg Rowland
Luc Sante
R.K. Scher
Toni Schlesinger
Matthew Sharpe
Jim Shepard
David Shields
Marisa Silver
Curtis Sittenfeld
Bruce Sterling
Scarlett Thomas
Jeff Turrentine
Deb Olin Unferth
Tom Vanderbilt
Matthew J. Wells
Joe Wenderoth
Margaret Wertheim
Colleen Werthmann
Colson Whitehead
Carl Wilson
Cintra Wilson
Sari Wilson
Douglas Wolk
John Wray

CHRIS ADRIAN ROB AGREDO KURT ANDERSEN RA
MATTHEW BATTLES CHARLES BAXTER KATE BERNHE
MEG CABOT TIM CARVELL PATRICK CATES DAN CHA
HELEN DeWITT STACEY D'ERASMO DOUG DORST MAL
GIBSON MYLA GOLDBERG BEN GREENMAN JASON
DARA HORN SHELLEY JACKSON HEIDI JULAVITS BEN
KUITENBROUWER NEIL LABUTE VICTOR LAVALLE J
LIPSON ROBERT LOPEZ JOE LYONS SARAH MANGUS
NEWTON ANNIE NOCENTI STEPHEN O'CONNOR STEV
PERCY MARK JUDE POIRIER PADGETT POWELL BOB R
ROSENFELD GREG ROWLAND LUC SANTE R.K. SCH
MARISA SILVER CURTIS SITTENFELD BRUCE STERLING
MATTHEW J. WELLS JOE WENDEROTH MARGARET W
WILSON SARI WILSON DOUGLAS WOLK JOHN WRAY
ROSECRANS BALDWIN NICHOLSON BAKER MATTHEW
BROCKMEIER MATT BROWN BLAKE BUTLER MEG CA
DAVIES KATHRYN DAVIS MATTHEW De ABAITUA STA
MARK FRAUENFELDER AMY FUSSELMAN WILLIAM GIB
MICHAEL HECHT SHEILA HETI CHRISTINE HILL DARA HC
KOESTENBAUM JOSH KRAMER KATHRYN KUITENBROU
TODD LEVIN LAURA LIPPMAN MIMI LIPSON ROBERT
MIRANDA MELLIS LYDIA MILLET MAUD NEWTON AN
PANTER ED PARK JAMES PARKER BENJAMIN PERCY
REINES NATHANIEL RICH PETER ROCK LUCINDA ROSE
SHARPE JIM SHEPARD DAVID SHIELDS MARISA SILVER
DEB OLIN UNFERTH TOM VANDERBILT MATTHEW J. WE
WHITEHEAD CARL WILSON CINTRA WILSON SARI W
ANDERSEN RACHEL AXLER ROB BAEDEKER NICHOLS
BERNHEIMER SUSANNA BRESLIN KEVIN BROCKMEIER
CHAON SUSANNA DANIEL ADAM DAVIES KATHRYN DA
MARK DOTY BEN EHRENREICH MARK FRAUENFELDER
GROTE JIM HANAS JENNIFER MICHAEL HECHT SHEIL